Thistle in the Mistletoe

by

Margaret Izard

Stones of Iona Series

Thistle in the Mistletoe

Cover Art by *Lisa Dawn MacDonald*

The Wild Rose Press, Inc.
PO Box 708
Adams Basin, NY 14410-0708
Visit us at www.thewildrosepress.com

Publishing History
First Edition, 2024
Trade Paperback ISBN 978-1-5092-5541-2
Digital ISBN 978-1-5092-5542-9

Stones of Iona Series
Published in the United States of America

Dedication

To my family for tolerating my obsession with decorating everything for any holiday. You know it's fun even if it's a lot of work. To my husband and my true love, who believed in me, told me never to give up, and showed me that anything is possible. To my kids for showing everyone how to chase their dreams. Thank you for your love and support. I dedicate this book to you.

Chapter 1

"Stop, don't kill anyone." Breaths echoed in the silent church as Mary's heart lurched from her chest. A blade held at her father's throat. Another at her clan's long-time enemy, the MacDougall laird.

The newest laird stood proud, eyeing her from across the pulpit. He'd tied his jet-black hair in a queue at his nap leaving a lock that fell over his eye, making him seem handsome and vulnerable.

Damn him. She shouldn't find her enemy attractive.

His expression held malice and disgust, reflecting her father's. The expression the MacDougall wore, her father well earned. The glare her father settled on Laird MacDougall, she knew, was not.

She took a deep breath. "Certainly, there is some other way."

The king's agent spoke in a flat voice. "Marry, or they both die."

Her gaze shot back to the MacDougall laird. While not old, he wasn't in the budding of youth. His enormous frame filled out his clothing well, and the muscles on his exposed thighs flexed as he fought to remain still. Her eyes traveled back to his face, and his mouth quirked a half grin.

The king's agent raised his hand, and Mary grabbed his arm. "I'll do it. I'll marry Laird

MacDougall." One of her mother's sayings echoed, *a journey of a thousand miles begins with a single step.* One step toward peace, and it started with her.

The king's agent chuckled. "Lass, you are the wisest in the room."

She fingered her cross necklace, knowing a knife hid inside. But her pin knife, compared to the swords the king's guards carried, remained useless. The moments before the confrontation ran through her mind.

Why was she here for a meeting between the king's agent and her father? At Iona Abbey, of all places. Prior to entering, the king's guards disarmed her and her father's men. They wait, but for whom?

A scuffle from the back of the church alerted them that the guests they had waited for had finally arrived.

A long curse echoed in the sanctuary. "Son of a bitch, the Comyns."

Mary turned, and the worst sight greeted her. Her clan's long-time enemy stood at the back of the church. His plaid was similar to her Comyn's, green and red. But the dominant color of the MacDougall's was red, whereas hers had more green and blue.

Her eyes connected with the large warrior's, much as they had weeks before in battle. She wasn't supposed to be with the war party, but she came, the men needing her. Her father, too focused on the attack, didn't notice or maybe didn't care. She spotted the MacDougall on the ramparts as he called orders to his men, who responded as they tried in vain to protect their home. When his eyes found hers, they both stopped as the fighting continued. The blue of his eyes captured her. The intensity of his glare rooted her to the spot. She took a breath, then another, and he still stared as awareness washed over her. *He's your match, your soul mate.* She shook the sensation off, breaking eye contact. When her gaze tried to find his again, he had gone.

Now facing him here, those deep blue eyes held her in place.

What did the king have in mind?

That was earlier; the memory rang in her mind as the surrounding people shifted and prepared for a wedding ceremony. Had she known this morning, today would be her wedding day, she would have prepared better. A blue handkerchief, a token for her shoe, her grandmother's veil she'd kept wishing to wear it on her wedding day. Something old, something new, something borrowed, something blue, and sixpence for her shoe. Silly, but traditions all the same.

Her eyes roamed the church. At least greenery decorated the pulpit and pews, ready for the Christmas season. If they hadn't forced this upon her, she might find a holiday wedding romantic. She always wanted a husband, home, and children. *Be careful what ye wish for,* echoed—one of her mother's sayings. Here she was, a bride-to-be only mere weeks after a bloody clan battle. The king threatened the two lairds to meet or die. Demanding Mary be present. She should have known this was not good. Nothing good came from the English king.

The reverend turned to his place before her, and her stare met Laird MacDougall's again. His stern expression did nothing to calm her nerves, and the tick in his jaw reminded her of her father's fast fists. She glanced at her hands as a shiver shook her body.

"Trust me, lass, this isn't to my liking either," the

laird growled.

Her eyes shot to his, and she spoke without thinking. "Such romantic words from the groom."

"Too bad that sharp tongue doesn't match yer soft beauty. And here, I had hopes." His mouth quirked in almost a smile as the edges of his eyes crinkled. Was he jesting with her?

Her father pushed beside her and grabbed her arm. "Ye will mind yer tongue, Mary. Use it wisely for once."

Laird MacDougall barked a laugh, but when her eyes met his, he appeared somber again. His gaze focused on where her father painfully twisted her arm as tears gathered in her eyes.

The laird's glare traveled to her father's as he growled, "Ye will unhand my wife."

Her father leaned forward as he dropped his hand from her. "Not yer wife yet. Still my daughter and only child." He turned to her, kissed each cheek, and held her shoulders. "Well, ye finally are serving a purpose, lass. Do the clan a favor and stab him after ye fuck 'im?"

Her father's crudeness always chose the worst time to surface, his humor not helping. She glanced down as a tear fell. The reminder that she wasn't a son cutting the deepest, unable to fight as her father wished. At least she served a purpose, ending the clan war. She glanced between the two lairds. She hoped.

Laird MacDougall huffed a laugh. "If she kills me, the king will kill ye. Not a wise plan, Comyn."

The king's agent cleared his throat. "I will reread the king's orders so all will know and understand what he expects." His gaze traveled over the room. "And the consequences should either clan fail."

She lifted her head as she told herself to be strong and met Laird MacDougall's stare. His eyes roamed her face, then his expression changed. Was that caring she saw?

When the king's agent spoke, Laird MacDougall's expression vanished. "All Highland clan wars are to end by order of the king. As to the MacDougall and Comyn clans, the king orders Lady Mary Ann Comyn to marry Laird Alexander Roderick MacDougall to ensure peace."

Alexander Roderick. Does he go by Alexander or Roderick?

"Laird MacDougall's youngest brother, Malcolm MacDougall, must live with Laird Robert Comyn and train as a fighter serving him. Laird Comyn and Laird MacDougall will regulate visits to show the good health of both visitors. Should anything happen to each *guest* while in the other clan's care, consequences will be swift, and death the result."

Her father snickered beside her. "Try not to get killed, Mary. But if ye do, I shall enjoy watching Roderick die for it." *So, it's Roderick.*

Roderick's focus drifted to her father's, his voice deep and menacing. "Mary Ann Comyn shall be Mary Ann MacDougall and will never come to any harm. This I vow." He took a deep breath, shaking a little. "I, unlike others, hold to my vows."

Her father stiffened, the insult cutting. Her father had betrayed and killed Roderick's father in the last battle. They'd declared a truce to meet and discuss peace terms, but her father tricked Roderick's father and killed him. The war began before each became laird. Rumor claimed it started over a woman.

The king's agent spoke over the exchange. "To ensure peace continues into future generations, the king expects Roderick and Mary to produce offspring within a year. When Malcolm MacDougall reaches his majority, Laird Comyn will betroth him to a close Comyn relative at the approval of Laird MacDougall."

She'd heard all this before the guards drew swords, but hearing it over again brought the full meaning back to her. To fail meant death for either laird. She couldn't have that, not for her father, horrid as he was. Enemy or not, she didn't want to see the handsome MacDougall killed.

The king's agent stepped aside, and the reverend droned on about the sanctity of union in Christ. Her head spun. Was this really her wedding day? No flowers to hold, no traditions honored. Her friend Rose wasn't even present to be her maid of honor. Was this to be her life? Heat flashed over her, and her stomach turned.

She wavered, and a hand caught her. "Easy, lass, I have ye."

Her gaze met Roderick's. His eyes crinkled in concern, his hands on her arms firm. He stepped closer, wrapped an arm around her waist, and held her up.

He nodded to the reverend, who addressed her. "Lass, do ye take Alexander Roderick MacDougall as yer husband, to have and to hold from this day forward, for better, for worse, for richer, for poorer, in sickness and in health, to love and to cherish, until parted by death? Please repeat, this is my solemn vow."

The reverend blurred before her, and a hand squeezed her waist. She could do this—for the clan.

She needed to speak, shook herself, and stood taller. "This is my solemn vow."

The reverend turned to Roderick, who still held her. "Milaird, do ye take Mary Ann Comyn as yer wife, to have and to hold from this day forward, for better, for worse, for richer, for poorer, in sickness and in health, to love and to cherish, until parted by death? Please repeat, this is my solemn vow."

Roderick turned to her. His voice soothed as he spoke. "This is my solemn vow."

His eyes stayed on her as the reverend announced, "I pronounce you husband and wife. Laird, ye may kiss yer bride."

He turned, facing her. His hand still on her waist, holding her steady. The other rose and cupped her cheek. He leaned in but stopped when their lips neared. Their breaths mingled, and he inhaled through his nose and released it in a hum.

This close, she noticed the features of his eyes, blue like the deep ocean with flecks of silver.

His thumb caressed her cheek, then trailed to her chin as he tilted her, calming her. She closed her eyes. His lips brushed once, then again in light teasing strokes. She sighed, and he covered her mouth. His tongue slipped in and teased hers.

Her world spun as shock waves shot through her. No one had ever kissed her like this. His tongue danced with hers, swirled like her head. He ended the kiss as he sucked her lower lip. As he pulled away, she stepped forward, but he held her firm as a chuckle escaped. She opened her eyes, and Roderick held a sly grin.

Her father's voice boomed. "Damn, boy, don't take her here. At least wait for the bed…"

Roderick's expression turned so fast that Mary wasn't sure what he would do. "Enough, Comyn, ye will no longer insult *my wife*."

The king's agent stepped forward. "There's more to the command."

More? Wasn't this enough? What would the king have from them now?

"Two guards and I must witness the bedding and hang the sheet for all to see. There will be no trickery, and the king expects a wean in a year."

Shouts erupted around her as Mary gulped in large amounts of air. Witnesses? She was a virgin. God, this was *not* how her wedding was supposed to go. Where was her knight in shining armor?

Roderick's voice boomed overall. "I will not embarrass my wife so. I vow to honor the marriage and deliver a bloodied sheet."

"Silence!" The king's agent allowed his gaze to move to each person. "I have orders. You will obey." He turned to her and Roderick, who held her close. "This way. We have accommodations ready for you."

Leading the way down a corridor, they followed the king's agent with two guards who followed close behind. Roderick's eyes connected with his warrior beside him. They exchanged a nod as Roderick progressed still holding her waist.

As they marched, Roderick pulled her closer and whispered, "Mary, do not fash. I have a plan. Trust me."

She couldn't stop the snort from escaping as Roderick chuckled. Trust in her enemy.

They neared a door. The agent opened it as he waved them in ahead. Little furniture decorated the room, a bed, and a bedside table with a candle lit. A chair with a table and a carafe with two goblets sat before a blazing fire that created most of the light in the room. The agent and two guards followed in. One slammed the door shut. The thud announced the end of her dreams of a blissful wedding night.

Roderick stood beside her as his intent gaze roamed the room. What plan did he have?

The agent sat in the chair, poured himself red wine, and took a slow sip. "Disrobe, now."

Roderick stepped before her. "Ye cannot be serious. She's a virgin." He glanced over his shoulder. "Ye are, are ye not?"

She hit his back and connected with a wall of muscle that almost hurt her hand. "Of course I am. What about ye?"

His smile went wide. "One of us needs to ken what we are doing."

A sword sang from its scabbard and interrupted their banter. "Disrobe or a guard shall do it for you."

Mary groaned, sat on the bed, and removed her boots and stockings. The chill of the room brought forth a shiver.

Roderick kicked his boots off and chuckled as they landed at the king's agent's feet. His sporran flew off and his belt followed with a snap as his tartan fell to the floor in a heap that left him only in his shirt.

Mary stood beside the bed as she fidgeted with her hands.

Roderick came to her and turned her away from the other men in the room. As he slowly undid her laces, he whispered in her ear, "Have ye a blade or needle on ye, lass? Something I can cut myself with?"

It was her turn to chuckle. She removed her cross necklace and pulled out the pin knife as she secreted it in her hand. She placed the chain on the bedside table, beside a tied spring of mistletoe or *nuadhulig* the Gaelic word for all-heal echoed in her mind. The plant was an age-old charm against poison and witchcraft, with the power of rendering people fertile. Was it left as a sign or a joke? She wasn't certain.

Roderick turned her to face him and methodically slipped her bodice down and let it fall to the floor. He undid her skirt and allowed that to fall as well. When she stepped from the pile of fabric, their hands connected, and she palmed him the knife.

His eyebrows shot to his forehead, then a smile creeped over his face as he whispered, "Why, wife. Ye are full of surprises." He bent and kissed her full on the mouth as he let his intentions be known. He moved closer and kissed his way to her ear and licked it. "Leave it to a Comyn to come to her wedding armed."

His breath blew the wet spot and sent chills to her toes. "Had I known today was to be my wedding day, I wouldn't have come."

The king's agent's voice broke them apart. "Enough. Strip bare and get into the bed. I wish to sail this evening."

With one hand Roderick pulled his shirt over his head as he bared himself. His body was full of muscle; each movement undulated the masses in harmony that made her knees weak. He pulled the tie of her shift loose and lowered it over her shoulders. As the garment slid to the floor, his gaze roamed her body.

"Perfection," slipped from his lips.

Mary slid into the bedcovers and Roderick soon

followed. When he came close, he whispered, "Follow my lead and cry out when I say."

His eyes met hers as he pushed between her legs and spread them. She knew what sex was, had witnessed multiple couplings in her father's hall late at night. Knew how all the parts came together, but faced with the act now, she wasn't certain she could do it. Or even enjoy it as maids claimed they did.

He shifted, intimately brushed against her, and she jumped.

His head rested on her shoulder as he let out a groan. "This will hurt me more than ye, lass."

He brushed a kiss on her neck, then another at her ear as he sent another set of tingles to her toes. The warmth of his body pressed her into the mattress, and she found it comforting. Roderick kissed her full on the mouth as his body rubbed against hers. His hips pushed her legs farther open—his hand thrust between them. With a quick jerk, he groaned again. Wetness spread over her.

He whispered in her ear, "Cry out like I've pierced ye."

Mary gave a slight yelp as a guard chuckled.

Roderick nudged his hand again and covered him between them. "Louder lass, like I've truly hurt ye."

She jolted and loudly cried out as the king's agent sighed.

Roderick rocked back and forth as their bodies bumped and the wetness became sticky. He froze above her, groaned, then fell on her and panted as if he ran a long distance. Well, that was short, and he hadn't even done it right.

The agent stood at the foot of the bed. "Up with

you both. I'll take the sheet now."

Roderick growled as he pulled himself away from her. His free hand grabbed her wrist and pulled her out of bed with him. He flung the covers aside and exposed the bloodstained bedding as he stood tall regardless of his nudity.

Mary grabbed her shift and covered her nudity as she noticed blood on her woman's area. A glance at Roderick's body confirmed he had blood as well.

"Take it and begone. Now that ye have humiliated us, leave us in peace."

A guard gathered the sheet as he leered at Mary's body.

Roderick stepped in front of her and blocked the men's view as they filed out. The click of the door declared they were finally alone.

Roderick moved to the far side of the room near a dresser she'd not noticed before. Water splashed, and he returned with a cloth. As he reached for her, she backed away and grabbed the square from him.

His hands went up, the pin knife in one. "I was only offering to help."

She cleaned herself and offered the cloth to him. He handed her the pin knife in trade and eyed it. She rolled her eyes and gave him her back as she slid the knife in its case. They dressed, not speaking, the sound of rustling fabric the only noise in the room.

When Mary pulled her bodice on, hands rested on her shoulders that made her jump. "Easy, lass, I only aim to help."

Roderick made fast work of her laces as she glanced at him over her shoulder. "Ye know yer way around a woman's clothing well."

A chuckle was his only response.

Once finished, he turned her in his arms and held her. "Mary, this isn't the best of beginnings. But I vow to ye, I will do my best to make this marriage a true one. I want to make ye happy."

She nodded. "I appreciate that." Her gaze went to the bed. "The bedding, that was a smart trick. I, I thank you for saving our first intimate moment, for us." Another of her mother's sayings flitted into her mind. *A good beginning makes a good ending.*

He stepped closer, his hand on her cheek. "Mary, I would never force ye to do anything ye didn't want. King's order or not, I will not bed ye till ye say ye are ready. I promise." He bent and kissed her lightly on the lips.

Bam! Bam! Bam! A pounding came from the door that nearly knocked it in.

Not taking his eyes off hers, Roderick responded. "Enter."

The man she recognized from earlier entered. "The ship's ready to sail."

The man bowed to her. "Lady MacDougall. I've loaded yer bag, and yer companion waits."

She glimpsed from the man to Roderick. "My bag? I brought no bag, and Rose is not with me." She reached for her cross necklace, grabbed the mistletoe sprig, and tucked it in her bodice figuring she would need a little luck tonight.

Roderick took a deep breath. "Seems yer da is in with the king and came prepared. Wish I could say the same." He bowed to her, and she progressed through the door as they followed his man out into the corridor.

Roderick spoke as they strode down the hall. "This

is Archibald MacArthur, my first."

The large auburn-headed man tilted his head as he turned back, then proceeded on as they turned the corner.

Roderick guided her with a hand at her back as they exited the church. "We sail tonight. I do not trust the king's agent and yer father even less."

They exited the postern gate and descended the hillside to a beach where a rowboat sat in the surf. Roderick scooped her into his arms and waded into the water then set her in the boat. He climbed in after Archibald, and soon two guards rowed them out to a ship.

A bellow echoed from the church she recognized as her father's.

Roderick turned from the sound and addressed Archibald. "Ye delivered the private message as I asked?"

He nodded. "Aye, the blood isn't hers. Ye vowed not to force her."

****

Much later into the night, Roderick's ship clipped at a fast pace as they made good time to Dunstaffnage. He tipped his whisky flask and took another gulp as he stared into the night.

Memories of her body, naked before him, plagued his mind. Her softness and fresh scent haunted him. She was a beautiful woman unclothed. His attraction was undeniable.

Her face flashed in his mind's eye. Her expression reminded him she didn't want him. An unwilling bride from his clan's enemy. How in the world could he make this work? She was a pawn in the game of men, used for the good of the realm. He snorted. Adding insult to injury, the king ordered her to produce an heir like a brood mare.

Roderick stared into the sky. A lone lass dumped among a clan who hated her for her name, for the colors she wore, and she'd never lifted a hand in battle. How in the world would he keep her safe? He'd have to be crafty, convince the clan she was a necessity, that they needed her. He'd have to enlist help, and a plan formed quickly that he hoped worked. Both their lives depended on it.

Mere hours before dawn, Roderick carried his sleeping wife into her new home. No cheers greeted her. No one lined up, eager to meet the new Lady of Dunstaffnage. The only greeting were the snores of his men bedded down in the great hall. He moved to the side to avoid waking any, and her companion, Rose, followed on silent feet.

In her room, he placed her in the bedding and covered her. She moaned as she turned on her side, and a mistletoe sprig fell from her clothing. Roderick picked it up curious why she carried it. He held it and kissed her softly on the lips.

As he set it on her nightstand, she snuggled into the soft pillow and let go a soft sigh as Rose went into the adjoining room.

He caressed her cheek and whispered, "Poor lass. She's headed into the lion's den to be slaughtered."

Chapter 2

"I still can't believe my father told no one. He knew!" Rose handed her a head covering, something she needed to get used to now that she'd married. Roderick's smile flashed in her mind, bringing flutters in her belly. Maybe she needed to break her fast.

Picking up her cross necklace, she adjusted it on her neck. "Ye said he carried me to my bed?"

Rose sighed. "Aye, like the perfect groom."

Mary snorted. Perfect groom, he was not. She needed to get Roderick out of her mind.

Rose adjusted Mary's skirts. "Even kissed ye under the mistletoe."

Mary's gaze went to the sprig on her table. She'd wondered how it found its way there. Now she knew. Her hand went to her lips as they tingled. He'd kissed her again.

Rose crossed the room and opened the door to a guard standing outside in the hall. Rose glanced back at Mary, and her eyebrow raised.

Mary stepped into the hall and on toward the stairwell as Rose followed. Before descending the stairs, she glanced behind her, and, for sure, the guard followed. Oh, not even one day in enemy territory, and they already didn't trust her. Is this what life would be like, a prisoner in her own home?

At the top of the stairway, she froze. The great hall

fell silent, and all stared in her direction. Squaring her shoulders and vowing not to shy away from the challenge, she descended as one of her ma's sayings popped into her mind. *The road to hell is paved with good intentions.* When she reached the bottom, she tried not to make eye contact, but with the glares, the obvious evil intent in each expression, it was difficult not to look.

Mary had to walk through the lower tables to make it to the dais, and it was the longest trip of her life. Whispers came to her as she passed each table. *It's the Comyn whore. She's come to kill us all. She's a witch, I tell ye. Poor Roderick, married to the devil.*

Let them speculate. Mary would win them over. How much different could this group be than the hardened warriors that filled her father's hall? As she approached the dais, an attractive blonde woman in an expensive gown stared her down. A chill washed over her; this was an enemy for sure.

Roderick jumped down and met her near the raised table. "Good morning, wife, please break yer fast with me, with us." He waved to the clan members, who gaped at him.

He took her hand in his and led her the rest of the way, placing her in the seat next to his. Rose sat to her left and Roderick to her right. Archibald sat on Roderick's other side and the glaring blonde beside him. Her guard positioned himself behind her, so close if she pushed her chair back, she'd hit him.

She leaned in close to Roderick. "Is the guard necessary? I am not here to harm anyone."

Roderick glanced at the guard as he replied, "Mary, the guard isn't to protect ye from the clan. It's to protect the clan from harming ye." His eyes connected with hers. "Till they get used to the shock of having a Comyn in their midst."

He rose, meeting every eye in the hall. "May I introduce my new wife. Mary Ann MacDougall." He reached for her hand, pulling her to stand next to him. Instead of cheering for the newlywed couple, they received silent stunned expressions.

The reverend was the first to clap and call out, "Congratulations are in order, hear, hear." Her stare met his across the sea of angry faces, relief that someone had a heart.

Archibald banged his cup on the table. "Aye!" As he stood and clapped. He eyed warriors who all stood and clapped. Some women rose, applauding. But some sat in apparent defiance, like the blonde beside Archibald.

When the hall quieted, Mary moved to sit, but Roderick squeezed her hand.

He observed the hall as his voice rose. "By order of the king, we have wed. Hear me, clan MacDougall. There will be no mistreatment of yer new lady. To injure her will only guarantee yer laird's swift death. And I am fond of my head where it is."

Huffs of laughter flitted through the crowd as he raised her hand to his lips, kissing the back. "I look forward to the chance to get to know my beautiful wife, learn from her, and grow our clan together." He raised their clasped hands in the air, and the hall erupted in cheers.

Roderick released her hand, and they sat together.

She leaned over, whispering, "Impressive, but did it work over yer clan's hostility?"

He grinned. "Time will tell, lass." A maid set a bowl of oats and ale in front of her, spun, then marched away. Well, at least Roderick's speech seemed convincing.

"Break yer fast, Mary. I am certain ye are famished." She was hungry and noted a larger portion than she would have found at her father's table. She spooned the first bite to encounter oats so salty her lips puckered. She carefully set her spoon down, trying not to draw attention, and took a sip of her ale only to encounter something inedible. She smacked her lips, trying to think of a way to continue eating foul food.

The blonde woman leaned over, her whiney voice loud. "Lady Mary, how does the fare at our table meet with yer expectations?" So, was this who was behind the spoiled food? She can play a harder game than this. Her mother always said, *appearances can be deceptive*. Who was this woman?

She picked up her spoon and ate more, surprised she swallowed it. " 'Tis wonderful and a larger portion than my father serves. We've had hard winters for years with the war between the clans. Someone kept fouling our food supply. We've rationed for the past few years. Yer table is a bounty compared to what Rose and I are used to, Lady…" She waved her spoon, emphasizing the woman had not introduced herself before addressing her, the lady of the home, bringing the slight to everyone's attention.

Archibald coughed. "May I introduce my cousin, Lady Constance Ross. Lady Ross, Lady Mary MacDougall, and her companion Lady Rose McIntyre." He waved to each of them as he said their names.

Constance sneered at Mary's title. So, was she his

broken betrothal, or was she his mistress? Certainly, Roderick wouldn't parade his paramour in front of her. He had to have better sense. He knew she was armed, and she'd take great joy in pricking this bitch.

Constance's sneer did not fade as Mary took another bite of salted oats out of spite.

Roderick cleared his throat. " 'Tis good ye are here, Constance. Mary must take her rightful place as the lady of the house. Ye may hand the keys over now."

Constance spit out her ale. "Ye want me to hand over the keys to our stores to a Comyn? Yer mother is still alive. I will give them to her."

Roderick placed his cup down hard on the table. "My mother is in mourning, and ye and no one else will disturb her." He glared at Constance, and Mary knew that expression on any man meant to do as yer laird commands. Constance couldn't be that stupid.

Constance rose, knocking her chair, and yelling, "I will not turn the keys over to the Comyn whore."

She did not call her a whore. In front of the clan. Her gaze slid to Roderick. Would he defend her or allow it to slide? She held her breath.

Roderick gripped the table, his knuckles white. "Ye will first apologize to yer lady."

Constance stood rooted in her spot, silent.

Roderick turned but did not rise. "Apologize now." His voice brook no denial.

Constance whined, "Why'd ye go and get married? We were almost engaged. Ye love me, not that slut."

Archibald jumped from his chair, grabbing Constance. "Come, cousin, we need to chat in the garden." As he yanked her off the dais, keys flew at Roderick, who caught them with one hand. Cursing followed Archibald and Constance till it faded, and conversation resumed as the meal continued.

Roderick reached for her hand and placed the keys in them. "Some people will need to get used to this new unity. I apologize on her behalf." He wrapped his hands around hers. "Please take on the lady's duties. Archibald will help and introduce ye around later." He sighed as he stared into her eyes. "My mother is still mourning my father's passing. So, the hall needs preparations for the holidays. Please see to it and gather the maids to help."

Mary took the keys and nodded, knowing the responsibility of lady of the castle was no light task. She knew how to run a castle and knew how to do it well. Mary wanted to make him proud. She glanced down as Constance's declaration nagged at her.

Roderick's finger came to her chin and tilted her head up till their eyes met. "We were never betrothed. I refused to offer marriage, even though it was something she wished for. There is nothing between us. I allow her to linger till my mother recovers, but I can send her away if ye like."

Honesty, something rare between their clans. Here Roderick was, entrusting her with the care of his clan—an enemy, now his forced wife. She needed to trust him. They needed to trust each other.

"No, she can stay as long as she desires. I may need her help."

****

"Ye introduced her to the staff? Did she settle into her tasks?" Roderick paced the length of his study again.

Archibald sat before the desk, relaxed and

confident as Roderick glared at him. Wasn't he nervous as well?

"Aye, and her task will not be easy. Hostilities are high regardless of yer orders. Taking in a Comyn will take time, Roderick. We buried yer father only a couple of weeks ago."

Roderick stopped and leaned on the mantel. "Aye, and I could use his sage advice. God, I miss him."

His eyes slid to the *Fae Fable Book* in the corner of his study. The Fae had not been active since he was a child, and he prayed it stayed that way. Between the clan war, his father's death, and the ordered marriage, this was all he could handle now.

But what of Mary? She needed to get along with the clan, and soon. He couldn't risk anything happening to her.

Archibald sat back in his chair. "Yer spy arrived this afternoon. Her father left with Malcolm the following morning. Angered that the king's man allowed ye to take off in the night without a goodbye to his daughter."

Roderick barked a laugh. "The daughter he packed up with her maid, lied to, and trussed her off to a wedding he didn't mention? A union he declined until the king commanded it. I suspect he plotted this whole thing and relies upon Mary to kill me in my sleep."

Archibald raised an eyebrow. "What if that is his plan? What will ye do?"

Roderick pushed away from the fireplace and crossed the room, sitting at his desk.

He recalled Laird Comyn's abuse at the wedding. "Mary doesn't have it in her. I doubt she follows his orders outside of providing for her clan." No, there's no evil afoot from Mary, and after her comments about the conditions at clan Comyn, he suspected she was happier here.

He steepled his fingers as he set his elbows on the desk. "Ye have a spy set watching Malcolm?"

Archibald nodded. "Aye, first message comes via the tinker in a few days' time."

Nodding, Roderick ran everything through his head again. Spies on Malcolm—guard on Mary—Archibald sent out a message to ensure the clan follow his orders for Mary.

"Did ye send word out to the outlying villages? I've married a Comyn. We forged a new truce, forbidding anyone from attacking a Comyn unless shot upon first."

Archibald nodded. "Already sent. It will take weeks to cover the countryside, but two sets of guards set out to the outer villages, and rounds circulate information here. I say in a month's time all should know."

Roderick set his head in his hands. "Now we must face the leanest winter ever. The supplies dwindled from the siege. The clan hasn't rationed in years. Many don't know how to go without." He raised his head, staring at his long-time friend. "And how do I keep to the king's orders during this time?"

Archibald sighed. "How do ye plan to beget yer new wife with child if she's still a virgin?"

"I'll not bed an unwilling woman, but I plan to woo her." A picture of offering her flowers then sweeping her into a kiss crossed his mind. Then her reaction, a slap to his cheek. This was going to be harder than he imagined.

Archibald wiggled his eyebrows. "Did ye see her maid, Rose? Was she a commonly thing, eh?"

Roderick regarded his friend. "Maybe we can woo them together? I'll need all the help I can get."

Chapter 3

The cook, Bertha MacDougall, stood with her arms crossed, eyeing Mary. Her first act as lady, and it was with the most formidable cook she'd met. Well, she'd dealt with worse. Her father fired a cook, and they went months without one. Mary took over the running of her father's kitchen and learned many recipes.

She glanced at her guard, who leaned against the doorway and yawned. No help there.

Well, she could handle this woman. "Bertha, I am certain your planning is fine, but could you go over the meals for the week again? Roderick mentioned rationing, and I'd like to make sure we are using as few food stores as possible to save for the winter."

Bertha turned and gave Mary her back. "The meals are fine. Lady Constance has already approved the week's meals and will do so next week as well."

Well, the first slight wasn't so bad, but she kept at it. "I am sure it is, but as *Lady MacDougall,* I am now entrusted with the meal planning, and I'd like to ensure we are conserving as much as we can."

Bertha went about her duties as others in the kitchen followed her lead. Mary knew clan MacDougall rarely went without. Their stores shared between two castles, Dunstaffnage where she stood and Dunollie in Oban. They'd fortified both castles well, ensuring a prosperous clan.

Mary glanced around and noticed a full leg of lamb roasting, a maid chopping vegetables that were placed in a pot, and another kneading bread. Bread was a staple and flour a necessity, but the type of bread the maid made used other grains flavoring it, wasteful in times of rationing. Cook should cut the leg of lamb into a stew, so they used less meat per portion, saving the valuable ingredient to last longer and feed more. Her ma's voice rang in her head when they'd started rationing, *failing to plan is planning to fail.*

Mary tried again, "If I might point out—"

Bertha turned on her, raising her voice. "Out, that's right, out of my kitchen with ye. We don't need a Comyn telling us how to do things here. The only thing yer kind knows how to do is kill. So out with ye!"

Mary folded her arms. "I am yer lady. Ye will show respect."

Bertha barked a laugh. "Or what? The laird only has ye at the king's orders. Once yer father harms Malcolm, ye and yer father will die. And it will be sooner than ye think." Bertha turned her back to her, and the maids in the kitchen kept at their work.

So, rumors passed fast here. Mary guessed that was because of more women in this castle than her father's. Well, she would keep that in mind in the coming weeks.

Mary turned to the guard, who stood grinning at her. "Aren't ye going to do something?"

He shrugged. "My duty is to make sure no one harms ye. Settling yer squabbles isn't my job, Comyn."

She glanced back at the kitchen, all faces turned away—the slight obvious. She moved past Rose and crossed the room.

When she reached the door, Bertha exclaimed,

"Damn Comyn knows nothing."

Moving through the great hall, Mary encountered a group of maids preparing for an outing. They held large baskets and wrapped themselves up for the chilly weather.

As she approached, one said, "The greenery will be nice this year after an early freeze."

The other responded, "Aye, we'll make sure and gather much this season. We'll need it to make the hall nicer."

Mary stepped into the circle of women. "If you'll wait, Rose and I will gather our arisaids and join ye for the gathering."

Constance strode into the group. "No need. We have it all in order." Pulling on her gloves, she addressed the group. "This way. A guard has readied a wagon for us and a packed meal for the afternoon." The women curtsied to Constance, and an echo of milady filtered through the group who turned and proceeded out the main door to the bailey.

Constance turned to Mary. "I'm sure ye can find something else to occupy yer time. Like disappearing?"

Everyone cleared the hall, leaving Mary and Rose alone.

Rose turned to her. "Well, not so bad a morning? Maybe the afternoon will improve?"

Mary, dizzy, sat hard on the bench beside her. "Doubtful. The hospitality is as warm as the weather, which is colder closer to the coast." Her hand went to her stomach, which rolled in on itself in hunger. Her mouth pinched as acid rose, and saliva gathered when she swallowed. Her stomach cramped.

Rose sat next to her. "How are ye faring?"

Mary's stomach loudly growled, and one of her ma's sayings popped out of her mouth. "Empty vessels make the most noise."

Rose patted her hand. "I think that one refers to the brain, not the belly. Shall I try to get something from the kitchen?"

Mary nodded. "An ale, at least? Something. I am dizzy and ill."

Rose strode to the kitchen entrance as Mary sat in the hall. It was blessedly silent for once—something rare in her father's hall.

"Comyn! I see ye." Mary turned at the shout as an older man rushed her.

He waved his hand as he came closer. "My son, ye killed my son!"

He drew a dagger and lunged for her.

In a flash of movement, the dagger skidded across the floor and the man's arm was held high by her guard. "Alister, the laird's orders were clear. I know ye heard them, saw ye at the morning meal."

Alister crumpled, heaving sobs as her guard released him.

Mary moved to take his hand as he shied away. "Get away from me, witch. Ye will bring the devil down on us all."

Her guard helped him up and led him away.

Mary sat back on the bench, heaving a sigh. This was much harder than she thought. No matter what she tried, no one wanted her. Except Roderick, and that was because of the king's orders. In her father's hall, she was at least appreciated for providing for the clan. Here, she didn't have the opportunity.

Her guard returned and stood before her. "Are ye

hurt?"

Mary shook her head. "No, thank you… I'm sorry. What is your name again?"

She raised her face to his as he scowled. "Hamish. I'm one of five *awarded* with guarding ye. We drew sticks. I got the shortest, so the first shift is mine."

Rose came into her line of vision empty-handed. "Let me guess. Cook kicked ye out of the kitchen?"

Rose shrugged. "Said ye can eat grass. Ye've had yer portion like everyone else."

Mary hung her head. Yes, harder than her father's keep. They treated Mary like family there. Even though it was bad, it was better than the enemy.

Hamish chuckled. "Grass isn't so bad, but it gives ye the shites."

A group of maids came into the hall, resetting the tables for the midday meal. As one passed Mary, she gave her two fingers curled like talons, a sign to ward off evil.

Mary stood and pulled Rose to the side. "The midday meal is upon us. I will at least have something to eat, salty as it may be."

Hamish stood close but far enough to give them privacy. He might not help her with her struggles, but he took his duty seriously. He protected her and gave her space as a guard should.

Rose took her hands. "They shouldn't make ye suffer like this. Today we'll share. I'll insist on sitting next to ye, and we can trade trenchers. But I think it's time ye said something to Roderick. This is getting out of hand."

Mary shook her head. "No, I must make my own way with the clan. If every little challenge the clan gives me I run to the laird, I appear weak and whiney."

Rose snorted a laugh. "Like Constance?"

Mary smiled. At least Rose kept her spirits up. "Maybe, but the good news is she is out gathering greenery with the maids and a packed supper. So, she won't be here to spoil the meal."

Rose nodded. "Or yer food."

The maids quickly set out the trenchers and shared servings for the lower tables. Mary had to admit the castle ran efficiently, and the midday meal was soup with bread. So, rationing had occurred, but not for every meal. She would wait and see what they served for dinner and try to speak to Bertha again. Usually, three rounds of arguing would end any standoff. Bertha likely stood her ground as head of the kitchen, but she needed to show the lady of the clan respect.

Clan members filtered in and stood at their places. Mary waited for Roderick before approaching the dais, respecting him as laird. Guards filed in from the training field, and Roderick wasn't with them. Everyone seemed to be in their place, and there was no sign of Roderick.

Mary turned to Rose. "There's no sign of Roderick. I'll have to start the meal."

Mary made her way to the dais as Rose followed, mumbling, "This should be interesting."

Mary took her place at the high table, empty but for her and Rose, as a hush fell over the hall. She stood tall as her gaze roamed the room. All stared back at her with contempt. Well, she could keep them all waiting, starving like she was, but she wouldn't do that.

A guard approached her and whispered in her ear. "An issue detained Roderick at an outer village."

She nodded and announced, "Laird MacDougall's detained. Please, all enjoy the midday meal." Not seeing the reverend, she bowed her head, and led the prayer. "Lord, bless our food." Raising her head, she noted no one bowed theirs and all gaped at her. "Ye may proceed with the meal."

She and Rose sat, but no one else in the room moved, not even the maids whose duties it was to serve their individual dishes. Well, this was a serious slight. The whole damn clan?

Hamish yelled from behind her. "Ye heard the lady. Sit and eat while it's hot!"

The hall filled with the sounds of the scraping of chairs and the mumble of people beginning the meal. A maid strode by almost dumping Rose's bowl on the table. Someone else slapped a cup of ale beside it but set nothing before Mary. She hailed the maid, who turned her back to her. Maybe Constance wasn't behind the tainted food, but who was?

Rose stood with her bowl and cup and traveled to Mary's left, sitting beside her.

Rose grinned. "Share and share alike." Her ma's saying welcome as they openly shared the meal. But Mary could only eat a couple of spoonsful.

Hated by the cook, starved at every meal, nearly stabbed by a clan member mourning the loss of a son, and the entire clan ignored her—all before the end of her first day. The welcomes weren't warm here.

****

Roderick approached the dais for dinner, arriving back at the castle later than expected. The attack in the outer village took longer to clear than he thought. And he still couldn't believe the reports—the men attacking wore the Comyn plaid. Not even a week from the wedding and Comyn already broke a vow. Why should he be surprised? They were fortunate no one got injured.

He missed a chance to catch Mary and ask about her day. When he entered the main hall to see her standing in her usual place, relief washed over him. He looked forward to speaking with her. Archibald reported he introduced her around and left her in the capable hands of Bertha, the longtime cook at Dunstaffnage. He looked forward to hearing how she made friends and hopefully helped the staff learn to ration better. They were in for a hard winter.

When he drew closer, Rose stood on Mary's left, not her customary place. Archibald requested she sit with him, part of his wooing plan. Maybe Rose wasn't receptive to Archibald's advances. Too bad—they would have made a nice match.

He greeted the women warmly. "Lady Rose, Mary. 'Tis nice to see ye both." Rose glanced at him and smiled, but Mary kept her head bent and nodded.

Roderick noted Mary's guard behind her chair. Hamish had morning duty. Now it was Angus, an older, more seasoned warrior.

Hamish gave him Mary's day report upon his return. Alister attacked her in the hall. He'd planned, for each person who took issue with Mary being a Comyn, their punishment would be to spend time with her in hopes they'd get to know her better and see she was no threat. He didn't think it would take less than a day for an incident to occur, but it had. Roderick ordered Alister to return the following day to serve Mary for an hour.

He nodded to Reverend O'Donnell, who stood and spoke for all to hear. "I apologize. I missed the midday meal. But I understand Lady Mary blessed yer food." The reverend nodded to Mary, who stood staring wide-eyed. Was the encounter with Alister more than reported? He needed to ask her.

Reverend O'Donnell cleared his throat. "Thank ye, Lady Mary, and may we thank God for our food."

Roderick sat, signaling all around the room to proceed with the meal. Scrapes of chairs and the usual hum of conversation flowed as maids carried in plates for the high table. He noted the sliced lamb, boiled vegetables and potatoes, all individual servings. He glanced at the lower tables and noted the shared serving bowls filled with the same. He thought rationing had begun, which meant leaner meals that stretched the food supply among so many mouths to feed.

He turned to Mary, who sat picking at her food. "Mary." She jumped, and her fork clattered on her trencher.

She turned, smiling. "Sorry, Roderick, did you say something?"

He got his first glimpse of her face. Pale skin with circles under her eyes stared at him, not the bright flushed face from this morning. Alister must have frightened her.

He cut into his lamb, noting how tender it was. "How was yer day today, Mary?" He forked it into his mouth, and the spices rolled across his tongue. Spices that also needed rationing.

Her smile didn't quite fill her face. "It was fine, Roderick. How was yers?"

Constance snorted, and Roderick turned to glare at

33

Archibald's cousin. She seemed more and more troublesome by the moment. Archibald had spoken to her, reminding her of her place. Seems he also needed to have a stern word with the chit.

When he glanced back at Mary, he noted her plate seemed different, the portions larger. She cut a large piece of meat and ate it, then gulped some ale and sighed. It was good she ate well, seemed she worked up an appetite.

He ate more as he contemplated asking her about rationing but would mention it on the morrow. Tonight, he wanted to enjoy the evening.

After the meal was complete, he leaned back in his chair. "I noticed the greenery gathered in the bailey. It's good ye are ready to decorate for the holidays. We have much to be thankful for."

Mary froze, her cup halfway to her mouth.

Constance replied, "Yes, Roderick, the maids and *I* collected all the greenery. *We* will ready yer hall for ye." Maybe Mary assigned the task. It was good the women got along. The end of Mary's first day and all had come along well.

The dishes nearly cleared, he glanced at Mary, and a smile rested on her face.

He leaned over and whispered, "Would ye care to join me in the study?" Mary turned and nodded. Roderick took her arm in his as she rose. He waved off Angus knowing he would wait till Mary retired, follow her to her room, and guard her door.

Archibald approached Rose. "Rose, would ye sit with me by the fire in the hall? Tell me of yer first day here?"

Rose glanced at Mary, who nodded before turning

with him to go toward the study. Rose went with Archibald with a wide grin. So, she was attracted to him, but why move her seat at dinner? He'd have to ask Mary later. For now, he wanted to get to know his wife better. They passed Constance, who huffed and stormed away. Let her have her tantrum. Tonight, he needed to focus on Mary.

Roderick held the door open for Mary, who stepped into the room, going to the bookshelves. He stood back as she wandered the spines. Her profile was to him, and her color seemed better. Or maybe it was the glow of the fireplace, the only light in the room.

"Ye read?"

Mary turned, smiling. "Aye, my mother taught me before her death. Father wasn't happy. Declared it was a waste on the lesser sex, but she insisted. Claimed a woman's mind was just as smart, if not smarter, than a man's."

Roderick grumbled. Comyn didn't have the sense of a pea. Women had complicated minds capable of not only deceit and deception but such wonderful insight. He learned from his ma, it was best to use a woman's mind for good and not evil. His da always said, ye know nothing about a woman until ye make her angry.

Mary picked up a volume and flipped it open. "She taught some in the clan to read." She closed the book and set it back in the case. "I'd always wished to teach more of my clan to read, but my father wouldn't allow it."

Roderick would have liked her mom. Such a strange match for Laird Comyn, the gruff, crude, stern man he was. His father mentioned they were all friends at one time, before the feud. Mary's mom had been a

35

close friend of his ma's. But all that was before his birth, before the wars began. Strange how times changed.

He strode to the table of spirits and poured himself one.

Roderick turned ready to take a sip, and Mary raised an eyebrow. "Husband will ye not offer one to yer wife?"

His eyes met hers as he grinned, liking her banter. "Why pardon me, wife." He sauntered toward her offering the goblet to her. "Would ye like a dram, Milady?" Stepping close, he handed it to her, their fingers brushing. He waited for her to take a sip, expecting her to fall into a fit of coughs.

When she sipped and it went down smoothly, he chuckled. "A woman familiar with spirits. Shall I lock mine up?"

Her gaze fell to the cup. "With the warm welcome I've had, I'll need another." She stepped past him and sat in one of the richly upholstered chairs before the fire.

Roderick sighed and poured himself one, needing it for the conversation ahead. "Aye, well, I heard about Alister."

He crossed to sit in the chair next to hers, facing her, his drink between both hands. "Mary, while it will take some time for people to grow used to ye, I will not permit harm to come to ye. Ye must tell me, has anyone else done anything to ye? Something I need to address?" He glanced at her, hoping that things went well for her outside of Alister's outburst.

She sighed. "No, nothing I can't handle. As for Alister, I wanted to comfort him. We both have losses, and it's time for that to end."

Roderick sat back, sipping his drink then set his goblet on the table between them. She was a wise woman, one who understood loss from war. What all had the Comyn clan lost? What had Mary lost? His plan for her acceptance, she needed to know so they could work together to bridge the gap between his people and her.

"Agreed. Anytime a clan member does something against ye for being a Comyn, I'm having them serve ye for an hour."

Mary sat up, shaking her head. "It's not—"

"It is. Mary, it's not a punishment but a chance to spend time with ye, get to know ye. So, when Alister arrives in the morning, spend time speaking with him. Have him help ye so he's needed. Ye ken?"

Mary smiled. "Ah, befriending the enemy, show him my vulnerability." She sipped her whisky and peeked at him. "Yer plan has flaws. What if I am not a weak woman, Roderick?"

He slipped off his chair kneeling before her. "Mary, that's the best part of my plan. Ye are not a weak woman, and I want the clan to see it. To see what I see in ye."

He took her drink from her and set it on the table. Taking her hands in his, he stared into her eyes. "What I see in ye, Mary, is a strong woman who's had to fight for all she needed, provided for her clan in hard times. Forced to run a keep on her own at a young age must not have come easy and knowing yer father's warriors, must have been eye opening."

She blinked and stared at him. "It wasn't so bad. They are my family, my clan."

Tears gathered in her eyes. He was right. Her life under her father had not been easy.

He sighed as he spoke. "But what I see in ye is compassion, and I want, no, need my clan to see it too." He kissed her hands. "Give my clan a chance to get to know ye. Give me a chance as well. While we are ordered to, I want us to make this marriage work." He moved toward her, intent on a kiss. Her eyes closed, and a tear escaped. He brushed it aside with his thumb caressing her cheek and brushed his lips across hers. She responded in a sigh, and he shifted forward deepening the kiss.

Her kisses were the nectar his soul needed. No woman stirred him like her.

Her arms wrapped around his neck, and she whimpered into his kiss as their tongues danced. His desire raged, and he wanted nothing more than to take his wife into his arms. But he tried to win her affection first. He wanted this to grow into a true marriage, not the farce it started as.

He reluctantly ended the kiss, needing her trust first. "Mary, 'tis been a long day." He picked up her goblet; a sip was still left. "Finish yer wee nip, and I'll escort ye to yer room."

She gulped it down and set the cup aside. Maybe he really needed to lock up the spirits. Grinning, he stood and offered her his arm. She rose and took it.

They made their way out of the study into the hall. Clan members loitered around the hall in groups. Some stopped and took note of the laird escorting his wife above stairs, but no one commented. And they wouldn't with Roderick there, but what occurred when he was away… He needed the guards to keep a close watch. He feared the issues were only beginning for Mary.

They ascended the stairs in silence, and when they arrived at Mary's door, Angus moved farther down the hall, giving them privacy.

Mary raised an eyebrow. "Not yer room, Milaird?"

Roderick smiled. "I told ye the first night, we will take our time. I want a chance to grow our friendship. For now, it's good night, Mary."

He bent and brushed a brief kiss. If he took more, he would have backed Mary through the door and taken his husbandly rights. He pushed himself away stepping back, forcing his desire down. No, this was for the best, for them and the clan.

He bowed. "Good night, Mary."

She opened the door, crossed the threshold, and glanced over her shoulder. "Good night, husband." The door closed with a click.

Angus approached and stood beside the door at this post.

Roderick nodded. "Protect her. She's worth it."

Chapter 4

The following morning, Rose entered Mary's room fully dressed, with her McIntyre arisaid on that was bluer and greener than her red Comyn one, a bowl in her hand. "They served the morning meal in our rooms. I figured they gave ye nothing." She handed her the bowl, and inside wiggled wet congealed oats.

Well, at least it was food. Mary whispered, "A trouble shared is a trouble halved."

She'd spent the early morning lighting a cold hearth then sitting working through her mind ways to get the clan to accept her. The food was the first thing she must address, but without knowing if it was from the cook or someone else, she'd need to observe to figure out who was behind it.

She spooned the cold mixture into her mouth as Rose gathered her clothing for the day. "The sturdy one. I want to see the outside today, and based upon the chill of this room, it's cold again."

Rose set out the wool dress. "Aye, smells of snow."

Mary hummed. She loved snow, but today she wasn't as excited as usual. Handing the half-eaten bowl to Rose, she crossed and began dressing.

Rose proceeded to hand the bowl back, and Mary shook her head. "No, ye must eat as well. I'll need yer help today. The man, Alister, who attacked me is due to spend his penalty with me."

Rose snorted. "Shall I find ye a dagger?"

Mary fingered her cross necklace. "Maybe. The king's men took all the weapons and my favored dagger at the abbey. I only have my pin knife left." She sighed. She wondered when or if her belongings would come. Certainly, her father would send them. She picked up her Comyn arisaid and loosely wrapped it around her shoulders.

Fully dressed, both women exited the room. A guard stood in the hallway. Young, with fuzz for a beard, he tipped his head. "Robbie, Milady."

Mary smiled. "Short for Robert, like my father."

Robbie coughed and waved for them to proceed with him. Making the way down the hallway, Mary glanced back at her guard. "My husband, where is he this fine cold morning?"

Robbie skipped, catching up. "He's ordered training all day. Snow's expected, and he says there's no better time to train than in the cold."

Descending the stairs, Mary spotted many women gathered, and the evergreens spread across the tables. So, they proceeded without her. Tying the greenery for the holidays was a favorite task of hers. One she took joy in since it decorated the hall. Something her father didn't like but allowed at her insistence.

Roderick's hall, though, held many adornments without the extra décor. Tapestries hung in the walls warming the room, the clan shield hung above the grand fireplace, and even the bowls used for serving the lower tables had a weaved pattern in the wood. A woman's touch was evident in his hall. He had mentioned his mother was in mourning. Would she meet her?

She approached the group. "Tying the greenery is my favorite. Here, let me help."

Everyone froze and glared at her.

Constance's voice held an edge as she approached her. "Your type of help is not needed nor wanted."

She passed her, bumping her shoulder.

In Mary's weak state, Constance almost knocked her down. Mary took a deep breath and approached a table. All the women gave her their backs. As she reached for a swag, one snatched it away. Well, maybe she should try speaking to cook again.

She strode into the kitchen. All the work stopped.

Bertha turned from her pot. "Well, the Comyn is back. Go on with ye, we have work here."

Mary stood taller. "I must speak with ye about my food."

Bertha snorted and turned to the pot. "Ye got what everyone else got. Out with ye."

Mary stepped closer. "Actually, I had nothing this morning, yesterday's dinner was salted beyond consumption, and nothing was served to me for midmeal. My hearth is cold, and no one delivered water to my room."

Bertha turned, waving her spoon. "See here, this is not the queen's castle. A maid set up yer room as Lady MacDougall likes hers. As for food, we are rationing. Ye'll get what ye get. This morning it was oats like everyone else."

Mary stepped closer. "Speaking of rationing, ye served sliced roast lamb. Ye should have it in a stew, use the meat sparingly across many meals. And the bread, save the oats for meals and use only ground flour for yer bread. The spices, ye are using too much. Soups or stews are a better choice to feed many, and ye would use less meat and vegetables. I have recipes I can share. Lamb stew, cured ham soup, and vegetable soup."

Bertha raised her voice, shaking her spoon. "Ye dare come in here trying to force yer Comyn ways upon me. Lady or not, I'll not have it. Accusing me of neglecting ye, ye're a liar! Out! Out with ye!"

Chased from the kitchen, Mary and Rose stumbled into the great hall, shadowed by a smirking Robbie.

A few giggles came from the women at the tables as they bent, whispering. She guessed Bertha's voice carried.

A cleared throat had her turning to come face-to-face with a stern-faced Alister. Already it was time? She shook herself and went to greet him.

He backed away with his hands up.

She sighed. "Come, Alister, walk with me outside."

As they passed the women with the evergreens, she leaned over to Rose. "Stay and see if ye can befriend them, maybe help. We can speak over the midday meal."

As she strolled away, Rose greeted the woman who engaged her in conversation. Her arisaid must have let them know she was not a Comyn but a McIntyre.

Mary proceeded through the large hall doors with Alister on her heel and the shadow of Robbie behind. A cold wind blew, and she wrapped her Comyn arisaid closer happy to wear familiar colors and made her way to the outer gates.

Robbie jogged up beside her. "Milady, ye cannot leave the inner bailey. Orders from the laird."

Mary drew up short. "Orders? What is the meaning

of this?"

Robbie, out of breath, puffed between words. "The laird…not without him."

She eyed the gate, open for anyone to come and go, except her.

Alister spoke from beside her. "A shame, a prisoner in yer own home." She'd almost forgotten he was with her.

Robbie pointed to the side. "Mom MacDougall's garden's this way. Frozen, but a nice place."

They strolled on, and Alister kept pace with her. "Tell me, Alister, what do ye do?"

He stared at her. "What kind of question is that? Daft are ye? I farm like everyone else."

Mary smiled. "Well, ye could have been the butcher, or the smith. Maybe a cobbler?"

Alister huffed. "The butcher is Archibald's brother, Aaron, and can carve yer heart out. The smith is Bert, and the cobbler died last year. We need a new one, but the tinker comes once a month, and he brings us shoes."

They arrived in the garden, which was nothing more than an open space with frozen twigs. An early snow that already melted had killed the flowers. She bet it would be lovely in the summer.

"Seems yer keep is much like mine, a farmer, a smith. Our butcher died, and the cobbler moved on when times got tough. I learned to mend shoes."

A bench sat under an oak tree. She went to it. When she neared it, she glanced up. The leafless oak rose like frozen dark arms into the sky. When the snow came later, the dusting would cover it in white, making it seem like a wizard or Merlin from the King Arthur stories.

Mary sat and patted the bench. "Sit, Alister."

He hesitated.

She patted again. "I won't bite."

He sat next to her and took a deep breath.

She studied the castle wall. Her eyes traveled up, landing on a window. A woman in black stood staring, gray wisps of hair coming from beneath her head covering. Mary leaned to get a better view, and the woman turned away from the window.

Probably Roderick's mother, another in mourning. At least here they had the chance to mourn. Her father's hall was always too busy burying the dead and her too busy managing a keep of warriors bent on war to stop for remembrance. An endless cycle that she gladly left behind.

She waited for Alister. In her experience, people in grief needed an outlet, someone to talk to. Mary gazed at the clouds, white and billowy, close to snow. She'd not sat like this in a garden since before her mother died.

With Alister, it didn't take long.

He blurted, "I've got no one since my son died. Edith, my sweet Edith, died a couple of months ago. My farm takes more hands to maintain. I supply the lamb for the keep. I need help and have none."

She nodded. "Who is the taxman for Laird MacDougall?"

He turned to stare at her. "Ye know a lot about a castle, lass."

She glanced at him, then away, almost laughing.

She knew everything about running a castle. "Aye, I ran my father's keep. My mother died when I was young. There were few women and many warriors."

Alister grunted. "Aye, well, the Laird's taxman is Roderick's sister Ann's husband, Thomas. Newlywed, they live on an estate in a village not far. We only see him for collections. He makes the rounds to us, so we don't have to take time away from work." That was nice and efficient. Her father made all come to him, even made them wait the whole day without refreshments.

"What about judgment day, and why haven't ye appealed to the laird for help?"

He stopped pressing his lips together, obviously not wanting to speak but dying to tell someone. He groaned. "Estelle, the widow, and her son live close to me. But no, it wouldn't be right. Estelle is a right sweet woman and shouldn't have to do more than she can handle."

Mary grinned into the wind. His voice when he spoke of Estelle spoke of much more. The widows help one another, likely needing each other. They'd founded marriages on less, hers coming to mind. Her plan formed quickly, the process a welcome distraction from her own woes. Another of her mother's sayings came to her. *Actions speak louder than words.*

She rose and strode to Robbie at the entrance to the garden. "I need to see my husband now. Take me to him."

Robbie's eyes nearly bulged from his head. "Ye what?"

Alister came up beside her. "Milady, there is no need. I'll get along fine."

She marched past Robbie, a prisoner in her own home. Not today and not ever. Heading for the gates, a wave of dizziness hit her, and she stopped. She took a deep breath as Robbie and Alister caught up with her.

Robbie took her arm. "Milady, come inside the keep."

She pulled away and marched through the gate. "The training field can't be that hard to find. A bunch of grown men hitting each other. If I follow grunts and the stench of sweaty men, I'm likely to find it."

Alister caught her arm. "Allow me, Milady, this way."

Robbie followed. "I'll be cleaning a latrine shoot by dinner for sure."

Rounding the corner, soon they came upon the field. Close to the keep beside the stable within the outer bailey. Grunts and yelling came from the large group of men. It seemed there was a sparring match. She shouldered into the circle, and the men gave her space.

Before her, Roderick battled shirtless, sweat dripping from his face and chest. He fought a rather large man. Her husband moved with agility and grace as he led an offense with his broadsword. The larger man, stockier, had a harder time moving as fast. With a spin and an upward thrust, Roderick disarmed the man.

The sing of a dagger drawn from her right alerted her that someone had removed a blade. She spun to her left, passing before Robbie, and grabbed his knife. Stepping forward again, she knocked the oncoming knife from the attacker as it came at her middle.

The warrior stood stunned as his blade tumbled, landing at Roderick's feet.

His gaze rose slowly and met hers. "Greetings, wife."

Roderick waved to Archibald, who grabbed the

warrior. "Well, well, Bruce, seems ye earned not only an hour with the lady tomorrow but an evening cleaning a latrine shoot."

Bruce struggled. "She's a spy, here to kill us all. Did ye see her with the blade?"

Mary stood taller, speaking loud enough to ensure all the warriors heard. "I am no spy."

Roderick picked up the blade and walked toward her. "That I know, but the blade?"

The closer he came, the more she had to tilt her head back. The scent of him assaulted her, male musk with sweat, heady and sweet making her knees knock. Her eyes kept moving from his face to his broad chest, his naked broad chest. Her heartbeat was hard, and her breaths came short.

He asked her about the blade—*focus, Mary*. "In a keep of men, I had to learn to defend myself."

He held the blade between them. "Nice move." Without taking his eyes from hers, he called to his men. "Men, back to practice."

The men moved away, allowing the laird and his wife some privacy, but not too far. Eyes roamed to them as they stood there.

His gaze still on her, he handed the blade to Robbie. "Explain why my wife is out of the castle gates without her laird. Defying a direct order."

Robbie huffed as Mary quickly replied. "I came to seek ye. He had no choice but to follow—to protect me." True, but the statement, she hoped, protected Robbie from cleaning the latrine shoot. Her ears caught Robbie's sigh of relief.

Roderick smiled. "What is it ye want of me, wife?"

She glanced back at Alister, who shook his head.

She turned, and the muscled chest filled her sight. "Alister has a farm."

Roderick folded his arms over his chest, the muscles undulating, making her mouth water. Her view filled with his naked chest, and she wondered what it would feel like to touch, to caress.

Roderick chuckled, and her eyes snapped to his. "Yes, well, he needs help. The widow Estelle has a son, and her son is too young for hunting. And well, Alister needs help tending his farm. I came to ask if they could help each other. An exchange."

Roderick stepped closer, unfolding his arms and taking her hands in his. "Ye come to seek me out to propose help for a man who attacked ye yesterday?"

Close like this, she could whisper her response. "I suspect he has feelings for Estelle and is too embarrassed to ask. One widow, helping another. A match made, and both problems solved."

Rubbing his thumbs over her hand made chills move down her spine.

He stood and regarded her momentarily, a smile growing on his face. "Angus!"

Her guard from yesterday approached. "Milaird?"

Still rubbing her hands, Roderick spoke. "Take Alister to widow Estelle's. My orders are Estelle and her son will help Alister with his lambs. In exchange, Alister will provide them with meat. And they shall share their meals."

Alister bowed. "Thank ye, Milaird."

He came close to her. "Milady, thank ye!"

She glanced his way and nodded, but Roderick squeezed her hands, bringing her attention back to him. "Still, ye disobeyed an order."

She pulled her hands, and he gripped them harder, not releasing them. "Ye ordered me nothing. I did not know about leaving the castle. Why am I a prisoner in my home?"

His expression changed, his eyebrows creasing. "Ye are not a prisoner. Ye are my wife, and I must protect ye." He gripped her hands harder. "If ye go running around, I cannot ensure yer safety. A man near stabbed ye just now, another yesterday. Tensions are still high. It's mere weeks since yer father killed mine."

As he spoke, his voice rose, and his grip tightened on her hands, making her cry out. "Roderick, please, ye're hurting me."

He dropped her hands and stepped back.

Her gaze met Roderick's.

His face flashed a mask of anger. "Go back to the keep, Mary. Stay there where ye are safe." He turned, giving her his back, and strode away into a group of men.

She backed away, tears gathering in her eyes. Some men sneered at her. They all seemed like her father's warriors, hard, angry men eyeing a vulnerable woman.

She turned and ran for the keep, tears flowing now. Rounding the corner, her stomach cramped, and she fell to her knees, dry heaving. There was nothing there. Her stomach folded in on itself, and she stayed on her hands and knees for a moment. Trying to recover, trying not to pass out.

After some time, boots came into her vision—the ever-present guard.

Robbie's voice was soft. "Come, Milady, let's get ye inside."

He offered a hand, but she refused to take it. She leaned against the wall and lifted herself up like she always had. Same life, new place. Mary moved to the gate and passed through it. They could have closed it and locked it. The feeling was the same. A prisoner in her own home, the hated enemy. How would she survive? Like she always had, by sheer will alone.

****

Mary sat on the pew in the chapel in the woods, a private family chapel saved from the clearances which took many religious buildings. The stained-glass windows cast colorful afternoon shades upon the interior, reminding her of Iona Abbey. Her wedding came to mind and all that the king's orders entailed.

She sighed, and her stomach cramped, reminding her the midday meal was the same as yesterday, nothing. With an absent Roderick and nothing for her to eat, Rose tried to share her trencher again, but a maid took it before she could eat any. Cook must be the one behind it, the main person in command of the maids. She wanted to deal with it but needed a plan first.

Her head wavered, and she sat straighter. Passing out in the chapel would be a bad omen. She'd given the clan enough fuel for that fire. It took an argument with Robbie to come to the chapel outside of the inner bailey. With the reverend in the village and her begging time for worship, she'd won Robbie over.

Mary glanced over her shoulder another time, making sure she was alone. Bringing the rosary from her pouch, she bent her head in prayer as she fingered the beads. Keeling would be obvious, and she might not get back off the floor in her weakened state.

Mary made the sign of the cross small on her chest,

bending in case anyone spied on her. Despite its ban, many still practiced Catholicism. Not knowing the MacDougall clan's faith and based upon the fact they had a reverend, being caught as a bloody papist would not improve her reputation here. Then again, maybe it would.

Holding the crucifix, she began the Apostles' Creed in her mind, too scared to say it aloud.

I believe in God, the Father almighty, Creator of Heaven and Earth, and in Jesus Christ, his only Son, our Lord, who was conceived by the Holy Spirit, born of the Virgin Mary.

Mary kept the creed running in her mind. Her eyes closed, taking comfort in the familiar words. Near the end, she whispered it aloud.

I believe in the Holy Spirit, the holy Catholic Church, the communion of saints, the forgiveness of sins, the resurrection of the body, and life everlasting.

Amen.

As she prayed in her mind, she fingered the first bead. *Our Father.* Then one *Hail Mary* on each of the next three as they warmed in her fingers, the touch comforting. *Glory Be.*

Why had God sent her here? Why treat her this way?

She fingered more beads while meditating and continued her prayer, moving to each bead as her prayers calmed and soothed her.

Coming to an end out of habit, she spoke it aloud. "O my Jesus, forgive us our sins, save us from the fires of Hell; lead all souls to Heaven, especially those who have most need of your mercy."

"I suspect, Milady, out of everyone in my

congregation, you are the one who has the most need for God's mercy."

Mary turned, and a wave of dizziness overwhelmed her from the sudden movement. Her hand shot out to steady herself on the pew.

Reverend O'Donnell stood near her, smiling.

She hid her beads in her skirt.

The reverend moved forward, sitting next to her on the pew. "Milady, please never fear practicing yer faith in my presence. I welcome all who worship in the house of God." He chuckled. "But ye are right to hide it from the rest of the clan, barring Roderick. He and his mother still practice, but in secrecy."

Mary's eyebrows shot up as he huffed. "I suppose ye will learn of yer husband's faith soon. Sunday is coming, and the family holds a private service besides the clan's."

Mary sat back, shoulders down. "I am not welcome here. Not even by my husband."

It was the reverend's turn to lift eyebrows. "I doubt that. I see him with ye. He's caring and considerate. I know what he did for yer wedding night. Came to me in confession."

Mary gasped, and the reverend grinned. "Sharing a little won't hurt, and ye need to know more…more about this truce."

Mary rubbed her forehead, a headache coming on. "The truce is in the king's order, his guarantee the clans will stop the fighting, stop the killing. Both of us forced into a sham of a marriage."

He sat forward, tapping her knee. "Aye, but what ye don't know is Ian, Roderick's da, proposed this very thing months ago. When Robert rejected the marriage proposal, Ian wrote the king about it trying to find peace."

Mary glanced at the clergyman. Was this true? Did Roderick know, and was he agreeable before being forced?

The reverend nodded. "Yer father declined the offer. He claimed Roderick wasn't good enough for his only child. His jewel he called ye."

Tears welled in Mary's eyes. She'd not heard the endearment since before her mother died. It was what her mother called her, her jewel.

The man of God patted her hands. "Donna fash, Mary. It all came out in the end, and Roderick was willing, regardless of what aspirations Constance had." He turned to the side. "Something must be done about that one." His eyes came back to hers. "She's troubling ye?"

Mary wasn't sure if she should confide in the reverend. Was he an ally or not? Man of God, for sure, but he was a MacDougall, saw her as the enemy.

She shook her head and sat staring as everything rolled over in her mind—Roderick's father's death at her father's hands, the truce, her marriage. She sighed as tears gathered anew. Trying to get an entire clan who saw her as the enemy to see her as their lady and ally was no mere task. Even harder was figuring out who was behind her lack of food and confronting them to bring it to an end.

He patted her hand again. "Mary, I see yer doubts written all over yer face. I understand yer concerns. A member of the enemy trying to find trust amid people filled with hate and hopes of revenge." He sighed. "Trust will take time, but know ye are always welcome here. I am someone ye can trust, with yer life even. I used to be one of Ian's warriors and took to solace and prayer when my wife died. Would you consider me…a friend?"

She stared at him. His sincere expression gave her hope—a friend. "Aye, I'd like that very much. But I must return before I am missed."

She rose and stumbled. Would have dropped to the floor if the reverend hadn't caught her. "Ho, lass, I've got ye."

He set her back on the pew, concern lining his face. "Let me get ye some wine. Wait here."

Mary sat and took a deep breath, her head still spinning. When the reverend returned, Robbie was in tow.

The reverend helped her sip some wine. At first it turned her belly, but after the second sip it settled.

He turned to Robbie. "Escort the lady back to the castle, ensure she rests till evening meal."

He focused on her. "If ye are ailing, call for Agatha, the healer in the village. Any maid can fetch her for ye."

She couldn't do that. Concede to weakness and rely on another to fight her battles. The food war with the cook was something she needed to work out on her own to establish her place in the castle. No, she'd gone with little food before. Another few days wouldn't hurt. The wine made her feel better already. A little here and a little there, and she'd make it through like she had before.

Restored and fortified with wine, Mary stood and took the clergyman's hands in hers. "Thank you, Reverend O'Donnell. Your guidance and faith are needed and appreciated."

The reverend exchanged a glace with Robbie. "Ye are most welcome. And I'll have a chat with Roderick. There is no reason ye cannot come pray when ye want, and making ye stay inside the gates, 'tis absurd."

Mary moved to the chapel doors, Robbie opened them, and a brisk chilly wind wrapped around her. Snow was in the air. Mary always thought a new snow brought on new beginnings. Things were finally looking up.

****

At dinner Roderick sat next to his wife, eyeing her plate, not fully filled with food. She wasn't aware he observed her, but he did. Reverend O'Donnell's conversation echoed in his mind.

"Roderick, I fear the lass is having a harder time than she admits. She near fainted in the chapel."

They were in the study. Not even Archibald was present, Patrick O'Donnell having insisted on a private meeting.

"Fainted? The lass is sturdier than most of my aged warriors. What could ail her?"

The clergyman, an old friend long before becoming their spiritual leader, sat in a chair before the desk. "The clan has not taken yer marriage well."

Roderick huffed. That was an understatement. He took away an ale ration from all warriors for the last two attacks on Mary, hoping to convince them to leave her in peace. Reasoning with those in mourning was impossible, and he hoped an overall punishment delivered his message.

Movement caught the corner of his eye again. The maid removed her plate before she finished eating. If picking at one's food made up eating, he'd eat his best bonnet.

Leaning to her, he said, "Mary, ye did not finish eating. Shall I ask Cook for something else?"

She jumped at his inquiry. "No, Roderick, I am not hungry."

He waved to a maid. "Really, it's not a problem."

She grabbed his arm. "I'm fine."

He slid his hand into hers, his gaze searching hers. Mary's face appeared pale and drawn. Shadows appeared under her eyes when she turned to the side. Maybe she wasn't sleeping and was nervous over the attacks?

His eyes roamed the hall, searching for Agatha. Not finding her, he recalled a difficult birthing summoned her to an outer village. She'd be gone for some time.

He vowed after the meal when they were alone, he'd address the attacks, hopefully let her know she was safe in his home. He needed to apologize as well. Today he was angry with himself, with his warriors, and he took it out on her—something he loathed, hurting a woman. It was something he hated in her father and something he would never resort to, even pushed to the limit as he was now.

She pulled her hand from his and stood. "If I may, I am not feeling well. I'd like to retire early."

He stood with her, and all in the hall stood as his action signaled the meal was over. "Continue with yer meal, please."

He turned to her, whispering, "Please join me in the study. I, I have something I must say to ye." He gazed at her in earnest. "Things I need to say, please."

Mary nodded, and he took her hand, placing it on his arm. As they passed Archibald and Rose, Rose pushed to stand, but Mary waved her off. Based upon Rose's wide grin, it seemed Archibald's wooing went well. He hoped by the end of tonight he could say the same.

When they stepped down from the dais, she leaned on him, then sighed. She really wasn't well. He guided them into the study and led her to a chair in front of his desk.

Stepping behind the desk to the spirits, he held up a goblet, and Mary shook her head. Roderick poured a generous amount and took a large gulp. He refilled his cup and came around the desk sitting next to her.

Placing it on his desk, he leaned forward, taking her hand in his. "Mary, I, I owe ye an apology."

"Roderick, no, ye don't. I shouldn't have disobeyed. Although it would be nice if ye told me the rules before I defied them rather than after."

He huffed. She had him there. "This truce is new for all. My clan was hurt and angry but will adjust immediately. But it's not for them I owe an apology, it's me."

She tilted her head and stared at him. He continued, "I hurt ye today. In my anger and frustration with my clan, I hurt ye. I never intended to, and know I will never do so again."

Mary sighed. "I suppose this truce is hard for us all. Two attacks in one day, why I almost feel at home."

Roderick cringed at her attempt at humor. It spoke of the harsh life she'd had, and here where she hoped for a better life, so far it was no different. "Was it truly so bad?"

She rubbed his hands in hers. "Not always. Once Herbert, an older warrior, taught me to use the blade and everyone knew, the advances stopped. Then my father found out, and, well, after his punishments all the men looked to me as their provider. I mended, healed, saw they ate. Especially when times were lean." She shrugged. "I provided."

So much for someone so young. How many years had Mary endured, and how many more before it took its toll on her? She was such a sturdy lass in such a cruel world, all because of her sex. His heart went out to her—he wanted nothing more than to care for her and allow the comforts of the Lady of the Castle, his lady wife.

His hand rose to her face, caressing it. "Mary, who provided for ye?"

She blinked. "God."

Ah, another topic he had to discuss and at Patrick's insistence.

His hand moved away, and he picked up his whisky, taking a generous gulp. "Reverend O'Donnell spoke to me today." Mary's swift intake of breath had him turning to her. "Please don't worry, ye may practice yer religion. But Patrick is right. Some in the clan have converted. I'd like it if ye joined me in Sunday service, private in the chapel, tomorrow."

Mary smiled. "I'd like that."

He sat back in his chair, picked up his cup sipping his whisky. So far, he met his goals for this evening, his apology given, Mary's religion discussed. He took his ease with her, enjoying her company.

Her gaze went to the window, then back to him. She sighed and closed in on herself.

"Aw, now I sense a question the lady wants to ask but won't. Mary, ye can ask me anything."

She stood holding the desk for support and walked to the *Fae Fable Book* in the case by the window. Ah, it had caught her notice, as it did with many who encountered it for the first time. Thankful the Stones of Iona were hidden and safe, the Fae inactive for years, he felt comfortable speaking of his duty to the magic Fae stones. He had never seen one and hoped to never have to.

She bent over the book. "I noticed it the first time I came here seeking some reading. The book is magnificent and the story, or the part we can see intriguing, but the case doesn't open. I want to finish the story."

Roderick set his cup on the table and went to stand next to her. "Aye, the key's lost. The *Fae Fable Book* is an enigma of the family. Given to us by the Fae centuries ago and kept here. But what ye need to know is the quote it left open to."

She bent over the text, and Roderick grabbed a lit candle from his desk.

Mary smiled as he held it for her. "Corinthians?" she bent reading from the book. "And now, these three remain, faith, hope, and love. But the greatest of these is love."

He set the candle down and took her hands in his. An opportunity gifted and one he'd take. His chance to show Mary his intent for their relationship, their marriage.

Her eyes glittered in the candlelight as he spoke. "For love to bind, faith is a prerequisite. Ye must have faith, Mary. And one must also have hope. Please have

60

hope, Mary. The greatest of these is love. I have faith and hope we shall grow to love."

He took a deep breath, wanting her to understand his intent. "But understand, love shall always protect, always trust, always hope, and always persevere." As he spoke each one, he leaned closer to her lips. After whispering the last, he brushed his lips against hers. When she whimpered, he deepened the kiss, taking her into his arms.

Mary wavered, and if she hadn't been in his arms already, she'd have fallen.

He scooped her into his arms and relocated to the chair sitting with her in his lap. Her head fell against his shoulders. "Mary, are ye well, lass?"

She shook her head. "Tired. I need to sleep, so tired."

He caressed her face, noting how pale it was. "I shall call Agatha."

Mary shook her head. "Nonsense. This day has taxed me. A good night's sleep is all I need."

She slipped off his lap and stood stable on her feet. "Please escort me to my room."

Satisfied she wouldn't fall over again, Roderick complied. Taking her hand, they moved out the door. The hall was quiet as it was later than he thought. A maid walked past him, and he bent and whispered, "Douse the candles and fire in the study. I retire for the evening." She nodded, moving past them.

At the top of the stairs, they turned, and her door wasn't far down, his a few steps farther.

At her door, he stopped. "Till tomorrow, lass." He kissed her and stayed till her door closed and the guard positioned in the hall.

Faith, hope, and love—he had faith that Mary and their marriage would work. He held hope that his clan would grow to like her. He already knew, with their first kiss, he loved her.

Chapter 5

The air blew cold on her face. Fresh snow crunched beneath her boots as she took the path to the Chapel in the Woods. The chapel itself was a beautiful creation, a building nearly as regal and gorgeous as Iona Abbey. Rose claimed Archibald said there were few private chapels left and something the MacDougalls treasured. Yesterday the building's beauty had stunned her. As the sun rose and peeked over the chapel's roof line, today she sensed its spiritual connection with the Lord, and she looked forward to the solitude and guidance she'd receive in prayer this day.

Her belly was somewhat full of half of Rose's oats she'd shared this morning. Her ma's voice rang in her mind, *enough is as good as a feast*. She'd been used to living on little, but nothing would deter her from today. Her anticipation welled inside her as she looked forward to a morning of worship. Well, worship with him, Roderick. Mary and Rose stepped near the chapel doorway as the sun glinted off the roof near dawn on this early Sunday morning. The dew sparkled like gems in the morning light, like fairies coming to pray with the humans. Mary loved the stories of the Fae.

A grumbling Fergus, her guard today, trailed behind. "No one in their right mind attends church this early. I doubt God is even up this early."

Mary smiled to herself. God was always with her.

Fergus opened the door, and candlelight lit the room. The scent of the wood fire mixed with the tallow of candles hung heavy in the air.

Roderick stood inside the doorway. "Welcome, Mary, Lady Rose." He bowed to each and offered his arm to Mary. "Mary, join me please? Reverend O'Donnell has marked passages for us to read together." When she stepped into the nave and placed her arm on his, warmth embraced her. She nodded to Rose who retreated to the back of the chapel where Archibald waited. That was nice, someone to pray with Rose as well.

Roderick guided her to the altar where a gold cross with a blue diamond-shaped gem rested in the center. Before the altar the family bible lay open on an ornate stand with a large green jewel in the arm and a quill and ink well nearby.

Roderick stopped her before the large volume. "Ye must record yer name in the family bible." Mary smiled as she shifted her Comyn arisaid from her head and removed her gloves pocketing them in her skirt.

Roderick handed her the quill with a grin. " 'Tis a tradition we honor, one I hope ye honor as well." She dipped the end in ink and moved to sign the paper.

Roderick pointed to the right of the page. "Next to mine, Mary, I've already marked it for our marriage. Space is below for our bairns."

The mention of children brought on a full blush as she stepped closer to the tome. Touched by his care, Mary carefully wrote her full name next to his in formal swirly script as Roderick looked on. Mary Ann, she stopped at her last name almost marking a *C* but slowly wrote MacDougall, matching his name.

She returned the quill to the stand, and when she pulled away, Roderick took her hand in his and kissed the back. "Our marriage, our union recorded for the family." Her gaze connected with his, soft and reassuring.

He escorted her to the front pew and sat with another Bible to his right, her on his left. He picked it up and held it out for her to see. "My Bible from my youth." The small book seemed worn. Creases on the spine marked places he'd opened to often. She wondered what passages moved him and would they be the same as hers? Papers stuck out the top, marking locations in the text. He mentioned Reverend O'Donnell chose some passages for them to read together, pray over. Which ones had he chosen, and what message lay within?

Roderick leaned over and whispered, "Patrick, being a reverend cannot preside over catholic sermons, but he advises and accepts any confession. As an older warrior plus a steadfast advisor and friend to my father, we trust him with our religious guidance." He took her hand and held it on his Bible. "I trust him in his spiritual advice and hope ye can find the same."

Touched by his care Mary placed her other hand over his holding hers. "I shall look forward to it, his trust and yers."

He paused and beheld her face as a smile rested on his. The sun advanced through the window above the altar, lighting them in a halo of sunlight. His black hair reflected purple in the early dawn's light as his grin grew wider. They sat suspended in time as dust flurries danced around them. The moment spoke to Mary, a new beginning for them both.

Roderick was the first to move, pulling the Bible free and flipping the cover aside to the first marked page for them to read and pray over. "Let's see what wisdom Reverend O'Donnell has to share this bright sunny morn."

He held the book a little farther away and read the tab placed on the page. "Mathew 6 passages 14 and 15." He cleared his throat and read on. " 'For if you forgive other people when they sin against you, your heavenly Father will also forgive you. But if you do not forgive others their sins, your Father will not forgive your sins.' "

Roderick glanced at her then back at the book. She felt his apprehension at the chosen quote as he tensed next to her. The quote she was familiar with having read it many a time, praying for forgiveness for her father's actions in the clan war.

He lowered the book and closed the cover as he sighed heavily. Wanting to ease his concern, Mary reached for his hand.

He immediately linked his fingers with hers as he spoke. "Seems Patrick doesn't want to mince words and asks we get straight to the heart of our clan's issues. Forgiveness." He sighed. "Mary, we don't have to discuss this."

She halted him with a squeeze to his hand. "No, I want to discuss this. This quote is most fitting and one I have often prayed over begging forgiveness, praying for an end to the war."

She let go of his hand as her gaze traveled the chapel's interior. One much nicer than the room in her father's castle reserved for prayer, the reverend leaving shortly after her mother's death for a better assignment.

Forgiveness. Could Roderick forgive her father, her clan? Could his clan do the same? She glanced at him, and he stared at the stained-glass window above the altar, the one with a clear cross in it. The sunlight shone through and cast the cross pattern on his body. In him could she find salvation?

"Salvation."

His eyes slid to hers, and a smile creased his face. "Ye just whispered salvation." At her gasp he turned slightly to her. "In my prayers I find the way forward is to show our forgiveness for each other. Our union shall guide the way to healing and salvation for all."

His request seemed so simple yet still a large challenge. Could two people really be the path to peace? Could they forge ahead and prove forgiveness was possible?

She responded with her heart. "I hope we can."

Roderick brushed her cheek, then raised his Bible again. "On to the second quote. Tell me, what do ye think Patrick has chosen?"

Mary shrugged as Roderick flipped his Bible and read aloud for them. "Proverbs 3, passages 5 and 6. 'Trust in the Lord with all your heart, and do not lean on your own understanding. In all your ways acknowledge him, and he will make straight your paths.' "

He hummed as he closed the Bible and set it on the pew beside him. As he gathered her hands, he turned, fully facing her. "Mary, please lean on me, on my understanding. I want this truce to hold. Our union to bind our clans and us." He caressed her cheek. "Trust in me, in us, lass?"

Mary grinned. She'd seen him flip the page to an

unmarked area, a place in his chosen Bible. So, he knew his scriptures well enough to thumb the pages and find what he wanted. A learned man and a caring one as well—to beg for trust when he had all the reasons under the sun not to trust her spoke of his desire for peace—the same as hers.

"Husband, I shall uphold my vows. Trust and honor ye." She sat back, removing herself from his embrace. "But ye shall have to be truthful with yer wife to earn her trust."

Roderick's gasp did not go unnoticed, and she continued before he spoke. "Tell yer wife true. Was that the reverend's quote or yer own?"

Roderick glanced down as a laugh came from him.

When his face returned to hers, his eyes sparkled in mirth. "Well, it seems my wife is wise and canny. Aye, the quote was of my choosing, but my request is in earnest all the same." His hand returned to her face, brushed softly as he gazed into her eyes. "Please trust in me…" His face came closer to hers. Their breaths mingled as he bent for a kiss but stopped short. "…in us?" And brushed his lips against hers.

She whispered her reply. "Truth above all else."

He whispered into the kiss. "Aye."

He deepened his kiss, and her hands grabbed at his coat, gripping to find an anchor in the whirlwind of emotions his kisses ignited.

Reverend O'Donnell's chuckle filled the chapel. "I see my choice in scripture has inspired peace in yer union."

They both broke apart—caught kissing in the chapel. Mary brushed her hair and wondered if it was a sin.

Roderick rose and pulled Mary to stand next to him. "Aye, Patrick, it has." He crossed himself, and Mary did the same. Roderick pulled her from the pew and caught Mary's hand as they walked past the reverend. She paused, curious about what the reverend had to share.

He leaned in close and whispered, "I'm glad for ye both, and the Lord welcomes a kiss from yer husband, Mary." She blushed to the roots of her hairline as Roderick laughed and escorted her from the chapel.

Rose and Archibald followed behind, and Fergus and the reverend brought up the rear.

Mary moved to put her gloves back on, the cold stinging her hands. Roderick switched hands and held hers close as they strolled down the trail to the castle. "Now, we go to the service for the clan, the protestant service." He squeezed her once as they walked side by side, close.

She reveled in his warmth. "Aye, I'm always ready for prayers, no matter the type."

They came through the outer bailey, nearly empty of all. Something Mary hadn't seen since her arrival, the space which usually bustled with activity sat silent and still in the mid-morning light. They climbed the stairs to the wooden double doors, and a guard opened them. Roderick guided her into the great hall, and the clan sat ready for the reverend's Sunday service.

Reverend O'Donnell strolled past them to the front and waved Mary and Roderick to their places at the dais table. Roderick released her as they stepped to their chairs. He nodded to the reverend and sat.

Mary followed, only to have something pierce her backside. She yelped as she jumped up, her hand reaching her stinging rear. As she turned to see what she'd sat on, Roderick held up a small thistle.

She eyed her husband. "Tricks, Milaird?"

He growled, "Not from me, wife. I'd never hurt ye. I vowed it." He threw it into the fire.

She sat gingerly and made no other comment as the reverend began his sermon.

First, the food, then the thistle. What other trickery did her nemesis have? Whatever it was, she was ready. She'd not permit clan MacDougall to take her down without a fight.

****

That afternoon, Mary had just finished her hour with Bruce—the man who drew a knife on her in the training field. Much more subdued than before, she found her time with him well spent. It turned out to be only a rumor that she was a spy. Stern words whispered in haste. The source was unknown to Bruce and quickly dispelled by her actions helping Alister.

She and Rose strode into the main hall as her guard Fergus trailed behind. The maids sat weaving the greenery together. Mary glanced around, not seeing Constance, and winked at Rose as they approached the women. Mary stood back allowing Rose to greet the women, then invite her into the group.

Rose greeted them warmly as she sat and picked up some greenery. "Hello, Mabel. How's the wean this morning?" Rose nodded to the swaddled bairn in the basket. The babe let loose a loud wail that shook the rafters.

Mabel dropped her greenery and scooped up the babe. "Still complaining something fierce, and with Agatha away at a birthing, I'm left to deal with a foul belly." She rocked the baby, holding the infant in a feeding position. *Well, that's not what helps a foul baby's belly.*

Mary stepped up and spoke to Mabel. "Have ye tried holding him upright, like sitting?" Mabel jumped when she spoke, but the baby's loud cry caught her attention. As she bounced the babe, she tried to hold him upright, but the crying continued.

Another maid spoke. "Mabel, yer boy is fit to give us all headaches again."

Rose's gaze connected with Mary's as she nodded to the babe. "Mabel, let Mary hold wee Nal for a bit. Maybe she can help." Mabel gasped as wee Nal wailed loudly enough to call all to the great hall.

She thrust the babe into Mary's outstretched hands. "If a Comyn can calm my babe, I'd thank ye. No one's been able to keep Nal happy."

Mary took the baby and laid him on the table as he huffed a hiccup and fussed, but the crying stopped. She moved his right leg to his chest, allowing him to push her hand back. When she lifted the left one, wee Nal let loose a loud gas blow, startling him. His wide eyes popped open at the sudden burst from his rear end. Then he broke into a wide smile. Mary tickled him, and the babe laughed aloud.

She scooped the infant up and held him, so he sat in the crook of her arm. She rocked back and forth as she spoke to Mabel. "He's gassy, that's all. Likely from ye going without in rationing times." She smiled at the maids, who all stared at her with mouths agape. "Happened to many in my keep. Have ye tried fennel seeds seeped into yer tea?"

Constance stormed the group. "What is she doing

here?"

Her screeching sent wee Nal into a fit again, and Mary handed him back to Mabel. "Nothing more than woman's talk, Constance."

Constance eyed the table filled with greenery. "Ye maids still aren't done weaving the greenery? Back to work!"

She rounded on Mary. "Comyn, ye aren't welcome."

Mary's gaze rested on the maids, who all bowed their heads, none making eye contact. Why should they? Until now, Constance ran the household, and it seemed she still did.

She stepped back and waved Rose off as she made to stand. She addressed the maids. "I didn't mean to keep ye from yer chores. My apologies, please continue yer work. I love the greenery on the holidays and look forward to seeing it in the hall. Thank ye for all yer hard work."

She turned to leave, stopped by Mabel's side, and whispered, "Go to cook for fennel seeds, tell her it's for wee Nal." Mabel nodded and patted her arm but pulled back as Constance cleared her throat.

Another of her ma's quotes came to mind, *A friend in need is a friend indeed*. Mary would win them over, even if it had to be one at a time.

Chapter 6

Roderick entered the great hall for the morning meal, looking forward to spending time with Mary. The clan stood, awaiting his signal that everyone could eat.

He leaned over, speaking to Archibald. "Where are Mary and Rose this day?"

Archibald glanced around. "I have not seen them yet. Last night Rose said I'd see her at the morning meal."

Constance approached and stood behind her seat. "The ladies went to pray in the chapel. They won't be here for the morning meal."

Roderick searched the hall for Reverend O'Donnell, not finding him. He figured the reverend prayed with Mary and hoped to catch her at the midday meal. He hadn't seen her in two days, being called to an outer village, and wanted to catch up with her, see how she was settling.

As he sat signaling the beginning of the meal, he admitted to himself he wanted more than to ask her how she was. He wanted to see her, speak to her. Hell, he wanted to take her in his arms and kiss her senselessly. Sighing as a maid set a bowl of wet oats in front of him, he resigned himself to a day cooped up in his study going over correspondence.

Constance leaned over Archibald. "Roderick, would ye like to stroll with me today in the garden?"

Archibald placed a hand on Constance's shoulders. "Constance, not today. We have a pile of letters to go through since we've been away tending to other matters."

She sat back glaring at him.

Roderick didn't care. It had snowed a couple of days ago and stuck to the ground good. Everything was a muddy mess or covered in snow, not to mention freezing air wasn't his ideal "strolling weather."

He ate, contemplating what Mary might pray about. The clan taking her in. Guidance on how to go about the duties of the lady of the castle, or maybe him? He hoped the latter. Reverend O'Donnell supported the match and promised to help in any way he could.

Constance clanged her spoon in her bowl. "Roderick, ye have not had yer portrait painted as every laird has. I'd like to offer to paint ye, if I may?" The last came out leisurely.

He turned, staring at her. "Paint me?"

Constance huffed. "Aye, a portrait." She ticked off her fingers. "Yer da had one, yer grandfather, and all the lairds before all had a portrait. Ye need one, and I shall be the one to paint it." She stared at him, a twinkle in her eye.

His gaze slid to Archibald, wondering what conniving Constance was up to this time. Over the last year, she'd tried many tricks to get him to marry her. The first was a ride in the countryside last summer where she fell from her horse. Scared him half out of his wits, thinking she hit her head. Turned out it was nothing. The fall was on a picnic, and she tried to kiss him without invitation. He'd stormed off. The last before his leaving for the king's agent's meeting, he found her in his bed, in her chemise leaving nothing to the imagination. He'd started using the lock again and hoped now he was married; her antics would end.

Archibald nodded at their stare. "Constance, Roderick has many duties now that he's *married*—to Mary. I suggest ye find other ways to *entertain* yerself from now on."

Constance leaned over Archibald again. "But Roderick…" Her whiney voice grated on his nerves, bringing on a headache.

Archibald pushed her back into her seat. "Constance. I have warned ye repeatedly. Do I need to send ye back to yer father?"

She sat back, her hand going to her breast. "Ye wouldn't!"

Archibald sat staring at her, and she turned the other way, a sniffle escaping. Let her cry. She'd nearly worn out her welcome, and if his mother wasn't still in mourning, he'd send her home this instant. But with Mary being new, the clan having trouble accepting her, Roderick feared Mary needed all the help she could get.

Frustrated and tired already, Roderick stood and waved to everyone to finish their meal as he strode to his study. Archibald stood and followed. Maybe a day buried in correspondence would take his mind off pressing matters.

****

Four hours later, over a dozen correspondences responded to and Roderick did not feel any better. His worry for Mary increased as the day wore on. What was she doing? How were things going?

"Yer brother-in-law has sent over the reports and monies from the rents this month." Archibald waved a parchment in the air.

Roderick pinched his nose, his headache getting worse. "Let me guess. Times are still tough for the tenants. No one has money and even less to live on."

Archibald tossed the document on the desk as Roderick rose and crossed to the window. "I wonder where Mary is." He glanced out, and the snow fell again. Christmas was a week away, and he hoped the snow would stay. He always enjoyed a snowy holiday. A chance to gather with loved ones, celebrate the birth of Christ, and exchange gifts with those he loved— *Mary's gift*.

He rounded to Archibald. "The tinker is due today, is he not?"

Archibald nodded as he stood and stretched. "Aye, he will have our gifts and a full report." He yawned, then sat down. "I suspect he'll pull in around the midday meal as he usually joins us, then set up his wares. Thank goodness we sent word to my da and caught him for our gift orders."

Roderick turned back to the window. "Ye'll give him our full report?"

Archibald sighed. "Just as we discussed. Everything here is going well. Mary and Rose are adjusting well. The clan has set aside their differences. She and ye are getting along well."

Roderick huffed. "Ye got a spy on the tinker the entire time he's in the keep? As we discussed. In case anyone approaches him about anything? I need to ken if we have spies among us."

He turned as Archibald chuckled. "Ye know there are spies here, Roderick. Just as ye have spies in Comyn's keep, it's been that way for years."

Roderick crossed, sitting at his desk. "Aye, it wouldn't surprise me if they didn't all camp together, share information, and then have a good laugh."

A knock sounded at his door, and Roderick spoke loudly. "Enter."

A guard, Angus, opened the door. "The tinker's arrived, and midday meal is ready, Milaird."

Roderick stacked his papers, placed them in the drawer, and locked it, pocketing the key in his sporran. "Come, Archibald, enough of clan business. I'm hungry."

Both men followed the guard into the hall. Everyone stood ready for the midday meal. The tinker caught his eye, smiled, and waved. Good, his gift was ready. He hoped Mary liked it. He had it made especially for her. Archibald had something made for Rose but had been secretive about what it might be. Roderick suspected he knew but would wait to guess, not wanting to ruin any surprise his long-time friend planned.

As they approached the dais, he noted the women were absent again. "Where is she?"

Constance replied, "Mary and Rose are keeping to their rooms. They've just returned from the chapel. Frozen they were. Cook sent some warm soup and tea. They wish to stay there, undisturbed."

Roderick hadn't realized he'd spoken aloud until she replied. Well, at least they were safe in the castle, away from the chill and behind the gates.

He nodded to Archibald, who spoke loud for the hall as the reverend was not at the meal. "Bless our food."

He sat as a maid set his plate before him. He

stopped her with his hand. "Have ye seen Mary?"

She shook her head. "Not since yesterday, Milaird."

He nodded, then stopped her again. "Rose?"

She shook her head again. "Rose said she'd help us with the hanging of the greenery. Said Mary would love to help as well. I was keen on it. Mary's done some nice things for people lately."

Constance shifted in her seat, her spoon clattering.

The maid jumped, then bowed. "Milaird."

He waved, dismissing her. Strange, he knew Mary mentioned she loved the greenery, had wanted to be part of the decorating of his hall. Rose as well. He bent into his soup, the rich flavors of potatoes, leeks, and onion filling his mouth, reminding him of his childhood—warm soup on snowy days after working in the cold.

Archibald stood, signaling the tinker.

Roderick stood. "Everyone, finish yer meal, enjoy at yer leisure." He strode, following Archibald into the bailey, deciding to be present for the update. The tinker was already beside his wagon, retrieving their orders.

Archibald clapped the tinker on the back. "Joseph, how are ye this fine cold day?"

Joseph turned, holding out three fabric bags. "Good and well, thank ye for asking." He passed one small bag to Archibald. "As ye asked. I made sure the size is right."

Archibald said, "Shhh, 'tis a surprise. Not even Roderick knows." He winked at the tinker, who winked back. Joseph handed his bag over, coins jingling at the exchange. Well, Roderick supposed Rose was going to have one joyous holiday.

The tinker turned to him, his smile wide. "I know ye asked for tin. But being the laird and all, I got a great deal on silver. I had the smithy in Oban make it as ye requested."

He handed Roderick the first bag. "The same as who yer da used, the price lowered because of the smaller size. Sends his best to ye and wishes ye wedded bliss." Roderick opened the bag and upended the pendant, a duplicate of his mother's and grandmother's. The chain and pendant of high quality spilled into his hand. He rubbed his thumb over it, hoping Mary liked his gift and the meaning behind it.

The tinker handed him the second bag, his expression somber. "I had him make it to yer specifications, a small heart the length of my finger as ye wrote me." A perfect size. Now. His da's stone would have a resting place his ma could treasure.

Every captain on Loch Etive carried an Iona stone, a good luck charm from the old fable of the fisherman using a Gaelic charm to ward off a Fae spell. His parents had matching stones, each in the shape of a heart his father had carved. One for each to hold while the other was away, to hold each other's heart. His eyes watered, and he blinked as he closed the locket and placed it back in the bag.

He pulled a coin bag from his sporran and handed it to Joseph.

He took the coins and nodded as he spoke. "Yer da was a right great man, Roderick. We all miss him."

Roderick nodded. "Thanks, Joseph. What news do ye bring?"

Joseph's grin went wide. "Good tidings from the common land to the east. The laird, while put out from losing his maid, servant, and housekeeper, is right happy with a new guest. Calls him his second chance son or second son."

Roderick's eyebrows rose.

The tinker nodded. "Aye, it surprised most at first, but those close to him… Well, they knew he pined for a boy instead of the girl."

Archibald blew a huff, and Roderick agreed. Mary's father was an idiot. Mary was so much more. Malcolm as his second son, not likely. He probably kept him close and brainwashed him. Roderick sighed. He hadn't had a chance to warn the lad before they took him, but he'd ensure they had a private word on his first visit.

Roderick stared at him. "The second son. How does he fare?"

Joseph clapped him on the arm. "Taken into the bosom of the clan, he was. Given the girl's room and trains with the warriors daily. He's faring well, Milaird."

Roderick breathed a sigh of relief. Malcolm fared well and did not suffer. This was good.

Joseph smirked at both men. "So, the devil's bride, how does she fare?"

Roderick barked a laugh. "Devil's bride? Try devil's daughter, and she's faring very well."

It was Joseph's turn to laugh. "Aye, so ye say. I have yet to speak to yer people. Let's hope they say the same since I don't see the pretty lass at all. Whenever I stopped by the Comyn's, she was always the first to make it to my wagon." He glanced around the bailey. "Strange, she's not around."

Roderick folded his arms. "She's resting, as is

Rose." He needed to get Joseph off the subject of Mary. "What's the talk around the devil's clan?"

Joseph shook his head. "Talk of reviving the wars, even with the king's orders. It's not good, Milaird. Peace between ye both again, after all these years, would be welcomed by many."

Roderick glanced at Archibald, then back at Joseph. "The talk, is it from my villages or the devil's?"

Joseph leaned in, whispering, "Both, Milaird. But yers comes from the north. The devil's is everywhere. Seems the Comyn clan is still itching for war."

Archibald raised his eyebrows. "The north? That border is my clan. Is it my clan poking the snake in the bushes?"

Joseph shrugged. "Hard to tell, but I'd check into it if I were ye." His eyes moved past the men. "Gossip time's up. Here comes a gaggle of women I hope are heavy with coin." He rubbed his hands together as a group of maids approached the wagon.

Talk from his own clan and the Comyn to go against the king's orders. This wasn't good. He needed to keep control of his people.

Roderick pulled Archibald aside. "I don't like it. Talk from our own. Tensions are still high, and it would take a minor incident, then control would falter—the wars renewed. I don't want to leave Mary for more than a day being a Comyn amid MacDougalls."

Archibald nodded. "Agreed. I'll send warriors to my clan to find out who's stirring the pot. Put an end to it now."

Roderick nodded. "Pick three guards to send. Ensure one is familiar with yer clan."

Archibald nodded and strode to the warrior's area,

where some gathered waiting for a turn with the tinker, giving the women first choice.

He glanced around the bailey. Why wasn't Mary here for the tinker? He said she always visited him, and where was Rose? A sense of unease skidded down his spine. Something wasn't right. He couldn't place it, but there was that offset feeling.

Where was Mary?

He strode through the bailey, through the great hall doors, not stopping for the many people who greeted him. He took the stairs, hurried up them, turned the corner, and arrived outside Mary's room.

Everything seemed normal. Robbie stood in the hall, leaning against the wall.

Roderick approached him, and Robbie took notice and stood tall. "Milaird."

Roderick nodded. "The women, they are inside?"

Robbie grinned. "Been here all morning."

Roderick glanced at the door. "What do ye mean all morning? I was told they visited the chapel."

Robbie shrugged. "Nope, had a maid visit three times. She left in a huff the last time. But the women, they've not been out all day."

That can't be right. Constance said they went to pray.

Roderick knocked on the door, waiting for permission to enter.

Rose cracked the door, peeking out with one eye. "Roderick!" She glanced behind her, then back at him, keeping the door cracked.

He tried to look past her, but all he could see was the bed's edge. "I've come to check on ye. Where's Mary?"

Rose stepped from foot to foot. Roderick's heart sped up. Something was wrong.

Roderick pushed the door open. Rose squeaked and jumped back as the door banged against the wall. The sight that greeted Roderick knocked the breath from him. Mary lay in her bed, still not dressed for the day. Her head lay near the side, her hair disheveled and her face pale as the full moon. A bucket sat beside her on the floor.

He went to her, brushing the hair from her face. She turned into the caress and moaned.

He came close to shouting. "What is wrong? What has happened?"

Robbie followed him in. "She looks ill, Milaird."

Roderick glanced back. "Out in the hall, Robbie, close the door. No one comes in without my permission. And Robbie…"

At Roderick's growl, Robbie stopped halfway, closing the door. "Ye will tell no one, not a word. And we'll discuss yer *guarding* shortly."

Robbie gulped and closed the door.

He turned back to Mary, her skin pale and cold to the touch. No fever. He glanced into the bucket, drops only, no vomiting. What could make her ill?

He stood and turned to Rose. "Explain. What ails her?"

Rose put her hands on her hips. "Oh, don't be acting like this is my fault. I tried to help and begged her to come to ye. But she wouldn't, stubborn as she is. What's wrong with her! The question is, what's wrong with yer cook, yer maid, and yer whole clan?"

Folding his arms, he questioned her again. There had to be more to this. "What do ye mean? Explain it to me and leave no detail out."

Mary moaned. Rose nudged past him, wetting a cloth and pressing it to her forehead. "Yer people, Laird, they're starving her."

He stood at the end of her bed, as Rose tended to his wife. "Starving her? I've seen food on her trencher every meal."

Rose patted the cloth over Mary's face as a grimace of pain crossed it. "Salted to the point of inedible is the food ye have seen. They refuse to feed her when ye aren't there, and when ye are, it's salted. The ale's rotten, and no water or wood comes to her room." She returned the cloth to the bowl and stared at Mary. "We tried trading plates, were successful most times. Other times a maid snatched it away before Mary had but a bite."

She stood facing him. "Yer clan, Roderick, is trying to kill her by starvation. She's so weak she couldn't get up this morning, and as the day wore on, her condition worsened."

His eyes moved to Mary, motionless now, her pale skin near translucent. "How long?" He nearly choked on his whisper. "How long has this been going on?"

Rose's gaze went to Mary. "Since we arrived."

"Two weeks? What of her maid, the one who's assigned to serve her?"

Rose huffed. "What maid? Her hearth she lights herself, and no one's changed her bedding. I've served her."

Rage boiled within him. His clan taking the wars out on a defenseless female. His wife, their lady. Against his orders. He must find out who the saboteur was. Punishment would be harsh and swift.

He strode to the door, pulling it open so hard he almost yanked it off its hinges.

Robbie leaped at the sudden appearance of his laird. Good, they all should be jumping because Roderick was just getting started.

"Send someone to the village, silently. No scenes, no panic. Tell Agatha to come to the castle and bring her healing basket. Tell her to make it like a social visit."

Robbie nodded and turned.

Roderick's growl filled the hall. "I wasn't done."

Robbie turned back, his shoulders near his ears that Roderick wanted to box hard. "Ask Archibald to come to Mary's room now. Cook, send her to me immediately."

Roderick turned to the room, then glanced back. "Robbie, the five chosen guards for Mary."

Robbie nodded.

Roderick's voice held an edge of steel as he spoke. "Ye will await me outside my study. Ye will stay there, standing at attention till I come to ye. All of ye. Anyone who doesn't obey will get lashes, understood?"

Robbie's eyes went wide, and he nodded slowly as he backed down the hall. Roderick had never ordered lashes as punishment. The last time his father had, he was still a youth. Let that sink into the men.

Roderick closed the door and leaned his head against it, praying her illness was merely weakness from lack of food. As if the king's order wasn't enough to deal with, if Mary was truly ill…

He spun, going to the bed. He took Mary's hand in his and caressed her cheek. "Mary, can ye hear me?"

She moaned and turned her head, her eyes slightly

opened. "Rose, am I dreaming? I see Roderick."

He bent close, holding her hand in his. "Aye, Mary. I'm here, and we'll have ye better in no time."

There was a knock at the door, and Archibald peeked in.

Rose went to him, pulling him in. "Archibald, I'm so glad ye are here."

He glanced at the bed. "Why is Mary still abed? Is she ill?"

Rose whimpered with a nod, and Archibald took her into his arms. "Rose, why didn't ye come for help?"

She lifted her head. "I begged the maid. I begged for food, for a healer, for help." Tears fell as she sniffled. "She said no one cared."

Roderick stood, dropping Mary's hand, and roared, "No one cared? What is the meaning of this? Have I lost all control of my clan?"

A knock sounded, and the cook, Bertha, peeked in. "Milaird, ye called?" Her eyes fell on Mary in the bed as she stepped into the room. "What ails the lass?"

Roderick folded his arms. "What ails the lass, as if ye didn't know. Ye'rer starving her!"

Bertha fisted her hands. "I do no such thing. She's had the same as everyone else. Had a maid bring it to her each meal, whether here or in the hall."

She glanced at Mary, then back at him. "I've served this family since ye was in swaddlings, Roderick. I'd hurt no one here. Don't ye dare question me. I'll call yer ma I will."

Rose stepped forward. "We both came to ye, begged for help. Ye denied us."

Bertha barked back, "I sent everything to ye. Ye should have no need of more."

Roderick growled, "Which maid?"

Bertha shrugged. "She volunteered. No one wanted to serve her. I had a right hard time getting anyone to help."

Roderick was losing his patience. "Which maid?"

Bertha glanced between Archibald and Roderick. "Ester, Constance's maid."

Constance again—he would deal with her soon, but for now, he needed to tend to Mary, and quickly.

He pinched his nose, a headache coming on, and would likely not leave for days. "First, ye will assign someone to serve Mary. Someone ye trust yer life with and will do as told."

Bertha nodded. "My niece, Fiona. I'll send for her right away."

He turned, staring at Mary. "Broth, she needs something now. Ye will personally bring all her food until Fiona arrives, and only she will deliver it. Tell everyone it's for me. As a matter of fact, all her food is to come to me first."

Bertha turned to leave as Roderick turned his head. "Bertha, tell no one. Nothing is wrong. I'm spending time with my wife."

She nodded and left the room.

Archibald released Rose and pulled him aside. "I noticed no one guarded the door. The five guards?"

Roderick stood at the foot of her bed. "I put them outside my study awaiting punishment. Let them stand for an hour, then put them on cleaning the latrine shoots that haven't been cleaned already."

Rose moved to Mary, patting the cloth on Mary's head again. How did it come to this?

Roderick fisted his hands as he stared at his

captain, his longtime friend. "When did I lose control of the clan? Why would they do something like this?"

Archibald patted his shoulder. "I don't think ye have lost control. I feel it's one trying to gain revenge by tainting her food. The rest are only treating her poorly."

The door opened. Agatha strode in and abruptly came to a halt, her glance taking in the room. "Well, I can see why ye called for me, Milaird. Thankfully I was in the hall."

She went to Mary as Rose stepped aside. She placed her hand on Mary's forehead and set her basket on the bed. "No fever, yet her skin is pale. She's cold." She peered into the bucket. "Not vomiting."

Roderick spoke as Mary began shivering. "I checked for poisoning already, knowing what belladonna poison reactions look like. No poisoning, but there's nothing in her. Someone's tried to starve her."

Archibald stepped through the door. "I'll guard till we can figure out who to trust." He smiled at Rose before he closed the door. "It will be all right now, lass. Agatha's here."

Agatha sat on the bed. "I'll need broth for starters."

She turned to Rose. "Rose, is it?" And at Rose's nod, Agatha grinned. "Good, build up the fire, boil some water."

Rose shrugged. "No wood, no pot, no nothing."

Agatha huffed, but it was Roderick who replied. "They treated her like a prisoner. Barely gave her food and water, nothing to wash with. Nothing to heat her room." He sighed. "And all she did was marry me."

Archibald came in with the cook, who handed the

mug to Agatha.

Roderick held his hand out. "Wait." He stepped forward, grabbed the cup, and sipped it. No salt, only light chicken broth with a hint of spices. He handed it to Agatha. "I will taste everything. Bertha, from now on, we share a trencher at every meal."

Agatha took the cup and addressed Bertha. "This room is cold. There's no fuel for a fire, no pot, and no water. I trust ye can tend to that?"

Bertha eyed Agatha. They'd had their run-ins before but served without issue.

Bertha nodded. "I'll fetch it personally." She spun, exiting the room.

Archibald waved to Rose. "Come, Rose, we'll get ye something to eat and rest for ye. Roderick and Agatha can tend Mary."

To Roderick, he said, "Douglas, yer da's old advisor, is guarding. I'll check back soon."

Rose went to Archibald and then stopped speaking to Roderick. "She wanted to take care of this on her own, to earn her place with the women, the clan. She's gone hungry before. I don't know what's taken her so low." She glanced at Mary as a tear fell down her cheek. "She's my friend, the only one I have. Please help her."

Roderick nodded. Care for her, he thought he had.

Rose followed Archibald out the door, and he shut it quietly.

Agatha set the mug on the bedside table. "I'll need help sitting her up. Come on and use those muscles of yers."

Roderick moved to the bedside and carefully lifted Mary, propping her against the pillows that Agatha reset. When he set her back, she shivered harder, and her head lolled to the side.

Growling, Roderick rounded the bed, kicked his boots off, and crawled under the covers. He took Mary into his arms wanting to warm her. Her body felt like a rag doll, loose and weak. He set her head on his shoulder and reached toward Agatha, who handed him the mug.

He tilted it till some dribbled into Mary's mouth, making her cough. "Come on, Mary, I need ye to drink this."

She sighed. "No more salt."

Douglas opened the door holding it. Bertha marched in putting the bag of firewood beside the fireplace. She bent building up the fire and set the pot of water on the hook. She stood and nodded to Agatha, then marched out the door. Douglas closed it softly.

Agatha turned to Mary muttering, "That one's got to be dealt with." Her scrutiny came back to Roderick as he tried to get Mary to drink the broth. "Got yerself in a pickle this time, laddie." That was no understatement. Mary ill—should the king learn of it? What then? Would they come for him?

Mary drank a little of the broth. If her father, Robert, Laird Comyn learned of this treachery? Would he retaliate and hurt Malcolm? God, he hoped not. The "second son" sounded nice now; it protected his brother.

Agatha moved to her basket and began pulling herbs, setting them near the foot of the bed. Sorting her herbs, she hummed. "I can hear yer mind churning, Roderick. She'll be fine. She's heathy and used to going without. Her color's weak, but she's got no fever.

No powerful odor comes from her, no blackening of her nails, so no poison. I figure a day or two and she'll be up on her feet again."

He had her sip some more, then handed the mug to Agatha. "I can't lose her, Agatha. And not for the king's order and not for the clan."

The day he first spotted her flashed through his mind. Mid-battle and he turned to command the next wave to attack the Comyn wall. She came into his sight line, a lass on the ramparts who stood staring at him. He stopped and watched her as the battle waged around them.

She was beautiful, her golden-brown locks flying about her as she floated above him like a siren from mythology, half-woman, and half-bird. His heart thudded, and he sensed he drifted. She opened her mouth but said nothing. He felt a connection, something ethereal and unearthly. "My soul mate" floated through his mind. Someone passed in front of him, and Archibald ran someone through at his side, the yell startling him from his daze. When he turned back, she was gone.

His hand caressed her face. "*I* can't lose her."

Chapter 7

Awareness came over Mary, warm and toasty snuggled in her bed. She'd never been this comfortable before. Light musk mixed with clean bed linens came to her. A heartbeat sounded, and the pillow she rested her head on moved up then down as a faint snore came from above.

Mary's eyes snapped open to find herself lying on a man's enormous chest as he slept with his arms wrapped around her and his legs tangled with hers.

She let out a squeak and pushed away, shocked to find herself in bed with a man.

The arms tightened, stopping her movement as a husky voice came from the man. "Careful, Mary, I have ye."

Roderick, she was in his arms, in his bed. How did…wait. Her eyes traveled her room that was lit in early dawn's light. She was in her bed. Roderick was in her bedroom, in her bed. How did this happen? She didn't recall any of the previous day.

She tilted her head back, staring into Roderick's face. His expression soft in the early morning light.

"How did ye get here? Why are ye in my bed?"

His hand caressed her cheek. "Ye were ill, unable to warm or feed yerself. As yer husband, I took it upon myself to heal ye."

She stared at his naked chest, peeking through the

V in his shirt. It all came back. Yesterday she nearly starved. She'd woken so hungry. The rest of the day was a blur. She recalled seeing him in a dream. Him caring for her, feeding her. People came and went. She shook her head, and a wave of dizziness overcame her.

She must have tilted sideways since Roderick grabbed her shoulders. "Careful, lass, ye still seem weak." He set her aside and turned, retrieving something from the bedside table.

She curled her hand under her chin as she laid her head on the pillow, missing his warmth. His broad back shifted, and he turned back, holding a cup and bread. He extended his arms open in invitation to her. Blushing, she turned back to him, using his shoulder as a pillow, the warmth returning.

He wrapped his arms around her and brought the cup and bread together. "Break off a small piece of bread, dunk it in the ale, and eat."

She complied, the cold of the ale smooth on her throat, the bread settling in her stomach. She broke off another piece and sat up as her stomach growled.

Roderick chuckled, his chest shaking. "Careful, Mary, only a little for now. Yer belly's been empty for a while. Too much and it will come back up."

She ate another bite, slurping the ale from her chin.

"While I like ye eating from my hand, I like my shirt clean as well." He handed her the cup and bread, but kept her in his arms, holding her to him.

After a few more bites, Roderick took and set the items one by one on the table, not moving her from his arms.

She went with him, enjoying the feel of his muscles moving against her body. His warmth kept her toasty.

He stared at her for a moment. Under his scrutiny, she fidgeted. Was he angry? Would he yell and rail like her father? What had she done, and what would the consequence be? Her heart pounded. What was to come?

"Why didn't ye come to me, Mary? If my clan was mistreating ye, I'd want to know."

She shrugged and glanced down, picking at the bedding. "I wanted to do this on my own, not seem weak."

His thumb tilted her head till her eyes met his. "Mary, ye near starved. What would happen if ye became seriously ill?"

That's what he's angry about, the king's order. If she was not well, he'd be in trouble with the king unable to keep his promise.

She pushed away from him. "Well, I didn't die, so ye don't have to worry about the king. Ye can tell yer clan I'm stronger than they think. I'll live, no matter how hard they try to kill me."

His arms tightened on her, holding her in place as she spoke.

When he spoke, his voice came out hard. "Mary, that is not what I meant. Why allow yerself to suffer? I never would expect that from ye, and the people behind it will find only punishment."

His arms relaxed as he took a deep breath, his voice softer. "Mary, what I meant is, I don't want ye ill. Ye worried me. I want my wife by my side. I want to get to know ye. Make something of our marriage."

She peeked at him. Was what he said true? He wanted her. Wanted them? "Ye like me?"

He smiled, "Aye, very much."

She snuggled into his warm chest. "I enjoyed waking in yer arms. Ye are so warm."

He bent, brushing his lips against hers. "Ye can wake like this every morn. In my arms, to my kisses."

Her stomach growled, and Roderick chuckled into the kiss. "But, wife, we can't have ye hungry all the time." He reached for the cup and handed it to her. "Drink the ale. Yer belly is rattling something fierce."

Glancing back at the table, he reached for something.

When he turned back, settling her in his arms, he held the mistletoe sprig. "Ye kept the mistletoe from the Abbey."

She swallowed. "Aye, I always put it in the greenery for the holidays for luck. I wanted to here, but I guess that's not happening. The women tied the evergreens without me. It's my favorite part of the holidays. I'm sure they've hung it by now. I noticed no one gathered mistletoe."

He twisted the sprig between his fingers, allowing it to spin. "Gather mistletoe for the holidays?"

As the sprig twirled, she wished she had more for decorations. "My mother started the tradition. Each Christmas we cut greenery boughs and bring them indoors to symbolize life, rebirth, and renewal. She always spoke about it as we worked. The ancient people believed the Yuletide greenery had power over death because their green never faded. Thus, evergreens were used to defeat winter demons and hold back death and destruction."

She sipped the ale, finishing the cup. "'My mother said, the Yuletide greenery was to encourage the sun's return because of their strength and tenacity. The Druids held nothing more sacred than mistletoe and the tree on which it is growing, a hard oak. Druids considered mistletoe to be magical because it can grow without soil. We add the mistletoe to the evergreen for luck. We kiss under it at Yuletide to bring fortune and favor to the couple for the next year."

He hummed as he held the sprig. "Kissing under the mistletoe at the new year."

Roderick placed the mistletoe over her head and brushed a soft kiss. "For luck."

The door opened.

With a yelp, Mary hid under the covers.

Agatha's voice came to her as she closed the door and traveled about the room. "Enough, ye two."

Roderick's laugh shook her, and he shifted, holding her tighter. "I'm enjoying my wife's good health."

Agatha sighed. "Roderick, she's still weak. I hope ye didn't overtax her. She needs her rest."

He turned to her, and his body brushed against hers, letting her know just how much he enjoyed holding her.

She gasped, and he dipped under the covers, kissing her. She closed her eyes as he moved her, fitting them together, his body hard and hers soft. He deepened the kiss, opening her mouth with his tongue, and tingles floated over her entire body as his tongue danced with hers.

There was a loud smack. Roderick jolted, his teeth bumping into hers. "Ouch! Agatha, why swat my arse?"

Roderick tossed the covers aside, exposing both their heads, mussing their hair.

Agatha stood over the bed, her finger shaking at

Roderick. "Well, don't stick it out of the covers, bare as the day ye was born." She folded her arms. "Out of the bed, both of ye. I've ordered a bath and oats for the lass. Roderick, ye can bathe and break yer fast in the kitchens."

He snuggled into Mary. "I can break my fast here. Save water and bathe with my wife."

Mary gasped as Agatha raised her eyebrows. "I suspect yer wife might take issue with that, Roderick. Go on with ye now."

The door opened, and Angus hefted the half bath into the room, setting it by the fire. He bent and built up the fire as Robbie, Douglas, and Fergus, three of the other guards assigned to Mary, hauled in buckets of steaming water, each dumping them into the tub. Oh, a real bath. She'd not had one in so long.

Roderick pecked her on the cheek and rose from the bed. "I thought yer guards had a punishment coming."

Hamish followed, carrying folded sheets. "Turns out the latrine shoots are clean from all the other punishments. We must serve Mary until she's well."

Hamish's eyes roamed to Roderick's front, and he laughed. "Seems ye've had yer own kind of punishment, Milaird. Did we interrupt?"

Roderick picked up his tartan covering his front, but Mary got a peek, and the bulge was obvious. She blushed to her toes as she turned away.

The three with buckets marched out, laughing as Roderick wrapped his plaid around him, not bothering to fold it. He picked up his belt and boots from the floor.

Eyeing Agatha, he bent and kissed Mary on the

cheek again. "I'll see ye later today, this I promise."

As he strode from the room, Angus called back, "Kissie, kissie Roddie!"

Agatha turned on Angus. "Out with ye too!"

Angus huffed and moved out the door, closing it.

Agatha smiled at her. "I knew ye'd feel better by morning, but a bath and washed hair will make ye feel like a new woman. Up with ye, lass."

****

Roderick strode through the hall half-dressed, not caring what anyone saw. On a mission to right the wrongs to Mary, his list grew in his mind.

Bertha approached with a tray of food. "For yer lady wife. Would ye like to check it, Milaird?"

He scooped a spoonful of oats into his mouth. The sweet taste of honey and the warm oats brought a growl from his belly. Good, the kitchens were now more mindful of Mary's food and should have her fully healed by dinner.

Ah, tonight, which brought him to the next item on his list. "Bertha, gather the maids. The greenery is to come down."

At Bertha's snort, he patted her arm. "Temporarily. The men will gather mistletoe, and then the maids will weave it into the greenery and rehang before Christmas Eve. 'Twill be a new tradition."

Bertha grumbled. " 'Tis a bad omen, Milaird, to take down the greenery after it's hung."

Bad omen or not, the days of thwarting Mary's attempts to run the keep as a lady should, to be a part of the clan, end now.

He strode away calling over his shoulder, "And ye will ensure Mary oversees it."

He moved toward the kitchens, and Archibald fell in step. "Yer five guards are working overtime helping with Mary. I set Rose to rest. Is Mary better?"

The memory of their shared moment this morning came back to him. Her sweet kisses stirred him again.

"Aye, she's recovering."

He went through the doorway to the vacant kitchen, and the screen for the bath sat in the corner. Moving behind it, he found a steaming tub of water, clean tartan, shirt, and woolens for his boots.

Bertha knew her job and worked hard to prove her dedication to her laird. He hadn't lost full control. Dropping his load with a thud and stripping his shirt, he climbed into the tub, lowering into the heat with a sigh.

Archibald grunted. "A little yelling and they treat ye like a woman. The water's even scented." He sniffed. "Sandalwood."

His favorite. Ignoring the jab at his bath, he lathered up as he recited the rest of his list to his captain. "Gather some men, using the five guards still serving punishment. Go to the north oak grove and gather mistletoe, as much as ye can carry but leave some to grow the next year."

Archibald folded his arms. "Mistletoe? Ye want warriors to gather mistletoe?"

Roderick bent forward and dunked his head in the water, came up, and splashed some at Archibald who jumped back with a chuckle.

"Aye, mistletoe. Mary will oversee the weaving of it into the greenery for Christmas. A new tradition that we will honor each year."

Archibald nodded and turned to leave. "Done."

Roderick turned to him. "Archibald."

At his quiet command, his captain stopped.

"Constance, she returns to her father. Her maid Ester with her."

His captain cleared his throat. "I've already learned she is behind Mary's condition and was going to summon her when ye are ready."

Archibald stood a moment as he soaped his hair. He sensed what subject came next. It was the next item on his list.

He dunked his head rinsing it and came up without splashing his captain. "I'll speak to my ma today. Ye are right. I need her help, with Mary, with the clan. I should have gone to her when the summons came, but I didn't want to upset her."

Roderick sighed. "She will take it hard, but I'll need her help." He ran a hand through his hair. "How do I tell her...her wish for grandchildren will come true but only by a Comyn, the clan who murdered her true love."

Archibald shook his head. "I do not envy ye, Roderick. Yer ma was a lot to handle before her confinement. Now, she's nearly impossible. Bereft in grief." His captain sighed. "Picking mistletoe is a better duty than yer ma."

****

Roderick stared at his mother in her chair before the window. The room was dark, and the warm fire and the window were the only light casting her in shadow. He'd allowed this to go on for too long. She needed to join the living again.

She spoke from her chair, her commanding voice reducing him to youth again. "Ye seek my help. The Comyn girl had a run-in with that nasty Ross chit. I always disliked her."

Roderick blew a huff. "My ma, with spies in her own home. I should learn from the best." He stood chastised by the only person still living capable of it. She humbled him.

She rose and turned, her age not marring her beauty. "Ye should have come to me when the orders came from the king. Yer father and I discussed this idea of a wedding as a truce. It was my idea ye know. Ye and Mary."

He smiled. "I knew about the proposal but not about it being yer idea. Mary's mom was yer best friend. Until…"

She sucked in a breath, and her hand went to the heart pendant at her breast, a gift from his da to her, his true love. What rested inside was an even greater treasure, a magic Iona Stone, the Stone of Love. Today it did not glow. Her true love was not near.

She fingered it as she stared at him. "We were true loves, yer father and I." She sighed. "I would rather have a few years of wonderful than a lifetime of nothing special."

Roderick stepped forward, his hand going out to her.

She took it and held it closer to her. "Ye are such a gift in a son, and already a great laird."

Patting his cheek, she grinned. "Time to join the world again? I suppose I'm finished feeling sorry for myself. And I couldn't leave Mary's daughter alone, in a sea of the enemy." She huffed. "Her father, yes, but Mary's bairn, now a grown woman, no."

His ma was a remarkable woman. He should have known she'd already figured all this out. She was the brains behind every tactic the clan used. He should have seen it at the beginning. This was more a battle of wits to get his clan to accept Mary.

She stepped past him, heading for the door. "I can hear yer brain from here, son. Yer first mistake was not placing her in yer bed from the start. The clan sees it as ye rejected her."

He gasped. "Rejecting her! Ma, I *respected* her and allowed her time. The king forced us to bed *with witnesses*."

She stopped at the door. "Aye, heard about that too. At least some of my cunning has passed to ye. But ye're still as thickheaded as yer da. Move her to yer bed, virgin or no. Ye need to consummate the marriage. I suspect it won't be too difficult. I've seen the girl. Her beauty is richer than her ma's." She opened the door and moved through it. Over her shoulder she called, "Get on with it, son. I won't get any grandbabies till ye do."

Roderick stood in the empty room stunned at all the information his ma had. He must find out how she cultivated all these spies. He needed some for himself. Women, they were the real backbone to the keep.

Chapter 8

Mary sat in the window seat in her room and gazed at the loch. The built-in seats, a comfort she'd not had in her father's castle, were a place for rest and respite. Feeling better after a bath and full meal of oats, Mary pondered her morning. She woke in Roderick's arms, a shock for certain but a welcomed surprise. His warmth and care touched her. As his body wrapped around hers, he woke sensations in her she'd not felt before. The flutter in her chest when he held her as he fed her nearly stopped her breath, and when he'd kissed her, her stomach flipped like the gypsy tumbler who visited her father's castle last year. Her finger went to her lips as they tingled in a reminder of Roderick's kisses, and if the bulge in his shirt was any indicator of him as a man, as her previous maid said, "The more gifted a man is, the happier the wife."

Mary giggled as a knock tapped on her door.

She rose and crossed to the door. When she opened it, Hamish stood there with a grin on his face.

She smiled. "Aye?"

He stepped back, and a tall woman in all black stood behind him. Strands of gray, well, more like silver, lined the woman's pulled-back hair. Her regal stance immediately told Mary this was Lady MacDougall, Roderick's mother. Mary knew she was in her fifties, but her face appeared younger, her father being close to the lady's age.

Roderick's mother lifted an eyebrow as she spoke. "Are we to stand here gawking at each other all day, or will ye invite me in?"

Mary stepped back and opened the door wider. "Apologies, Milady."

Lady MacDougall strode by as Mary gave a small curtsey—the lady moved gracefully as she strolled with purpose.

Lady MacDougall turned when she reached the center of the room. "Well, shut the door and invite me to sit."

Mary complied and crossed past her to the window seat. "Please sit, Milady." She stood beside the benches and waved to the one opposite.

Roderick's mother kept her gaze on her as she crossed and sat.

She glimpsed out the window as she spoke. "I always liked this room. It's the only one in the castle with these seats."

The lady turned to focus on Mary as she sat properly with her hands folded, her feet crossed, as she kept her back straight. The few lessons from her mother rang in her head as she wanted to appear as a lady for Roderick's mother.

"Shall I call for tea, Milady?"

Lady MacDougall waved her hand. "Midmorning? No, thank you unless ye want some. Though I suspect after this morning's events, ye'll be able to get about anything ye want from Bertha." She huffed. "I had a mind to kick that Ross chit out long ago. Good that she'll get what she deserves."

Mary tilted her head to the side. Ross chit. Did she

mean Constance?

The lady's laughter came brightly. "Aye, I can tell from yer expression ye don't know. 'Twas her maid that served ye this whole time. Volunteered and, I suspect, at the lady's instruction. Roderick will do right by ye, or I'll tan his hide."

Mary nodded at the admission but wasn't sure about kicking her out. She glanced down, wondering where Constance would go.

Lady MacDougall tapped her knee. "Ye need not worry over Constance. She has her own clan she can go back to. Her father will be mighty upset she failed at her attempts to wed Roderick, but her pursuit wasn't welcome, and her affections weren't returned. 'Tis high time she went back home."

Mary glanced out over the loch. Would Constance be punished for not fulfilling her father's wishes? She hoped not. Regardless of what Constance might or might not be guilty of, no woman deserved penance for another man not finding interest in her.

Lady MacDougall sighed. "Ye are just like yer ma. Yer thoughts are written all over yer face."

Mary's gaze shot to the lady's. She'd known her mother. Mary glanced down, and it took a moment to recall. Her mother had mentioned they knew one another. Her face lifted to the lady's as the memory came fully back. Laird MacDougall, the lady, her father, and mother were all friends before the feud.

"Ye knew each other, didn't ye?"

Lady MacDougall smiled wide. "Aye, we did. Ye are the spitting image of her, ye know. All beauty and grace. Even curtsied when I came in." She patted her hand. "Good it is that her kind soul lives on in ye." Her frown came hard. "Even if ye had to live with that bawbag of a man."

Mary gasped. Living in her father's castle, she knew full well what a bawbag was and what it meant, but she'd never heard a lady say it.

Lady MacDougall laughed again. "Oh, now I've gone and done it. Offended yer wean ears. I'd thought in that man's hall ye'd have heard more rabid terms than a man's balls."

Mary huffed opening up to the lively lady. "Well, aye, I have."

The lady folded her arms. "Aye, well I imagine Robert's hall wasn't all that nice a place for a lady after yer ma died. And the feud didn't help, did it?"

She nodded as she wondered what all Lady MacDougall knew about her father and mother.

The sudden urge to unburden her woes to a woman overcame her, and she spoke with little forethought. "Well, no, it wasn't, and times were lean often. But I learned well and at least kept a maid. When Rose came as my companion, well, things got better."

Lady MacDougall nodded. "Rose is from the McIntyre clan. Ye know that's my clan."

Mary sat forward. "I knew where Rose came from, but I wasn't aware ye were from the same clan."

The lady stared at her a moment, then smiled. "Why don't ye call me Elizabeth, Mary?"

Mary glanced down. "I am certain I am not what ye wanted in a daughter-in-law, a Comyn."

Elizabeth snorted. "Ye'd be surprised what I think, Mary." She cleared her throat. "Tell me more about Robert's hall."

Mary warmed to Roderick's mother as she missed

regular female companionship. Rose was a great friend and made the best companion, but having an elder's advice was welcome. Something more than her father's crude remarks and male dominated views, Mary craved.

Her father's hall was a joke. Mary rolled her eyes. "Where do I begin? We've rationed for so long; I forgot what a cut piece of meat tasted like without being soaked in broth. The men, I can't recall a time when it wasn't something akin to a brothel, not that I've visited, but I've read."

Elizabeth barked a laugh. "I imagine Robert's hall is a war raged pig stye whore house.

"So, yer ma made sure ye read. Taught ye herself?"

Mary laid her head back. It felt so good to speak to another woman about something other than war, food shortages, and needs to fuel the feud. "My mother, aye, she taught me to read."

Elizabeth hummed. "Ye know that's what she wanted to do, teach her people to read."

Mary smiled. "Aye, she told me. Desired to teach the whole village, much to my father's dismay. I tried the same but…" The day she'd asked her father if she could take up her mother's deepest wish, to teach all to read, came back to her.

"Ye want to do what?" Robert had roared, his voice reverberating off the hall as all in the room stopped, waiting for his wrath to let loose.

Mary stood firm in the hopes that her mother's wish would soften his temper.

Her father seethed between his teeth. "Must ye take on every little thing that woman did? It isn't enough that ye must enter every room and remind me of who I married. Now ye run around acting like her."

Mary blinked back tears and stared beyond his shoulder, knowing it looked like she looked at him, but she didn't.

"Why don't ye learn to take up the sword, be useful for once. Help fight the feud, take down the MacDougalls once and for all."

Her head went down as a tear escaped. "Be useful for once," echoed. That's what she tried to do, be helpful for the clan. Help those who needed help, make the clan stronger with better education, better resources, a better life than living from crumb to crumb all due to an argument over what rumor claimed was a woman.

A hand touched hers, and she blinked back tears, her vision blurred.

The hand patted hers, and she blinked again. Lady MacDougall came into focus. "No worries, dear. Ye are here and gone from Robert's hands once and for all."

A tear fell, and she wiped it away.

Elizabeth sat up taller and adjusted her skirts. "I understand ye wish to redecorate the hall. Something about mistletoe?" She hummed. "Ye know yer ma loved mistletoe."

Mary grinned. "Aye, I wanted to continue her tradition. Even in the hardest times, she made sure we had greenery and mistletoe for the holidays."

Elizabeth glanced at the loch then back at her. "Ye know for Robert's daughter, ye are all right. Being Mary's daughter, ye are a bright ray of sunshine." She nodded. "For a Comyn, ye'll do, dear."

****

Roderick stood in his study awaiting Archibald to deliver Constance. He wasn't looking forward to the confrontation, but confronting Constance was long overdue. Constance's tricks needed to end, and the only way that would happen was if he sent her home. Archibald's cousin or not, her welcome had worn out.

Archibald opened the door and waved Constance inside. Archibald led her inside, crossed to the mantel, and leaned on it. When Roderick's eyes found his, Archibald raised an eyebrow.

Roderick stood beside his desk, his arms folded, and feet braced apart, much as he'd seen his father do. Establish a dominating demeanor and don't take shite from anyone.

Constance waltzed into his study and flounced as she stood before him.

He waved an invitation for her to sit.

Constance lifted her chin.

So, this was how she wanted to play. That's okay. Roderick was ready.

"Constance, it is well known ye set yer maid to serve Mary to spoil her food and ensure Mary wasn't properly provided for."

Constance gasped as a hand went to her ample bosom and fingered the low-cut bodice. She trailed them away, ensuring his gaze lingered as she called attention to her assets.

Roderick maintained eye contact, ready for her games.

She huffed and dropped her hand. "It's not as ye claim. The twit acted on her own. Her obvious worry for me was her motivation." Constance hiccupped in an attempt to cry but no tears formed in her eyes. "She worried as she was certain our betrothal was to be announced upon yer return." She sniffed and whined, "Her place secured as the lady's maid, thwarted by that

Comyn bitch ye came back married to."

Constance sniffed and lifted her nose. " 'Tis her ye must punish."

Roderick saw straight through her and nearly laughed aloud. He'd already spoken to the maid, who wailed as she claimed Constance threatened to see her not only beaten more but banished. The visible bruising on her wrists and neck easily confirmed the maid's claims. It seemed Constance took up her father's treatment of servants and abuse—something Roderick loathed, like his da, who prohibited the behavior throughout his clan. His da issued any punishment swiftly if offenders were caught, and Roderick planned the same.

Roderick nearly growled his response. "I have spoken to yer maid. It seems her story is different than yers."

Constance threw herself at Roderick as she grabbed him in an embrace. "She lies, tries to keep us apart."

Roderick peeled her from him and set her away from his body. Her cloying nature made his skin crawl. Her lies and treatment of her servant turned his stomach.

"Constance, I have given yer maid a place here, away from ye."

She pulled her arms away and glared into his face. "Ye steal my servant? Ye aren't my *laird*."

Roderick's grin went wide. "Ye are on my land, Constance. Here I *am* yer laird. But better yet, when ye threw a fit over my ordered marriage, yer cousin contacted yer father."

Her eyebrows shot to her hairline, then her glare leveled at him, feral like a trapped animal. So, she planned to fight. He grinned, ready for her.

She fisted her hands at her side as she yelled, "My father can go to hell!" She turned and sat in a chair before the desk, speaking softer. "I have left his residence, never to return." She waved her hand. "He knows this."

Roderick's eyes met Archibald's across the room, who shook his head—another lie. This must end.

Roderick leaned on his desk. "Ye will return to the bosom of yer family."

Constance huffed.

Roderick kept speaking over her. "Where yer father will welcome ye. I understand he is most anxious to have ye home."

She turned away. "Ye lie."

Archibald spoke from the fireplace. "I received a missive last night." He pulled a scroll from his sporran. "Ye are welcome to read it. Says he has finally secured yer betrothel to a man who would reel in yer wild nature. Control yer wild ways and tame ye into the fine woman ye can be."

Constance rounded on her cousin her eyes wide as her mouth opened in shock. "No, not old man Graham." Her glare went between both men as she shook her head. "No, it cannot be so. I convinced him the man was too old."

Archibald opened the parchment and began reading. "Greetings, cousin. I am so happy ye have reached out to me. Constance assured me her attentions to Laird MacDougall were welcome, and a betrothal would soon follow. It seems my crafty daughter is up to her old antics again. Please extend my apologies to Roderick and my condolences on the passing of his father. Also, send my congratulations on his new wedded bliss. Ending that old feud with the Comyns is long overdue, and I hear Mary is a beauty like her mother. Aye, send Constance home. I have secured her betrothal with Laird Graham."

Constance's whiney huff filled the room, lacking the tears to back it.

Archibald paused and waved the page. "Shall I continue, or have ye heard enough, Constance?"

Her face shot to Roderick, and she bolted from her chair so fast he drew his dagger. But all she did was lie at his feet as she hugged his ankles. "Please, Roderick, ye don't know what life is like with my father." Her eyes lifted to him as real tears filled them. "He beats me. Ye know this."

Roderick sheathed his dagger and stared out the window. Damn, she was right. When she'd arrived, she spent a week on her belly, the lashes too new to lie on her back.

She bent and cried on his boots. "Old man Graham is no different. I'll be beaten daily." She lifted her eyes to his as a tear fell. "Just for being a woman."

God, he couldn't do it. No matter how bad Constance could be which was bad at times. No human deserved rough treatment.

His expression must have given away his thoughts. When he glanced down, Constance smiled. He needed more practice being a laird. His father was so much better at this. Roderick schooled his features and nodded to Archibald who crossed and picked up Constance. She reached for him, but Archibald pulled her to the fireplace.

Roderick rounded his desk and sat in his father's

chair as he drew strength from what he hoped was his father's spirit.

"Ye may stay for now."

Constance collapsed against her cousin. "Oh, thank God."

Roderick smiled. "I wasn't finished, and I wouldn't be thanking God but begging his forgiveness." He drew a deep breath. "Ye will befriend Mary, become a companion like Rose. Help Mary become part of the MacDougall clan. Support her as ye introduce her to all ye know."

Constance jerked from Archibald's arms. "If I do this, what can I expect in return?"

Roderick nearly laughed out loud. No one gets something for nothing was a saying his da used all the time. It seemed Constance knew it well.

"Yer maid will be someone from the MacDougall clan, not able to succumb to yer demands." He paused as he glared at her. "Ye will not mistreat this maid, Constance. She reports to Bertha, and all will be told. Ye will remain a loyal friend to the MacDougall or find yerself an outcast."

Constance stared at him. He couldn't tell what her calculating mind tried to plan, but he wouldn't have it. She'd find herself kicked out and her father's anger so fierce she'd likely end up homeless.

He nodded. "I will send a missive to yer da pleading yer desire to not wed such an old man. In the meantime, I suggest ye mend yer ways with Mary and find someone here in clan MacDougall who can be a replacement groom to appease yer da."

Constance stood tall as she nodded her head. "Aye, Roderick, I can do that." When she curtsied, Roderick's eyebrows shot up. No woman curtsied to him, not since he was young and jested with the girls. He nodded back and Archibald escorted Constance out of the room.

Roderick stood alone in his study and hoped he hadn't just secured a life of hell for Mary with Constance as her companion.

Chapter 9

Mary strode behind Lady MacDougall as they made their way to the kitchens. An elder guard followed, none of the original five chosen in sight. Apprehension filled her as they neared the doorway, but after the morning's rest and a lunch of lamb stew, Mary felt fortified and ready for the confrontation that waited for her with Bertha.

Lady MacDougall paused outside the kitchen door, out of sight of those within, and spoke lowly with a smile. "Ye go ahead of me, and let's see if Bertha still has a thorn in her side."

Mary nodded. "Aye, Milady."

Lady MacDougall touched her arm. "Elizabeth, call me by my familiar."

Mary smiled as Elizabeth brushed her cheek and nodded to the kitchen. Her ma's voice rang in her mind; *fortune favors the bold.* She squared her shoulders and strolled into the kitchen with her head held high.

All work stopped, and everyone stood as they glared at her. She blinked once and stared back, unsure if they were angry at her intrusion or only stunned by her appearance.

Bertha crossed from the fireplace, where a large pot hung over the flames. "Milady, so glad I am to see ye better." She hustled her over to the pot as the maids resumed work. "Lamb stew was for lunch, nearly gone already. Cullen Skink is what we will have for dinner—smoked fish from the last catch. I used only part of the catch, much less than usual. Packed the rest away for the harder winter months ahead."

Bertha spooned a sample and offered it to Mary. Rich, creamy flavors bathed Mary's mouth in onions, leeks, potatoes, and carrots with fish in a creamy broth hitting her taste buds just right. Not too heavy on the spices but hearty all the same. Perfect for feeding so many using little resources. Bertha took the spoon from her and ushered her to the wooden worktable. "The hearty oats we save for the morning meal as ye suggested and the fine grain cut with ground sand to make it last longer."

Mary's eyebrows raised. "Sand, ye grind sand to carry yer flour longer?"

Elizabeth's voice came firmly from the doorway. "Aye, an old trick from my ma." Everyone in the room stooped and curtsied to Lady MacDougall. Mary had to restrain herself from doing the same, but Lady—no, Elizabeth—was stern in her instructions. All were to bow to her now.

Elizabeth scrutinized the room and landed on Mary. "I see ye at least haven't forgotten yer manners, but I am no longer Lady of the Castle. I noticed not a one of ye bowed yer head for Lady MacDougall." She waved her hand to Mary, who blushed under the attention as all in the room turned to her and repeated the curtsey.

Elizabeth's voice carried a mocking tone. "I assume I shall not have to venture in this room again to remind ye all of whom is yer lady?" Everyone rose and went back to their tasks, not making eye contact.

Elizabeth strode to Mary and took her hand. "Let's check on yer holiday greenery, shall we?"

They turned, but Bertha's hand on her shoulder had her turn back. "The fennel seeds, thank ye. Mabel's had a time with wee Nal."

Mary blinked at the praise. "Of course, anything for the clan. Come to me anytime."

Bertha moved back to her pot as Elizabeth tugged her hand, and they made their way through the door into the great hall. "A friend in need is a friend indeed."

Mary gasped. "Ye know my ma's sayings?"

Elizabeth grinned. "She quoted them all the time. They echo often."

Mary smiled. "Aye, they do."

Rose and a group of maids sat at a table placed near the fireplace weaving the greenery into long strands. Mary noted as they approached that the maids had not yet hung in the hall the woven foliage.

The main doors burst open, and Hamish, one of her guards, marched in, followed by Robbie, Fergus, Douglas, and Angus each carrying a large bundle on their backs. Her guards were all smiling. When Hamish reached the table, he set his burden down carefully, and the men followed, placing each at Mary's feet. From the side, mistletoe peeked out.

Mary gasped. "Mistletoe?"

Hamish stood tall. "Aye, the laird commanded we collect as much as possible but leave some for growth next year. Said it was a new tradition."

Mabel rose and untied the cloth bundle, and mistletoe sprigs spilled over Mary's feet. "Dash, Milady. There's enough for everyone in the clan plus the greenery." Mary's eyes watered. Roderick did this—for her?

Mabel eyed her. "Ye will show us how to weave this into the greenery. I've got extra hay. Maybe we can finish soon and hang back up the greenery."

Mary blinked back her tears. "Hang back up?"

Mabel patted her hand. "Aye, the laird had us take it all down. Said yer ma used to weave mistletoe into the greenery for luck. Lord knows we can use all the luck we can get."

Mary's gaze traveled over the mistletoe, five full bundles in all. "Where is my husband now?"

She glanced at her guard, who nodded at her. "He's busy, Milady, with a special project. Said ye won't see him till dinner."

Elizabeth picked up a mistletoe sprig. "I always loved yer ma's traditions. As ye show the ladies how to weave it into the greenery, ye can share some of yer rationing ideas with the women."

Mary glanced back and forth between Mabel and Elizabeth's expectant expressions then landed on Rose's smiling face. "I'd love to." She examined the greenery, quickly estimating the total length. Then over the hall, mentally measuring the walls. "There's plenty of greenery for the hall, which leaves quite a few lengths…maybe we can decorate the chapel as well?" Her eyes fell to the sprigs at her feet, some larger and others a single grouping of three to four leaves and a couple of berries. "Mabel, you and another separate the larger sprigs from the smaller. We'll use the larger ones in the greenery about every hand's width. The smaller we'll wrap and gift to each person at Christmas dinner."

Mabel's eyebrows shot up. "Everyone at Christmas dinner, the whole clan?"

Elizabeth bent, picked up a mistletoe sprig, and twirled it as she spoke. "A fine idea and a wonderful way to start a new tradition, sharing with all."

She grinned at Mary. "I recall how yer ma weaved these. Let's get to work."

The women bent into their tasks, some on the single sprigs and others on the greenery. Mary sat among them, showing how to weave the hay around the sprig into the greenery. Elizabeth led the other group with the single sprigs, placing them into a large basket.

As the conversation rolled around Mary, a maid youngest in the group spoke up. "I had a hard time I did, rationing. How do ye do it?"

Mary spoke without thinking as she continued to weave the mistletoe. "Use all ya have, the bones, skin, meat. Pickle the vegetables, preserve the fruit. Salt or smoke the meat. The freeze helps the food over time but keep it in yer kitchen, not outside." She sighed. "Soups are always my favorite. Vegetables boiled down into a broth can be so filling and soaked in course bread, why it makes a meal."

The silence around her clued her to glance up. All stared at her with their mouths agape.

Mabel was the first to break the silence. "Ye, Milady, went without? Ye, a lady!"

Mary sat up taller and nodded to Rose. "Well, times have been hard for my clan. We had to adjust, learn to live with what we had. Survive." She huffed. "I even learned to make shoes." She lifted her skirt and showed off a sturdy pair of well-worn boots that kept her toes warm even in the coldest winters.

Mabel gasped. "Will ye look there now? Boots on a lady!"

Constance strode through the middle of the group. "How base, boots on a lady. Slippers are the proper attire."

Elizabeth lifted her skirts, showing both her feet, clad in petite ankle boots made of sturdy leather lined with sheep's wool, polished, not a scuff on them. "I love my winter boots. Keeps my feet warm."

Constance snorted and marched away as Mary scooted near Elizabeth, who spoke under her breath. "Poor woman doesn't know a good shoe if someone threw it at her."

Mary snickered with the maids but leaned over and whispered, "Ye shouldn't say mean things, even if she is deserving."

Elizabeth smirked. "Mary, I said to yer ma, and I'll say it to ye. If you can't say anything nice, come sit beside me."

Mabel held up the greenery with the mistletoe strung into it. "My, how beautiful is that?" She beamed at Mary. "Will look right nice at Christmas and over Hogmanay. The gift exchange is the highlight of the festivities."

Gift! She's got nothing to give Roderick. Her father had not sent anything of hers. She'd barely arrived with the clothing on her back.

She sighed and turned to Elizabeth, whose knowing expression met hers. "I have some fabric already cut for a shirt. Planned to make it for Ian, may he rest in peace. Please take it and make yer first proper gift—a shirt for yer husband." As she spoke, her hand brushed her pendant, a silver heart the size of her palm hanging from her neck.

Mary's eye drew to it. "That's such a lovely

necklace. Was it a gift?"

Elizabeth stared into the flames of the fire. "Aye, it was a gift, still is." She sighed. "My Ian, my true love, gave it to me with a love stone inside. He said I would always carry it as I carried his heart with me." She wiped a tear and glanced at Mary. "Ian's grandma, Katherine, was buried with hers, but the stone passed down from one lady to the next."

Mary smiled. "How romantic, a love stone."

Elizabeth leaned to her, whispering, " 'Tis romantic and blessed by the Fae. The stone, it glows when yer true love is near."

Mary scoffed, "Glows, a stone?"

Elizabeth patted her hand. "Aye, ask Roderick to tell ye the Fae Fable, the Stone of Love, and ye'll see."

****

The day passed in a blur, likely due to the fact Mary fell asleep over her mistletoe. Elizabeth had situated her in a chair before the fire in the great hall, where she curled up in a MacDougall plaid toasty warm as the light chatter of working women lulled her to sleep.

A slight shake woke her, and she looked upon Elizabeth's smiling face. "Rested ye are now?"

Mary stretched as her gaze roamed the room. The greenery was gone, and maids worked as they set up tables and benches for the evening meal.

Mary yawned. "I slept the day away. I've never been so lazy."

Elizabeth snorted. "Not lazy, rest earned and needed." She handed her a cup of ale, and Mary drank, thankful for the respite.

She wiped her face feeling refreshed. "The

greenery's done?" She glanced up. "But not hung yet?"

Elizabeth took the mug from her. "Not till ye are ready." Then pulled the plaid off her and folded it as she smiled.

Her guard stepped forward and bowed. "I am to escort ye to yer husband, Milady."

Unused to the bow, Mary's surprise must have been evident as the older guard laughed. "Yer special five have earned rewards for the mistletoe and drink the night away. I am Leod, at yer service."

Mary nodded as she rose. "Thank ye. How many guards will I have? So many names."

Elizabeth patted her arm. "A few for now, soon only one. Off with ye now. Roderick has plans."

As Mary strolled behind Leod, Elizabeth called after her with a large grin, "Have a nice night, Mary."

Leod led her upstairs, but dinner was soon. "Leod, 'tis almost dinner. Why are ye taking me to my room?"

He said nothing as he strode past her room, the door slightly ajar, the bed made, and the room clean.

Leod continued down the hall, rounded the corner to stop before a large wood door, the craftsmanship like the main door to the keep. *The laird's door* flitted through her mind as the door opened, and Roderick stood on the other side.

He nodded to Leod, who bowed, turned, and strode away. They stood there momentarily, her on the outside and him on the inside, much like their relationship, an invisible barrier between them. The reasons for the divide rushed through her mind, differences, the clan wars, her father killing his, and the king's demand. Their farce of a marriage. The start of their relationship, something still fragile. Memories of this morning flashed quickly, warmth, his arms wrapped around her, and his body, all muscle yet the perfect pillow.

Roderick huffed. "My ma is right. Yer emotions are easy to read, evident in yer expressions." He held his hand out to her. "Beautiful as they are. Please join me, wife."

She took his hand, and his thumb rubbed the back as he tugged her into the room. Mary easily followed his lead, curious as to what his room was like. Would it be like her father's—messy clothes spread about, a whore sleeping in his bed? Doubtful. She pushed the image from her mind, and as she crossed the threshold, inspected his room.

The largest bed she'd ever seen dominated the room. A box bed with posters and heavy curtains pulled back to reveal a stuffed mattress, not straw, piled with pillows and multiple coverings. On top was the MacDougall plaid. His dressing stand for his plaid and a chest of drawers sat to the left of the bed. His broad sword propped next to the head of the bed. Before her to the right was a desk with a mirror, reminding her of what her mother had described as a woman's vanity. A large trunk she didn't recognize sat next to it.

Roderick led her to the fireplace, where a small table and two chairs sat before the roaring fire. He released her hand and picked up two chalices so ornate she feared touching them. He handed her one, and she stood and stared.

He grinned. "Mary, please take the wine. I have a toast to make."

As she took the cup into her hands, she fingered the fine metal, likely gold. Roderick's fingers brushed hers, sending tingles up her arm.

He hummed as he removed his hand and lifted his cup to her. "The MacDougall chalices. Reserved for only special occasions."

Mary's thumb rubbed hers. "They are very nice."

He eyed her over the rim, his gaze riveting her in place. "My wish this evening is to begin anew. A new start to our union, our vow, and our marriage." She held her goblet to his, and he clinked them, the light sound ringing in the room. He sipped his, and she did the same. Warm mulled wine filled her mouth and easily slid down her throat.

Roderick pulled a chair out and offered it to her. "A private dinner. A tradition we were not afforded after our wedding."

She sat, and his arms rested on her shoulders as he bent and whispered in her ear, "A slight I had no control over, but now ye are in my home, something I can see to." He lightly kissed her ear, and she giggled as his lips tickled her ear.

He sat and set his cup down. "Ah, laughter, something I want to hear more from my wife." He lifted the tureen, and the smell of Cullen Skink soup filled the room.

Mary sighed in relief as she reached for the serving spoon, intent on serving her husband. "I am glad we are having the same as the clan. I'd feel guilty if we ate better during rationing."

Roderick caught her hand and returned it to her chalice. "Allow me, wife, please." He lifted the ladle and spooned a large portion into her bowl. "Aye, I figured as much, and I hear this is yer favorite." He served himself two ladles full and returned the lid to the tureen.

Mary bent her head in prayer, and Roderick did the same, crossing himself. She peeked and did the same, comfortable doing so in his presence. Mary picked up her bread and broke it into little pieces adding this to her soup. The bread soaked up the broth, and she spooned the fish and vegetables first.

Roderick's chuckle brought her regard to his as he stared at her. "Ye always soak up the broth, lass?"

She glanced down just now, realizing her habit might seem strange. "Well, many a time. Broth was all we had, vegetable broth." She spooned a soaked bread piece and ate it under his scrutiny. After she swallowed, she shrugged. "Coarse bread fills an empty belly. Wet stiff bread goes down easier."

Roderick's hand came to hers, stopping her spoon from reaching her mouth. "I am sorry. I didn't mean to bring yer bad memories to our dinner." He released her hand as he spooned his soup. "Under my care, ye will never go hungry again."

Mary shrugged. "Even salted, I've had more food in the last weeks than in my da's hall for a month."

Roderick grunted as he ate more soup.

Mary moved her wet bread around her bowl, wanting to ask about Constance. Elizabeth claimed he'd send her away, but her appearance that afternoon spoke differently. Maybe she should thank him for the mistletoe.

They spoke at the same time…

"I have to explain about Constance."

"I want to thank ye for the mistletoe."

Roderick laughed. "It was my pleasure to have the men gather mistletoe. It seems the idea has gotten the clan excited for the holidays. Ye will hang it tomorrow?"

She nodded. "Aye, I will." She sighed. "Constance came by as we worked the greenery. She's not happy."

Roderick set his spoon down and gulped his wine. "I wanted to send her home. I caught her in so many lies it made my head spin. But her da, he's a hard one—beats her. I can't abide that in any man. Friend or foe."

He set the chalice down hard. "She will not bother ye. If she does, ye are to report it to a guard to report to me at once. I will not tolerate her tricks and games anymore. She will not disrespect ye as lady. I commanded her to befriend ye."

It was Mary's turn to laugh. "I doubt she has the ability, but I will heed yer advice and try to be a friend no matter how hard she makes it."

He stopped and gazed at her. "Mary, I made a mistake. There's something I need to mend between us. Something we need to mend."

Concern crawled up her spine as she carefully set her cup down. What would he be referring to? Had she done something wrong?

He set his cup down as well and took both her hands into his. "Mary, the king's orders, the vow I made to ye."

He wanted his husbandly rights even after his vow.

Mary jerked her hands from his and stood. "This is nothing special. Why 'tis a trick, isn't it? To bed me for the king's orders!"

Roderick stood fast and bumped the table, clattering the dishes. "No! Ye didn't let me finish." He ran his hand through his hair, scooped up the chalice, and drained it. He took a few deep breaths and then stepped toward her.

He took her hand lightly into his and led her to the woman's vanity. He lifted the truck lid, and inside, on top of a pile of clothing she didn't recognize, sat her meager belongings. A comb, mirror, and brush on top of her favorite shift. All she'd brought with her, and the dress she wore now—the mistletoe sprig from the abbey on top of it all.

His finger rubbed the top of her hand. "It was a mistake not to place ye in my room. My parents slept together every evening. They were never apart." He huffed. "The clan saw me placing ye in another room as a slight, a denial of ye as my wife. As their lady." He brought her hand to his lips and kissed the back. "My vow I shall honor, Mary. I will refuse my rights till ye are ready, till ye say aye. But ye need to stay here, please, Mary." The memory of waking in his arms sent a hot flash over her body. A full flush warmed her cheek.

Roderick took her in his arms and kissed her lightly on the lips.

He whispered into the kiss, "Was it so bad waking in my arms?"

Mary giggled. "Such a burden. I guess I'll have to suffer ye in my bed." She kissed him, and his growl had her gasping. He took advantage, and his tongue danced with hers as his hands roamed her back. A fire ignited so fast inside her she stepped back. He released her from his embrace, and she returned to the table and sat gulping her wine. All so fast, could she trust him?

Roderick followed and filled both cups to the brim. He sat and eyed her as he sipped his wine. "Mary, I will honor my vow." He took a deep breath. "But I will pursue ye."

Mary grinned, liking the idea of being pursued by Roderick. She sat and ate the rest of her soup-soaked bread. Roderick smiled as he joined her.

Finished with his first bowl, he scooped another portion. "My mother mentioned ye wanted to teach the clan to read. Ye mentioned it before. Carrying on yer ma's wishes."

Mary's head shot up. Would he deny her and rail at her like her father? He glanced at her and stopped as his expression shifted. "Mary, have I frightened ye? Ye look like ye've seen a ghost."

Mary took a deep breath as she stared into her bowl. "No, I'd like to teach reading if it's all right by ye. To any who want to learn, even the servants." She kept her head low, waiting to see what his response would be. His spoon clattered in his bowl, and she flinched.

His hand rested on hers softly as he spoke. "Mary, please do not be afraid to ask for things ye want. While I may not always be able to say aye, ye should ask." Her gaze met his, and he smiled. "I'd like the clan to learn more. Being learned makes us a stronger clan." She returned his smile as he sipped his wine.

She sipped hers and rubbed her full belly with a contented sigh.

Roderick smirked. "Exactly as I planned, a satisfied wife makes a happy wife."

Mary scoffed. "Who said I was satisfied? A full belly, aye, but where's the entertainment for dinner, husband?"

At Roderick's smoldering stare, Mary nearly took her statement away. But his expression fired her flame. His kisses from this evening tingled her lips. As his body shifted in his chair, he reminded her of him moving against her this morning, only clad in his shirt. She rocked in her chair, his eyes still on her.

Roderick stood and pulled his chair aside. He set his goblet near the fireplace on the floor and went behind the table as he pulled it away from the fireplace. He crossed, stood before her, and offered his hand to her. She took it and rose. He took her cup and placed it next to his, released her hand, and slid her chair next to his. He strode to the bed, removed the larger pillows, crossed to her, and plopped them at her feet. He held his hand to her again, and she placed hers in his, only to have him bring it to his lips and kiss the back.

She giggled. "What are ye up to, husband?"

He stepped toward her and kissed her ear. "Yer entertainment, wife."

He pulled her down to the pillows and settled her in his arms as they lounged before the fire.

He bent, retrieving the cup, handed her hers, and brought them together. "To ye, wife."

She clinked them. "To ye, husband."

He kissed her lips. "To us." And sat back, sipping his wine.

She took a healthy sip and snuggled into his embrace.

He hummed. "What would be my wife's pleasure this evening?"

Mary fingered the chalice. Small red stones in the shape of hearts lined the top.

Elizabeth's necklace came to her mind. "I like stories. Yer mother said to ask ye to tell me the Fae Fable, the Stone of Love."

Roderick stilled, then blew his breath out. "She

did? Did she tell ye of her stone?"

Mary glanced up as the motion brought his gaze to hers.

She wondered what the stone meant, what the story entailed. "I noticed her necklace. She touched it when she spoke of yer da." Mary's regard slid to the fire. "She mourns him, called him her true love."

Roderick's sigh had her eyes connect with his. "They are, were. True loves."

Mary sighed. "That's so nice. But she said the strangest thing. She said her stone glowed when her true love was near."

Roderick laughed. "Aye, 'tis from the fable. Tuck in and let me tell ye one of our Fae Fables. Actually, ye asked about this one before."

Mary glanced down, trying to recall what he meant. So much had happened in the last few weeks her memory seemed a blur, but the Fae Fable book in the library popped into her mind.

She blurted the answer. "The story in the *Fae Fable Book* in the library! 'Tis the Stone of Love? Ye will tell it to me?"

"Aye, well, the first part ye know already 'tis exposed on the page now."

"The story starts with the Corinthians quote. 'And now, these three remain, faith, hope, and love. But the greatest of these is love.' "

Roderick sipped his wine and nodded. "Aye, so I'll give ye a shorter version than the text. The one my ma told me as a bedtime story."

Mary sipped her wine as he spoke and replied, "I haven't had a bedtime story told to me since my mother died."

Roderick cleared his throat. "Well, let me do the honors, wife.

"There was a prince who lived in the castle. The Fae gifted him with the Stone of Love. The stone was very powerful, and the Fae charged him with guarding it. He made a necklace with a heart-shaped stone and always wore it so that he would know when his true love was near because then, the stone would glow red."

"Wait, like yer ma's. She said she carried such a stone."

Roderick nodded. "Aye, but ye must listen to the whole story."

Mary settled into his embrace, looking forward to a Fae story.

His chest vibrated as he began the tale again. "Many maidens came from far and wide to see if the stone would glow for them, but it never did. The prince became depressed, thinking he'd never find his true love. He would sneak away to the village and sit at his favorite spot by the stream to contemplate the issue with the stone. It would glow every time he went there, but he was always alone."

"Why are fables so sad?"

Roderick whispered, "They start that way so the ending is happy. Hush and listen, wife."

She liked it when he called her wife. He squeezed her once when he said hush, making her feel comfortable and safe.

"One day, a beautiful woman came to the castle. Gorgeous and sensual, she went near him and made the stone glow. While physically attracted to her, the prince did not feel love for this woman. Confused, he snuck off to his spot by the stream. As he sat, he saw a maiden approach the stream.

"She had glowing cream-colored skin and an inner beauty he had not seen in a woman before.

"Her light-brown hair glimmered in the sunlight, seeming as if to cast the threads of a pure gold halo around her head. Her soul called to him in a way he had never felt before."

Roderick tilted her chin till their eyes met. "The day in the chapel when we prayed together. 'Tis what ye looked like as the sun shone on ye. Cast ye in a halo."

Mary hummed. "I saw the same. Ye—no us—cast in a halo."

Roderick kissed her, and as he deepened the kiss, Mary pushed back. "Wait, ye distract me. What happened next?"

Roderick grinned. "He kissed his wife senseless."

Mary swatted his chest. "The story, husband."

Roderick chuckled. "Can't blame a man for trying."

He picked up his wine, sipped it, and set it aside. "So caught up in his examination, he had not noticed that the Stone of Love glowed red.

"The prince must have made a noise because the village girl turned suddenly, startled, and she dropped her water bucket. Her face met his, and her shock was apparent. 'I'm sorry to disturb you, Prince.' Her voice sounded as if the angels sang for him alone.

"The prince rose and retrieved her bucket, handing it to her. 'I'm sorry I startled you.'

"The girl stared at the stone, pulsing red. The prince, so caught up in the village girl's enchantment, only now noticed the stone glowed. Shocked, he took her to the castle to see if the stone glowed for both women."

Mary sat up and set her wine cup down by the fire. "Both women, is that possible?"

Roderick took her back into his embrace as he continued the story.

"Upon arriving at the castle, he confronted the evil Fae. The Stone of Love burned his clothes and chest when he approached her. Angry that she was discovered, the evil Fae cast a spell upon the village girl and the prince, opening a portal to purgatory.

" 'True love or a lifetime in purgatory—choose yer fate,' she yelled at the prince.

"Confused, the prince asked, 'Why do you do this? Why do you hate so much?'

"The village girl answered the evil Fae. 'She does not hate; she is fearful. The opposite of love is not hate, but *fear*.'

"The prince offered the stone from his neck to his true love, the maiden from the stream.

" 'I shall live forever in purgatory so ye may live a full life. Take the Stone of Love.' But her love for him was so strong that she could not allow the prince to sacrifice himself for her, the village girl. When he handed her the stone, she thrust it into his hands and jumped into the portal, casting herself into purgatory, saving the prince.

"So angered by this, the prince turned upon the evil Fae and drove his sword through her heart while holding the necklace with the Stone of Love in the same hand as the sword. The evil Fae's blood dripped from the blade to the Stone of Love. Dropping his sword to the ground, the prince fell to his knees, gripping the

Stone of Love to his heart. He prayed to the Fae that his true love would return to him.

"Dagda, the king of the Tuath Dé Dannan, appeared. 'I am sorry, Prince, I cannot help ye. A spell cast by the evil Fae I cannot undo. But I can give ye a chant, and ye may call her back if yer love is powerful enough. But I warn ye, the chant will fail if she does not return yer love.'

"Roaring in his pain, the prince focused his prayer on his one true love. He chanted:

I want to see love's highest power
Take me now, not to my past
Right now, at this hour,
Bring my true love back at last

"He prayed over and over. He closed his eyes and poured all his love into his one wish. The Stone of Love grew hot in his hand, so hot he had to let it go. It floated to the center of the room, hovering above everyone, and glowed pure white. The prince kept repeating his chant. The Stone of Love burst into a million points of light, blinding everyone momentarily. When their eyes adjusted, they saw the village girl standing in the center of the room.

"Overcome with emotion, the prince threw his arms around her and kissed her. The sun shone through the glass window above them, casting them in a light halo.

"Dagda said to all in the room, 'The greatest power of all is true love.' "

****

Mary had nearly drifted off to sleep twice near the end of his story.

She sleepily repeated the ending. "True love." As

she drifted off to sleep, she mumbled, "Mm, love Roderick."

Roderick held her before the fire well into the night. Her sleepy declaration of love rang in his heart. Without knowing, Mary had professed her love for him, romanced by the Fae Fable planted by his ma who wanted nothing more than to help their floundering marriage. Mary had no idea the irony of telling the fable now. Or maybe she did. The *Fae Fable Book*, in truth, revealed the fate of each of the magic Iona Stones, Hope, Love, and Faith. The Stone of Love, the real story which played out in life was the very reason for the clan's feud in the first place, should be the one story to bind Mary to him. He prayed the end of their story came out happier, that no other man vied for her affections as had for his ma. While happy with his da, the clan wars started with the very fable he'd just told.

Chapter 10

Mary woke to the most wonderful sensations. Warmth embraced her as she lay on her side. A breath blew in her ear, sending tingles to her toes. A large hand gripped her hip as lips brushed her ear, making her catch her breath in a moan. A low hum vibrated her ear as the hand trailed to her breast, and his body pressed against her back as Roderick's scent filled her nose.

His whisper ruffled her hair near her ear. "Mary, please let me have a taste of ye. Sleeping beside ye is torture."

In her sleepy haze, she registered Roderick held her, but in the dream-like state, she drifted back into her erotic dreamland.

Descriptions from her father's maids rushed her mind. "He was all muscle and took me to the heavens with his man's rod."

The hand squeezed her breast, and his rod rubbed her backside as his groan blew her ear.

She moaned, "Yes, Roderick." The hand moved lower and cupped her mounds as a sigh escaped her.

He lifted her shift as he kissed her ear. "God, Mary, ye are so sweet." She rotated in his embrace as he stripped the garment from her body. His lips captured hers as he slid his finger into her wet folds. Reality and the dream blended behind her closed eyelids.

The maid's claims echoed in her head. "Why, I took him and pumped till he cried out."

Driven by his kisses, Mary reached for him and encircled her hand around his shaft. His swift intake of breath told her he liked the action. His fingers on her folds pulsed faster, and his mouth claimed hers, harder this time. She pumped like the dream said. His breaths came faster on her lips. He slid a finger inside her, and her world came apart. Her breath caught, and his fingers rushed as bright lights burst behind her eyelids like nothing she'd experienced before.

When she returned from her flight, he gripped her wrist and sped up her action guiding her hand as his tongue delved into her mouth. Faster and faster, he guided her hand. She gripped him hard to hold onto the rod. With an intake of breath, he froze and stayed rigid for a moment then a sigh escaped as wetness covered her hand.

He groaned. "God, Mary, *mo chridhe*. You truly are *my heart*. I'd wake like that every morn."

Sometime later, the bed shifted, and his kiss brushed her lips. "Rest, Mary, my true love."

She drifted to sleep, back in her dreamworld again.

Sometime later, a bright light flooded the box bed as someone drew the curtains back.

Mary rolled over, and a young woman she didn't recognize greeted her with a smile. "Good morning, Milady."

Mary rolled over, wanting nothing more than to drift back into her erotic dreamland. Something scratched her face, and her hand went there to encounter the mistletoe sprig. She lifted it, and the sunlight caught the greenery dotted with white berries.

Her dream flashed in her mind, Roderick holding her, caressing her, kissing her. Then their hands move in sensual play. His last words echoed from her dream haze, "Rest, Mary, my true love."

The Fae Fable flashed in her mind. "True love is the greatest power of all."

The maid brought her a mug. "Tea, Milady." She handed it to her as Mary sat up in the bed.

Mary took a sip, liking the light brew. "Ye're my new maid?"

The young maid turned and curtsied. "Aye, I'm Bertha's niece, Fiona." Fiona passed her a plate with half-eaten bread on it, dark with seeds on top. Mary sniffed; mmm, carrot bread.

Fiona nodded to the bread. "Left here by yer husband, half gobbled it up but there's a little for ye."

Mary took a bite of the bread, sweetened with honey that tasted good with the tea. "What about Rose?"

Fiona grinned as she set her boots aside, cleaned, and polished. "She's yer companion, not yer maid. She has a maid of her own and took yer old room."

Mary set the plate down as Fiona lifted the trunk lid and began pulling a garment from it.

Mary sipped the tea. "My husband, where is he this morning?"

Fiona shook out a dress Mary didn't recognize but liked the light blue color. "He's out with the men searching for the yule log."

Fiona laid the dress out and retrieved some stockings, wool that looked new, and laid those beside it. "Left specific instructions the laird did." She stood and smiled. "Ye were to have a 'lay in' since ye needed rest. Everyone was to await ye to hang the greenery. He mentioned to tell ye, he'd like to have the hall decorated by the evening meal. Says he has something special planned." She giggled. " 'Tis Christmas week. And here we have celebrations through till Hogmanay."

Mary choked on her tea. "Christmas week already?" Where had the time gone? She had so much to do. She flung the bedcovers aside only to find herself naked as the day she was born.

Fiona gasped.

Mary covered herself as her woman's parts tingled. Her erotic dream apparently wasn't that much of a dream.

Giggling, Fiona handed her a shift. "Roderick seemed quite pleased this morning, Milady. The clan's buzzing like the bee's talking, carrying on about new starts now that ye share yer husband's bed." Fiona helped her into a shift, and the dress efficiently followed.

Mary shoved the rest of the bread into her mouth and spoke around it as Fiona helped her dress. "I must hurry; the hall must be perfect."

Fiona quickly finished dressing her and smiled as she tied her shoes off. "Nothing like new love, makes everyone all romantic." She stood and took Mary's hands in hers. "I've eyed the young guard Robbie— he's a nice catch, ye think?"

Mary patted her hands, the girl's excitement rubbing off on her. "Aye, that he is." Robert, like her da.

Fiona pulled out the stool for the vanity and waved Mary there. "Let me set yer hair. Then we can get on with today's duties."

Mary took the seat, and her image met her gaze in the mirror. Wavy but still clear, her color looked good, and her eyes connected in the reflection, happy as Fiona brushed her hair out. A rash showed on her neck. Her hand went there recalling Roderick's kisses from the early morning and his stubble. After securing her hair at her nap and a covering for a married woman, Mary stood ready for her first actual day as Lady MacDougall.

Fiona followed her into the great hall and touched her arm. "I'll gather the maids and the greenery, Milady."

From across the room, Rose smiled and rushed to her. "Mary, ye look divine in that new dress."

Before she could respond, Elizabeth crossed the hall. "Glad I am that ye rested but time to get to work. That greenery must go up. Before ye know it, the men with be back with the Yule log and the drinking will begin and not stop till after Hogmanay!" Maids bustled in carrying baskets of the mistletoe laden with greenery.

Mabel stopped Mary with a hand. "Wee Nal is doing well, thank ye, Milady."

Mary turned to pick up a greenery swag, and another maid stopped her. "The soup recipe ye shared the other day, my husband loved it."

A guard came into the room with a ladder and held it ready for instructions.

A maid took the greenery from her and asked, "How do ye want them hung?"

Mary turned to a group of clan members' smiling expectant faces, all waiting for her command. Warmth spread in her heart as she started her instructions.

She waved to two full baskets at her side. "Take

those and a small group to the chapel and hang them along the tops of the windows."

She turned to the rest in the hall. "Of these, center the largest piece over the hearth. Then allow it to drape as we hang it in even intervals an arm's width apart, so the hangings dip a little showing the mistletoe for all to see." Maids and the guard hurried, and decorations soon started going up in organized chaos.

A few minutes into the process, a maid approached Mary. "Mom MacDougall said ye could read. That ye wanted to teach reading." She held a small book and handed it to Mary as her eyes connected with Elizabeth's across the room as she nodded and smiled. Mary took the book and rotated it, recognizing a Bible. She sat and patted the bench next to her inviting the maid to sit. Mary handed the book back. "Open it to any point, and we shall start there." The maid bent, flipped the pages, and started to read in broken words that Mary corrected every couple of words.

Constance entered the hall, and Mary stopped short on a word. Constance smirked at her and moved to help a maid hang the greenery. Well, one positive act makes for a budding friendship. One of her ma's quotes came to mind, *you can choose your friends, but you can't choose your family.*

Elizabeth approached the pair. "Mary, ye should teach them all, like yer ma wanted. Start Sunday after the holidays." Warmth and pride spread through Mary, her ma's dream now hers come true. Why 'twas the best thing that had happened to her.

****

Roderick rode with his men through the woods, intent on finding the fattest Yule log to date. He wanted this one to burn bright and long, lasting longer than the holiday season indicating to all good tidings, and a good omen to the clan.

Reverend O'Donnell rode on his side as Archibald rode on the other. The silence at the start of the ride was a welcome reprieve as "good omen" echoed in his mind.

Archibald was the first to break the silence. " 'Tis a good thing, ye moving Mary to yer chamber. The clan is already excited about the coming holiday season." He wiggled his eyebrows at Roderick. "My da said the time ye was conceived many in the clan followed suit. I suspect as with then, many new bairns will come around fall. Just in time for Samhain."

The reverend huffed beside Roderick. "Pagan ritual or not, 'tis good ye and Mary have reconciled yer fate."

Roderick nodded in agreement. "She is a right smart lass."

Archibald cleared his throat. "Smart lass is an understatement. Once she started telling all how to ration properly, well, many sought her guidance. Word spread quickly." Archibald nodded. "Aye, the kitchen took quick to her suggestions. The rationing is already started, and the winter stores grow preparing the clan for a lean winter."

Roderick pulled his horse around a fallen log, still not large enough to fill his hearth fully. "Already?"

Reverend O'Donnell weaved his horse past another log. "Well, I suspect yer ma had a hand in it. Her 'birds' as I like to call them fly fast."

Roderick chuckled at the reverend's reference to his ma's gossip group, likely large enough to form an army.

The reverend shifted in his seat as he was not used to long hours in the saddle anymore. "Aye, yer ma already discussed with me the revised Sunday schedule to allow Mary time to teach reading to those who want it." His gaze connected with Roderick's. "If that pleases ye, Milaird."

Roderick nodded. "Aye, I already told Mary teaching reading was fine. Something to progress the clan in these modern times."

Archibald steered his horse closer. "Aye, something to keep us entertained in the long winter days. Not that I need help with entertainment in the long winter nights!" Archibald's laughter echoed through the forest, Roderick's and the reverend's joining him.

Roderick smiled at his longtime friend and advisor. "So, yer pursuit of Rose is going well?"

Archibald's eyebrows wiggled. "Ye weren't the only one kissing a woman last night, Roderick."

Roderick sighed. "I only hope Mary's happy here. Life in Comyn's hall was rough, times hard. She deserves a better life."

The reverend's horse bumped alongside his. "Find solace in each other, Roderick. She's a bright and faithful lass. Together in yer faith, ye both shall find the way."

A guard called from the side. "Milaird, come, we found the largest log in the woods!"

Excitement welled in Roderick. With Mary planning it, the holiday season would be a good omen for the clan.

****

Mary directed the maid atop the ladder to get the

swag above the hearth just right. Each time the maid relocated it, each side became lopsided—this would not do. She wanted everything to be perfect. From across the room Constance spoke loudly. "Lopsided decorations are a bad omen."

Frustrated, Mary waved the maid down. "Come down, I'll hang it."

The guard holding the ladder turned to her. "Milady, I can't let ye go up there. The laird, he'd have my head if ye got hurt."

Mary took the first rung of the ladder. "Nonsense, was it Rupert?" The guard held the ladder closer and nodded.

Mary climbed the ladder. "Well, hold on, Rupert." The second to top step was as far as Mary could climb, and she had to stretch out to reach where the greenery attached to the top of the tapestry. She stretched farther, just a little more and she'd reach it.

A commotion at the hall doors shook her. She turned, and the men returned, hefting the largest log she'd seen over their heads, her husband leading the group. Cheers broke out in the hall, and the men progressed toward her. Only her feet secured her to the ladder, and when the men neared, the ladder nudged.

Her yelp had her husband's eyes connect with hers. As she teetered trying to catch her balance his roar sounded in the hall. The ladder fell from beneath her, and she dropped. Her breath caught, and her heart stopped as the world flew by, but it ended in a grunt as strong arms caught her and wrapped her into a hard muscular chest. Her husband's scent enveloped her as his strong arms gripped her harder.

He turned and roared at Rupert, "Why did ye let

her on the ladder?"

Mary's arm on his chest stalled him as she spoke. "I commanded it, husband."

Constance stood close by. "Aye, I heard her. Rupert only did as she demanded." Strange, when did Constance move across the room?

Roderick's gaze connected with hers, concern evident in the creases in his eyes. But as he lowered her along his body, each ripple ignited her memory from this morning. His growl as he set her on her feet had her glance at him again, his smoldering expression showing he recalled their play as well.

Mary stepped back, but Roderick held her close. "Now that ye are safe on the ground, show me all the work ye have done, lovely wife."

She turned, and he turned with her, keeping her in his embrace. "I have hung all the greenery, even in the chapel. That group should return soon. The task is complete." She glanced up above the fireplace, and the swag she had managed to adjust was even. Her husband's eyes followed and then returned to her.

She smiled. "Ye have a Yule log, I see?"

Roderick's grin went wide as he stepped to the log the men placed before the hearth and announced, "The biggest the clan has had to date." The men in the hall cheered. Roderick bent and kissed her full on the mouth before all the cheering rose in volume.

Roderick waved to them all. "One extra ale ration for all today. The log we light tonight, and celebrations shall begin!" Men and women filtered out of the hall. Rupert took the ladder, and maids took the empty baskets as the hall was set to order. Soon they were left alone.

Mary made to move, but Roderick held her close. "Mary, ye need to take care." When her gaze met his, she was nearly angry, thinking he meant to mention the king's orders, but his eyes brought her up short. He was genuinely concerned.

She patted his cheek. "I am fine, husband. Now tell me of yer Yule log. I haven't had one in years. Not since my mother died. She used to tell the story when we'd light it. I'd love to hear it again."

"Ahh, another tale my wife craves." He sat them in the large chair before the hearth, his chair, and settled her in his lap, still held in his arms. "Allow me to share our version."

He kissed her ear and spoke lowly. "The Druids started the tradition of the Yule log. They believed the sun stood still for twelve days in the middle of winter. During this time, they lit a log from the remains of last year's fire. They believed the light conquered the darkness, banished evil spirits, and brought luck for the coming year. Traditionally they used an oak log like the one ye see here.

"In an old Highland tradition, they connected the Yule log with Cailleach, the spirit of the winter months and the creator of our hills. While everyone completed their morning chores, the head of the house would slip into the woods on Yule E'en. He would proceed to chop down a withered tree. He would then cut this into the rude shape of a woman. The whole household would drag the 'Cailleach' back home. They placed the log on a peat fire and allowed it to burn over Yuletide."

Mary glanced at the log before the hearth. "It's not cut in any shape. Why not?"

Roderick grinned. "We decorate it instead. Each

146

family member places a decoration on the log tonight before I light it."

Mary turned to him. "But I have nothing to place on it to decorate it."

Roderick caressed her cheek. "Mary, the hall, ye decorated the hall." His eyes roamed the room. "And a wonderful job ye have done." Roderick's eyes rested on hers. "Why it's almost as beautiful as ye."

Mary blushed. "Well, I don't know about that, but the hall is lovely."

Roderick smiled. "Aye, ready for the special dinner I have planned."

Mary blushed. "Another private dinner, husband?"

Roderick took her hands in his and gazed into her eyes. "No, a wrong I must right. Ye will see."

Chapter 11

All stood at their places waiting for Roderick to arrive to begin dinner. Even Elizabeth attended the dinner tonight dressed in a colored dress, signaling her mourning period had ended. Rose stood next to Archibald's place, waiting for him as well.

Mary glanced around the room, noting that her first five guards and most of the clan's warriors were absent. Another elderly guard stood at her back. The ever-present guard Roderick insisted for her had become a comforting presence. Her husband not present, she turned to ask her guard if she should start the meal, but the great hall's doors opened. She turned as her husband strode through the doors, Archibald and the reverend behind him. Her first five followed, and the rest of the clan warriors. All marched in lines. When her husband stopped before her, the men stopped, and silence filled the hall.

Roderick turned and faced the clan, still on the floor, not the raised dais. "Clan MacDougall. I have made an error and forgotten a clan custom. An error I and the entire clan will rectify this evening."

The guard behind her whispered in her ear as he offered his arm. "This way, Milady." She took his arm, and he led her down the table to the end, rounded it, and took her before her husband. The guard patted her hand and stepped back.

Roderick bowed on one knee before her and spoke loudly. "I promise on my faith that I will, in the future, be faithful to my lady, never cause her harm, and will observe my homage to her completely against all persons in good faith and without deceit."

Fealty. Roderick swore an oath of loyalty to her, something she'd not seen in her father's hall since her mother's death. He ruled through fear and manipulation.

He stretched his hand to hers while keeping his head bowed. She stood stunned as the hall remained quiet. Roderick's gaze rose to hers. "Please, Mary, forgive me. Take my hand and accept my oath."

She took it as he rose, and she kissed the back. "Of course, husband."

He turned to the hall and nodded. Archibald stepped forward and repeated the vow. She took his hand as he rose. The reverend followed, and her five guards repeated the oath. Robbie blushed, and Hamish winked at her. Every warrior in the clan repeated the same, one by one. Soon each had sworn an oath bringing tears to her eyes. Roderick escorted her to their seats on the dais as a maid placed a single trencher before them filled with cheese, bread, and cured ham soup.

Roderick held her hand in his as he spoke. "The clan has done a great disservice to ye, Lady MacDougall. Ye have all awaited yer meal as the clan righted the wrong." He picked up bread and broke it in two, offering her a half. She raised an eyebrow. He smiled and winked as she took it. He turned to the clan and ate a bite. She followed suit, trusting his lead.

"I will share a trencher with my wife from now on.

Ye poison yer lady, ye poison yer laird. The punishment shall be swift and severe."

None moved in the hall, and Roderick turned and kissed her before all. When he finished the kiss, he announced, "Now, let's get on with the celebrations!" He sat, alerting all the meal could start.

As the meal ended, the reverend came before Roderick with a group of warriors hefting the Yule log between them. Roderick banged his cup on the table, and the hall quieted.

Reverend O'Donnell placed his hand on the log and whispered prayers. At his nod, the people at the dais table stood, Mary following. This must be the time when the family decorated the Yule log. Mary had secreted a mistletoe sprig into her skirts and fingered it now, ready to add her part to the family tradition. Constance was the first being at the end of the table. She stepped down and placed a lavender flower on the log but eyed Roderick as she placed it. Would that woman forever be a thorn in her side? She glanced at her husband, who stared ahead. That he did not acknowledge Constance's signal warmed Mary's heart.

Rose and Archibald followed. Rose, carrying the greenery they placed together. Rose blushed as Archibald smiled at her, and Mary was happy for the pair's budding romance. Elizabeth, or as all called her now, "Mom MacDougall," placed a woven vine in the shape of a heart on the log as she stood there a moment fingering her necklace. Mary imagined she thought of her husband Ian, her true love.

Elizabeth stepped back. Roderick took Mary's hand in his and led them to the log.

When he reached it, he handed her a similar heart-shaped vine. "Hold it with me, Mary, so that we can place it together."

She glanced at him, his fable story echoing in her mind. The Stone of Love was a heart-shaped stone that glowed for true lovers. The act touched her heart. She did and then placed her mistletoe on top.

Roderick picked it up and smiled. "Mistletoe." He held it over her head and kissed her full on the mouth as the clan cheered.

When he ended the kiss, he whispered in her ear, "For luck, Mary." Then placed it on the log.

The reverend handed him a stick that flamed on the end, and he lit the log. A small flame caught, and the clan cheered again as the warriors took the log to the hearth, signaling the beginning of the Christmas season.

Her first of what she hoped to be many to come. She whispered to Roderick, "Christmas began in the heart of God. It is complete only when it reaches the heart of man."

Roderick smiled at her as she said, "Thank you for this night, husband."

He grinned at her. "The night's not over."

Roderick served her each bite from their shared trencher, always offering her first bite, then taking two or more bites as the meal progressed. When she reached for the bread, he'd stop her hand and offer a ripped piece from his fingers, sometimes brushing the tips against her lips.

Mary glanced to the other side of Roderick, where Rose dined with Archibald. They, too, had their heads bent close, sharing bites between trenchers. A movement beyond Rose caught her eye, and Constance glared at her, then rolled her eyes and dropped her spoon.

A tap on her left arm turned her to face Lady MacDougall, Elizabeth, who beamed when their eyes met. "Such a lovely evening, Mary, and a wonderful start to the holiday season." Her eyes traveled the hall as she spoke. "The perfect time to end my confinement and join the living again." Her regard settled on Mary. "And ye were the reason for it." She patted her arm again. "Thank ye, Mary, for this early gift. The gift of life again."

Mary blushed. "I have to thank ye, Milady. If it weren't for yer help with the people, I'd still be an outcast."

Elizabeth waved her hand as the maids cleared the tables. "Nothing ye wouldn't have figured out on yer own being yer sweet self. Now, get back to yer evening with my attentive son. Tomorrow, we begin making the presents for the staff and clan."

Mary nodded. "Aye, and I must set some time aside for sewing. We've been so busy with other preparations, I haven't had time to make my husband's gift."

Roderick leaned in and whispered in her right ear, "Gift, did I hear my wife has a gift for her husband?"

Mary shifted aside. "Eavesdropping on the women, husband?"

He beamed when her eyes met his. "I thought my wife had a gift for me. Am I wrong?"

Mary grinned back. " 'Tis not yet Hogmanay, husband. Ye are impatient."

He cleared his throat. "Aye, I am." He rose and offered his hand to her. "Join me, wife?"

She took his hand as he pulled her to stand beside

her. To the clan, he raised his cup. "To Lady MacDougall and the beginning of our celebrations. Stay and take yer leisure."

Mary rose and whispered to Roderick, "Ye do not wish to stay?"

He kissed the back of her hand. "I have another surprise, wife. Come with me." He took her hand in his, waved her guard away for the evening, and headed up the stairs. So, they headed to their bedchamber for the night. What surprise could Roderick have in store? Mary was in their bedroom earlier, readying for dinner. She noted nothing unusual.

As they neared the doorway, two guards she didn't recognize exited the room. The last one nodded to Roderick as he closed the door. "All set, Milaird."

Roderick stopped before the closed door and took both her hands in his. "Mary, my first gift to ye, my wife, for this holiday." He kissed both hands on the back. "I hope ye like it."

He pushed the door open, stood back, and waved her into their room. At first, she noticed the room was lit with many candles, making it bright compared to the dimness of the castle. When she stepped into the room, her eyes drew immediately to the fireplace, where on the mantel sat the same greenery that graced the hall, complete with mistletoe sprigs. Her gaze roamed to the box bed, the covers folded open, awaiting their rest. Then rose to its canopy. Draped over the top in swags from poster to poster was greenery with mistletoe.

When she came a full circle, Roderick leaned against the doorframe with his arms folded. "I wanted ye to have the decorations here as well. Yer new tradition that I wish to honor, wife."

Tears welled in her eyes as her gaze connected with his.

He stepped forward. "Mary, this is to yer liking? Ye have tears in yer eyes."

She launched into his arms, and he took her close. "Aye, husband." She pulled back till their eyes came even. "Very much to my liking."

She kissed him, then did so again, but this time he stalled her retreat by slowing the kiss. His hands traveled to her lower back, pressing her closer to him, and with her gasp, his tongue delved into her mouth. Sweet tingles shot through her as his lips teased hers in a dance that sent flutters through her. He backed her into the bedpost and pressed against her, the bulge in his plaid reminding her of this morning's dreamy play.

She giggled into his kiss. "Husband, yer kisses remind me of my dream this morning."

He grinned as he brushed his lips against hers, his breath tickling her mouth. "A dream? Why I dreamed a fairy whisked into my bed and took me to an impassioned paradise."

She tilted her head to the side as her eyes rolled. "Must be a different dream. Mine was of a prince who came to carry me away to a sensual paradise. Must be someone other than my husband, then."

He kissed her hard, his hand tilting her head till he had complete control of her as he took her to passionate heights in a demanding kiss that repeatedly sent spark after spark through her. When he finally lifted his head, he whispered, " 'Twas yer husband who came to ye this morning, and make no mistake, I will be the only one in yer bed."

Mary caressed his cheek. "Always, and I will be

the only one for ye. Yer Fae come to enchant ye." Her hand drifted from his cheek to his chest, then to the front of his plaid, finding the proof of his desire and gripping it.

Roderick threw his head back in a growl. "Wife, if ye keep teasing me so, I will not be able to stop this evening, and I vowed to ye…"

Mary kissed him full on the lips taking the lead. Her tongue delved as he had to her, to show him she desired him beyond all else.

He gripped her shoulders and set her from him as he panted. When their gazes met, the fire in his eyes told Mary she'd affected him, maybe pushed him beyond his limits. After all he'd done for her this night, she wanted to be his in truth. Couldn't he see it in her eyes?

Her hand went to his cheek. "Roderick, I wish to be yers. I want to be yer wife in truth. Please let me show ye how much tonight has meant to me."

Roderick stood frozen as his smoldering expression held hers. His hands loosened on her shoulders as his look changed to something softer. His hand came to her cheek and caressed it.

Then progressed to her neck as his fingers brushed there. "My wife. I'd like that very much, Mary." Roderick's fingers brushed the top of her chest in a soft caress. Then he pulled the tie on her bodice front. His eyes shifted there as he slowly pulled the strings loose, allowing the front to fall open.

She reached to help loosen the garment, but his hand batted hers away. "No, I wish to take my time, not being afforded it the first time. I wish to savor my fairy wife."

She took a deep breath when the bodice's tension fully released, and she hummed as she dropped her hands to her sides, enjoying his attention. He slipped the bodice away, and she allowed it to drop to the floor.

Stepping closer, he drew the ties to her shift, and the garment fell open. His hand slid inside and cupped her breast, soft at first, then forming in his hand, his action making her head tilt back as a sigh escaped.

His lips brushed her exposed neck, and his tongue darted out, licking, then trailing to her breast as he pushed the fabric aside. He took her nipple full into his mouth and suckled, sending hot sparks through her. Her hands moved on their own and grabbed his head, her fingers threading through his hair. He quickly shifted to the other breast repeating the pull with a nip making her gasp.

Roderick's lips returned to hers and caught her gasp in a deep kiss. He pressed himself fully against her as she rested against the bedpost. He continued to kiss her as his hands fumbled at the ties to her skirts. They soon fell around her feet, and with a growl, he stripped her shift off her and exposed her to him. He stood back, her hands in his, as his eyes roamed her body in the candlelight. "Perfection," whispered from his lips, and he came swiftly to her in a heated kiss.

She grinned as she twisted and traded their positions, pressing him against the bedpost.

His grunt and raised hands aided her in the changed positions. "All's fair in love and war, husband."

She reached for his belt, and he undid it brushing her fingers aside. The belt clattered to the floor, and his plaid followed in a swish of material. She bent a little as her hands connected with his legs at the bottom of his shirt and traveled under against his naked skin. When her fingers shifted to the front and brushed his staff, Roderick's head tilted back and banged against the bedpost.

She continued traveling up to his chest with her hands beneath the material, her goal reached when she pulled his shirt off, bearing him to her in his full glory. His arms rose overhead as he removed his shirt and threw it aside in a growl. Her finger trailed down his sides, and a huff and a chuckle were his response to her tickle. The undulation of his muscled chest made her mouth water, and when he reached for her again, she stepped back to admire his form.

He stood before her as his eyes connected with hers in a heated glare. "Love and war, wife? Are we at war?"

She stood gazing at him. "No, I give ye my heart, Roderick."

He reached for her, and she stepped into his embrace as he kissed her fully, bringing her against his body. Heat rushed her when they connected as man and woman.

He lifted her as they still kissed, only breaking to lay her on the bed.

He traveled till he lay beside her. "And I give ye mine, *mo ghràdh, my love.*"

Her arms caressed his shoulders, then his chest as she had imagined the first time she saw him bare-chested. When she wondered what his bare chest would feel like under her hands. The reality felt even better than her imagination.

Roderick slid his leg between hers as his hand drifted from her knee to the apex of her thighs. His fingers tickled her woman's hair sending her stomach into flutters. Memories of this morning came back to her, and she shifted toward his hand. Roderick bent and kissed her as his hand covered her core. Heat suffused her body as his fingers slipped into her folds and her hands gripped his shoulders. Roderick spread her wetness, then slid a finger inside as her breath hitched.

His hand stopped. "Mary, are ye all right, lass?"

She sighed as she wiggled her hips. "All right? I am in heaven. What ye do to me." She sighed again as Roderick slid his finger deeper. He kissed her deeply and slipped his finger out, then slid in again, bringing forth a deep sigh from her.

He chuckled into their kiss. "My wife likes my attentions?"

Mary could only nod as she kissed him harder, encouraging him to play more. He took the cue, and his finger continued at a melodic pace as heat rose in her. She shifted and moaned as Roderick bent to suckle a nipple, his finger increasing its movement. This morning's activities flashed in her mind, and her hand gripped his rod. Roderick's hips bucked as he groaned. His hand maintained its rhythm. She matched his pace stroke for stroke as each panted. Heat consumed her, and her passage tickled and then tightened. With the next thrust of his finger, lights exploded behind her lids, and she called out.

Roderick removed his hand and went between her legs, dropping kisses down her neck. His weight pressed her into the mattress, a heavy comfort as he covered her with his body. His staff rubbed against her wetness, nearly driving her over the edge. Hot bliss burst from her, and he rubbed against her again.

Heat flashed over her body as Roderick's kisses trailed back to her ear. "Mary, my wife. 'Twill only hurt for a moment. But I promise ye sweet joy after." He rose and nudged till his tip pressed against her, then slid slowly inside.

His heat consumed her and threatened to tear her apart but with a kiss on her ear and a whisper. "God, Mary, love, ye are so beautiful."

She sighed into his embrace, and he slid the whole way in and stopped. At first, the stretching was almost too much. But soon, as he shifted, little tremors shook her legs as tingles shot from where he joined with her. She rocked her hips with his, and he kissed her hard as he began to move within her. Each push longer, driving harder. She caught her breath, and the tingles turned into waves of pleasure that burst with each of his thrusts.

His lips found hers again as he started at a faster pace. Mary's legs drew in, but his hips kept her open as he plunged in repeatedly, taking her higher and higher. She cried out as lights burst behind her lids and her hips shook.

Roderick panted with his exertion. The pace demanding her passion matched his. In a hard thrust that rocked her on the bed, Roderick froze above her, his breath held, and redness covered his body. He yelled her name and collapsed on her. His breathing came heavy. He rolled to the side, pulling her to him holding her as he caught his breath.

When he shifted her, her woman's area pinched, and wetness spread, but an overall satisfied feeling overcame her—one of relaxed joy.

Once Roderick controlled his breathing, he tilted

his face to hers. "Mary, ye are a joy to behold. That was wonderful, wife."

Mary blushed and tried to turn away, but Roderick held her face in his hand. "I meant it, Mary. Ye are such a gift."

Mary smiled. "As are ye, husband. And this time ye did it right."

Roderick chuckled as he lay back, stretching. "Aye, I suppose that first night was a shock. But we are truly husband and wife now." He turned and kissed her hard. "My wife."

He stopped and gazed at her momentarily, his finger trailing her cheek, then pushed her hair behind her ear. He patted it and disengaged himself from her. He crossed the room to the bowl of water. Wet a cloth and cleaned himself. He rinsed it out and returned to the bed.

She moved to take it from him, but he lay beside her as he held the cloth out of her reach. "Please, allow me. I wish to care for ye."

He cleaned her, and when she shifted and whimpered, he gathered her in his arms as he tossed the cloth, and it landed near the stand with the bowl. She placed her head on his chest, much as she had done when he healed her before. His heartbeat was steadily in her ear as he covered them with the blankets and plaids. They lay as the candles burned down, and his hand rubbed her back. She nearly drifted to sleep, and Roderick bent and kissed her. "Good night, sweet wife."

Chapter 12

The short week leading to Christmas Eve passed in a blur, each day nearly the same. Mary woke to Fiona's cheery smile and Roderick's half-eaten carrot cake with warm tea. The days filled with work readying the castle for the coming holy day of Christmas and the gift exchange of the new year brought a welcome bustle to Mary's daily life at Dunstaffnage. The nights she spent in Roderick's arms as they explored and discovered their newly wedded bliss. The soreness of the first night together quickly progressed to the repeated thrill of being a well-wedded woman.

As Mary worked on the mini soaps Elizabeth suggested she gift the castle staff with, the memory of last night's newest exploration that involved Roderick's mouth flashed in her mind.

Warmth spread through her as his tongue licked her folds. "Roderick, ye kiss me there?" The breath of his chuckle tickled her hair, sending tingles all over her body. His mouth covered her, and his licking and suckling pressure sent her to new heights as she screamed when she peaked.

Someone grabbed her hand. "Mary, ye near dumped the tray of soap."

Fiona had her hand as Bertha took the tray from her. "I have it, Mary."

She carried the tray away as she mumbled, "Lass

has her head in the clouds now that her husband is so attentive. 'Tis a wonder she's out of bed. He keeps her there longer and longer each day."

Elizabeth folded each cut soap into a cloth and placed them in a basket as they worked in the kitchen. "Aye, soon I'll have grandbabies to cuddle for myself." The group of maids in the kitchen giggled as Mary blushed. They were right. Her head was in the clouds.

Elizabeth tapped her arm. "Why don't ye go into the hall, sit by the window, and see if ye can finish yer husband's gift."

Rose set her soap aside. "Oh, I need to knit. I'll join ye so we can work on our gifts together."

Mary nodded and picked up her basket as she entered the great hall. Rose grabbed hers and followed. Some staff milled about setting this or that to order. She settled in a chair Elizabeth had set before the window so she could sew near the light.

Rose sat next to her, knitting her gift for Archibald, woolen socks. "Usually, I'm off with maids on errands, but today I'm glad I stayed to help with the soaps."

Mary smiled at her friend. "Aye. 'Tis good ye came into yer own life here at Dunstaffnage."

As she pulled out the partially sewn shirt, the incident only two days before flashed in her mind. When Mary had come to pick up her nearly finished shirt from her basket, the shirt fell to the floor in shreds bringing tears to her eyes. No one in the castle knew who'd snuck into the basket she'd left by the window, but someone had ruined her gift. Mary had an idea but decided not to raise concern over Constance. One of her ma's sayings echoed, *better the devil you know than the devil you don't.*

Well, it seemed all Mary needed to do was wait. Constance's presence grew less and less the closer they drew to the coming holiday. These days Mary had taken to carrying her sewing basket with her. With Fiona's and Rose's help, they'd redone the shirt in a day. She put on the final touches, Roderick's initials A.R.M. embroidered on the collar.

"Alexander Roderick MacDougall." She whispered his name as she started the first stitch to the *A*. Elizabeth's statement came back to her—grandbabies. Her hand went to her flat stomach. Would they have children?

Rose giggled as she looped her yarn over a needle. "It's the third time this morning ye touched yer belly. Some news, Mary?"

Mary was startled. "Oh, I don't think so. Too soon."

Rose smiled as she pushed together her knitting, checking the sock's length. "Certainly, with as attentive as Roderick has been, a babe could take root."

Mary shook her head and focused on her gift—the next stitch, the peak of the *A,* and another back down the other side.

Rose glanced at her sewing. "Initials on the collar. Nice and personal." She bent back to her knitting. "So, a babe. How exciting. Would the name start with an *A*? *A*, for Anabell or Alex, after his father. Imagine, Mary, a petite, dark-headed girl with a fierce determination like her father or a lad with yer soft brown hair and his father's broad build."

Mary sighed. "Would be nice, aye. At least with the birth of a babe, we would fulfill the king's demands." A life of their own that could become normal—without war, troubles, or shortages. A life of bliss like she'd felt for the last few days. She stitched the cross arm of the *A* and prayed for a babe—not just for the king but for her and Roderick, a family of their own.

****

Roderick sat staring at the stack of missives on his desk. Archibald sat across, entering notes into the accounting records. A huff or hum would come from him from time to time, but overall, the clan's first light part of winter had weathered the rationing well.

Roderick's mind wandered to last night, or was it this morning? His encounters with Mary blurred together into one erotic moment he spent each night in since they'd first made love.

The pink of her nipples peeked through the sheets as he dropped his head to the apex of her thighs. He breathed through his nose, her aroma making him rise to the occasion. He had plans for his wife this night—to take her to heights he'd only heard bragged about between warriors. He'd had a widow once, one his father sent to him to teach him the ways of a woman, but the couplings with her were physical and base, whereas, with Mary, there was more. He felt a desire to bring them together and join emotionally as well as physically. And tonight, he wanted her to soar through the heavens. He bent and licked her once. Her gasp came fast as she sat up. "Roderick, ye kiss me there?"

He chuckled as he bent to his task. The desire to have Mary scream his name before morning gave him extra energy he'd not had.

A slap on the desk brought him upright.

Archibald burst into laughter. "Less than a week in

yer bed, and ye are already daydreaming of yer wife."

Roderick blinked at him, the haze of his lust fading as he glared at his longtime friend.

Archibald waved a missive. "I asked ye three times, what reply do ye want to send Comyn? 'Tis his first formal message. His complaints and accusations cannot go unnoticed."

The letter in Archibald's hand he'd read earlier and tossed aside disgusted with Comyn. "He says he's enjoying his new second son and the laziness of peace."

Roderick barked a laugh. Second son and what the hell is lazy about peace? Work around his property still went on. The fight to live and survive took work. Something Comyn had no concept of, forcing others to work hard while he sat.

Then his accusations heated Roderick. "Aye, the bastard has the nerve to accuse us of raiding his villages when it's him doing all the raiding. Food stores were damaged but not a total waste to the people. All done by warriors in his plaid."

Archibald set the message down with a sigh of his own. "He claims the same. But the attacks from us have people injured. He says it's our plaid."

Roderick slammed his hand on the desk. "It's not ours!"

Archibald put his hands up. "I know, Roderick. My guards sent to yer northern borders returned yesterday. My da says he has no idea who's behind the prodding, but someone's spreading the word *ye* want the wars to start again."

Roderick stood and strode to the fireplace. "I have not. Ye know that." Mary came to his mind. "Why, I want, no *need* them to end." He turned, facing his old friend. "Mary and I have only begun our marriage. And off to a good start. I want this peace to work between our clans."

Archibald nodded as he pulled out a fresh piece of vellum. "Aye, start with yer reply to Comyn and craft it well. He's sending some of his warriors soon with Mary's belongings. Invite them to stay a while. Let them have some freedom."

Roderick started to speak, but Archibald cut him off. "Secretly guarded. Let them see for themselves, ye and Mary happy and how welcomed they are. Offer aid to help find who is behind both raids on the clans."

Roderick crossed to his desk and picked up a quill, liking the sound of Archibald's plan.

When he sat, Archibald grinned at him. "In the meantime, we send some scouts to his lands. Let us peek at what is happening in the 'common land.' "

Roderick began his letter, and part way through, his head shot up. "Mary, she doesn't need to know there are still issues. I want her at peace and comfortable in our new lives together."

Archibald smiled over a message he read. "Of course, and Rose as well."

Roderick chuckled. "Things going well with ye and Rose?"

Archibald laughed. "Ye aren't the only one who's not gotten much sleep lately, Roderick." At his chuckle, Archibald added, "It will be a happy Christmas this year, friend."

****

Christmas Eve morning came cold, but Mary didn't notice. Waking warm and well-loved in her husband's arms, she stayed and fell asleep again.

A shake woke her later, and she rolled over. "Fiona, 'tis Christmas Eve. Leave me to lay in."

A breath brushed her ear, then a kiss and her husband's voice whispered, "Not Fiona, *mo chridhe*. Mass awaits."

She rolled over and welcomed the day to a kiss from Roderick, the carrot bread taste fresh on his lips. "Did ye leave any for me to break my fast?" The plate of bread was set on her chest, and Roderick stood beside her with her cup of tea. She sat up holding the plate and wondered if her husband had steeped her tea by the hearth as Fiona did each morning. As she took the mug, the steam rising told her he had. He shook out her dress and wiggled his eyebrows at her. "We could stay here and worship each other..." Mary rolled her eyes as she finished off the bread and rose from the bed.

Her attentive husband dressed her and escorted her to the chapel. They knelt side by side, each praying over their rosaries.

As Mary prayed for Christ's birth, her conversation with Rose came back to her. Now more than a couple weeks spent in Roderick's bed, certainly she could be pregnant. As she counted her beads, she counted the days since her last cycle. They were always irregular. After spending so much time rationing and working hard in her father's hall, a traveling healer had told her under duress she'd skip courses but wouldn't be pregnant. Still, she counted again and came up with too many days. Her hand flew to her stomach as she gasped aloud.

Roderick stopped his whispered prayers and leaned over. "Mary, ye all right, lass?"

Mary bit her lip to stop herself from saying

anything. It could be duress. She'd wait another week or so before she'd assume anything.

She bent to her prayers as she shook her head, and Roderick returned to his.

That night Mary stood before the clan at Christmas Eve dinner. Her time to speak about her mistletoe tradition was now upon her, and her hands broke out in a sweat. She glanced at Roderick, who winked at her. Rose cleared her throat, and Mary regarded her longtime friend, who nodded to the clan sitting in the hall awaiting the special meal.

Roderick had asked her to tell her mistletoe tale so everyone in the clan would understand her gift of new birth and life. At each place setting, a small mistletoe sprig sat. Some people held theirs, others twirled them, and some watched her with anticipation of a great tale. She hoped she wouldn't disappoint them.

She turned to the clan and took a deep breath. "The Druids held nothing more sacred than the mistletoe and a tree on which it grew—a hard oak. On the sixth day of the moon, they gathered the plant with a great ceremony. The sixth day chosen for a rise in strength in the earth and not one-half of its full-size moon gave the plant extra potency. The moon, in their native word, means 'healing all things.' They prepared a ritual banquet beneath the oak tree. A priest arrayed in white vestments climbed the tree and cut down the mistletoe with a golden sickle, and they caught it in a white cloak." Some clan members held their sprig close to their hearts while others stared at her, awaiting the entire tale. All sat enraptured in her story.

"They'd pray to God to render his gift favorable to those he had bestowed it on. They believed that mistletoe given to each would impart fertility to any barren animal and that it was an antidote for all poisons."

Roderick took her hand in his and tickled her palm. She glanced at him, and he winked at her. His flirtation lifting her confidence, she turned back to the clan to continue her tale.

"Today, we gather and honor this tradition to spread 'healing for all' with the mistletoe strung throughout the hall."

Roderick stood and held his mistletoe over her head as she spoke. "A gift for each clan member. Yer own mistletoe sprigs. A kiss under the mistletoe at Hogmanay from yer love will bring good luck for the year through."

She turned to Roderick, their plan to kiss briefly, but his smile went wide. He grabbed her about the waist, bent her over his arm as he held the mistletoe over her head, and kissed her most thoroughly to the cheers of the clan.

Roderick and Mary sat, signaling the meal could begin. Their shared trencher a maid set before them, and the habit of feeding her between his two to three bites began. She wondered if she'd ever have a meal where she fed herself again and giggled at the thought.

Roderick fed her another bite of lamb, not stew, for the special meal. "What's funny, lass?"

She chewed her meat, tender and flavorful, before she responded. "Nothing, husband."

He leaned over, and his breath tickled her ear as he whispered, "Did ye like my kiss? The one under the mistletoe?" Mary blushed and nodded her head. Roderick's grunt of approval came as he took another bite of the lamb. She felt playful this evening, the celebrations and the holiday lifting her spirits.

She leaned over and whispered, "Did ye like my story?" She leaned in farther as her hand brushed his inner thigh. "Tell me, Roderick, will ye need to drink some wine soaked in mistletoe to help with yer fertility?"

He jolted in his chair and dropped his knife on the trencher as she leaned back. He coughed and had to drink some of his wine to settle himself. Good, she had his attention.

Roderick leaned close, his fingers rubbing the side of her breast. Even through her bodice, she felt the caress. She flinched as he whispered in her ear, "Trust me, wife. I need no...assistance."

The memory of last night's passion came to her mind. The emotions of Roderick's lovemaking filled her and brought a smile to her face.

Mary reached for her mistletoe, wanting to kiss Roderick under hers. Something stabbed her finger hard. She yelped and dropped the spring. Blood spread from the sprig to the tablecloth.

Roderick took her hand in his as he sucked her pricked finger.

His other hand picked up her mistletoe. "Mary, there's a thistle in yer mistletoe."

Blood dripped from her finger as the sting spread, bringing tears to her eyes. Roderick growled as he dropped her spring and wrapped her finger in his dining cloth.

He bellowed, "Agatha!" She jumped at his shout.

Mary waved her away, shaking her head as those in the hall closest to them turned and stared.

Mary didn't want the slight to be known as she tried to cover the incident. "No worries, Roderick, just a weed in the sprig. A mishap."

Agatha stepped between them and took her hand, removed the cloth, and examined it. "No harm, Milaird. The bleeding has already stopped." She dropped Mary's hand. "Hope it's not a bad omen, her good luck charm stabbing her." Agatha moved back to her place to finish her meal.

Roderick growled as he rose, strode to the fireplace, and threw her mistletoe into the fire. Her good luck charm for the year went up fast in flames as Mary stared on, hoping her dreams hadn't gone up in flames as well.

When Roderick returned to his seat, the swag behind them above the fireplace fell. All in the hall gasped, and a couple of women cried out.

Mary stood as Roderick waved a warrior to rehang it. A whisper reached Mary. "It's a bad omen, the greenery falling. The Comyn bitch should have never taken it down." When she glanced to see who spoke so near, the space behind her was empty.

Roderick patted her hand. "Ye have the mistletoe from the abbey, Mary. Ye have all the luck ye need, lass."

She hoped so.

Chapter 13

Snow crunched as Archibald approached Roderick as he stood watching his warriors practice fighting.

His captain warmed his hands over the small fire before Roderick. "Hogmanay and ye have the men out here fighting in the snow."

Roderick grunted. They needed to be on alert, no matter the day. And a holiday was the perfect time for a surprise attack from the enemy.

Archibald pulled out a flask, opened it, and tipped it up for a swig. "The report from the village said only a small raid." After smacking his lips, his longtime friend and advisor handed the flask to him.

He upended it as Archibald spoke. "No one was injured. Only food stores damaged."

Roderick handed the flask back. "We must be prepared at any moment for the wars to start again. I trust no one and Comyn even less."

Archibald pocketed the whisky and toed the snow. "Ye have the women worried. Mary questioned Rose, who had to lie."

Roderick growled, "I told ye not to say anything to the women. Why would Rose have to lie to my wife?" Damn Archibald.

His captain blew his breath. "The women aren't stupid. They see ye send scouting parties, see ye in council, see us prepare." Archibald glanced at the castle and back at him. "They've lived with war enough to know what preparations look like. Even on holiday."

Roderick looked to the sky, overcast with deep white clouds. Mary standing at their window this morning as she gazed out came to his mind.

"More snow, husband, I smell it." She rubbed her stomach and smiled. "I loved snow on the holidays." More and more, she caressed her belly. His ma asked if they had news to share, but Mary had said nothing to date. She'd even admitted to asking Mary after catching her with her hand on her stomach. Who denied it. Said she even questioned Fiona, Mary's maid, about her courses—nothing since Fiona took over. Elizabeth claimed her hand action was involuntary, that Mary might suspect she carried but said nothing till she was sure. His ma's list of symptoms ran through his mind. Sickness in the morning, no. Dizziness when she stood, no. A healthier appetite, yes, but he'd attributed that to his kitchens being better fortified than her da's hall.

The clang of swords brought him out of his thoughts. Nothing would disrupt the newfound happiness of his marriage. Not war, not rationing, not troubles. Nothing would harm his Mary, and no one would harm his family.

He hardened his resolve as he spoke to Archibald. "We stay vigilant." His gaze roamed the skies. "Seems the heavy snow comes early, blocking the passes as winter sets in." He nodded as his warriors fought before him, their grunts echoing. "We can't fall into a false sense of ease. Comyn is too crafty. I must protect all."

****

It didn't snow that day, but that didn't deter Mary's excitement for the evening's celebrations. Snow still dotted the ground, adding to Mary's excitement. Hogmanay was upon them, the new year and the present exchange after dinner. Roderick served her another piece of roast lamb, a pause in rationing for the holiday dinner commanded by her husband, much to the joy of all. His attention to her seemed more these days. He checked on her food regularly, asked how she felt often, and even today sent Agatha to her even though she'd not complained. A maid filled their cup, and she reached for it only to have her husband snatch it and sip it first, then hand it to her with a smile.

She glanced about the hall; the present exchange would start soon. She ran her list through her mind, the mistletoe at Christmas, her gifts to the clan, soaps distributed earlier today to the castle staff, and her present for her husband sat under her seat.

Movement from the corner of her eye caught her attention. Constance sat with a young warrior as she tossed her hair and nibbled from his offered food. Next to her, Rose and Archibald whispered to each other over their trencher. Well, it seemed everything had worked out well for all. Still, she couldn't dispel her nerves, and her hand went to her stomach. Was it nerves or worry? She wasn't certain. She glanced to her right at Mom MacDougall, who watched her with a smile.

Her husband's whisper in her ear startled her. "Ye feel well, Mary?"

She turned to him and smiled. "Well, husband."

His gaze went to her hand and back to her face. "Almost time for presents. I hope yers is grand." She might not call his shirt grand, but she'd made it herself and would give him a proper first gift.

He took her hand in his and kissed the back. " 'Tis time."

Roderick stood and banged his cup on the table. The hall quieted, and all turned to their laird. His gaze traveled the hall, landing here and there on different clan members. Some Mary recognized and others not.

His eyes landed on her, and he winked. "Clan MacDougall, this new year has brought many new opportunities to our clan." His regard went back to the crowd. "The clan wars ended, a new hope with a new bride." He glanced at her and caressed her cheek. When his face returned to the clan, his expression went hard. "Newfound peace for our land. And I will see we keep it that way for all our generations."

He paused a moment, took a breath, then let it out. "The snow holds off, suggesting a light winter instead of the heavy one predicted. With that, spring harvest should be bountiful. With it we should see the end of our lean times." He grinned at her as he spoke. "If the spring's bounty is high, extra rations for each household." The clan cheered as the men pounded the tables and women hugged their children. At first, Mary worried over his promise, but she'd heard the reports from the farmers the bounty would be higher this year.

Roderick pulled her hand, and she stood next to him. He raised his cup, and she followed as he yelled over the cheers, "To our new family and new year!" They drank together, and Roderick banged his cup on the table. "Take yer ease and to yer gifts!" They sat together, and clan members filed past, wishing their laird and lady a new year. A member from each household approached and set presents before Roderick: small trinkets or handmade tokens of devotion to their laird.

Mabel set a spring of dried lavender before Mary. "For ye, Milady."

Another maid she'd help read passed a basket to her. "Figs, from me own garden." Even Constance came forward with her new man on her arm. She set a cloth before Roderick, who didn't acknowledge her.

She turned to Mary and offered a wrapped loaf of bread to her. " 'Tis carrot. I hear ye like it."

As she set it before Mary, Roderick snatched it, broke a piece, and shoved it in his mouth. When he chewed and swallowed, he nodded to Mary.

Now that Constance's offering had passed his test, Mary smiled. "Thank ye, Constance. Happy New Year to ye." Constance moved off on the arm of the man, and they left the hall.

Most had filed out of the hall, leaving the family alone. A large pile sat before Roderick while only a few items were before Mary. No matter. This was more than she'd ever received in her father's hall. Roderick stood and went to his mother's side. He sat beside her and took her hand in his. "For ye, mother." He placed a small bag in her hand. Elizabeth patted her son's cheek and then opened the bag. A smaller version of her silver heart necklace fell out.

Roderick fingered it in her hand. "It's for yer Iona Stone, the one da made for ye to carry that matches his."

Elizabeth grinned and patted his cheek. "Oh, Roderick, thank ye. But my gift to ye is the stone he carried." She pulled a small white stone from her pouch and handed it to her son. She curved her hands over his as he held the stone. "It was his stone he carried for luck. And now ye shall carry it."

Roderick tried to hand it back. "Ma, I can't. Ye carry the mate."

Mary leaned over and asked, "Is this the Stone of Love from the Fable?"

Elizabeth took another stone from her pouch and held it up for Mary to see. Between her fingers she held a small heart-shaped white stone about the size of Roderick's thumb. "Not the Stone of Love, but an Iona Stone. All sea captains carry them for luck. My Ian had matching stones carved, so we each carried the other's heart when away." She placed hers inside the silver case and pocketed it as she smiled at Roderick. "Now Roderick carries his father's for luck."

Roderick cleared his throat. "I shall with honor."

Archibald stood and announced, "My turn!" He turned to Rose and handed her a bag. Rose gasped. "Archibald, for me?" She upended the bag, and a bracelet with a round blue stone glittered in the firelight. Her face met Archibald's, and she smiled as she held her wrist out for him to put it on.

Rose stood and handed Archibald a packet. He untied the strings quickly like a child, and inside were the socks Rose had worked hard to knit. Archibald pulled them onto his hands. "So warm!"

Mary withdrew her gift out from under her chair and handed it to Roderick as he sat. "For me, wife?" He opened it slowly as he eyed her. Not sure if he'd like it, she felt butterflies tickle her stomach. He pulled the shirt out, and the collar caught his attention immediately.

His finger slid over the embroidered initials. "I've not had something so personal. My initials." His gaze met hers. "Ye made this?"

She nodded. Roderick bent and kissed her full on the mouth. Her focus shifted from person to person—a new start to a new year with a new family and life. Archibald stood. "Well, that's it. Off to bed."

He grabbed Rose's hand, who pulled back. "Wait, what about Mary's gift? From Roderick?"

Mary blushed. "I have the gift of family. Like every year, it will be enough."

Elizabeth snorted. "Not in my household and not with my son!"

His mother picked up her gifts, strode by Roderick, and batted his head. "I'll leave ye to give yer wife a proper gift, son."

Archibald took Rose's hand in his as they gathered their gifts. "Aye, Rose. Leave them to their own." He followed Mom MacDougall out of the hall.

Roderick hummed as he took her hand in his.

She eyed him. "Ye planned this, didn't ye?" Roderick grinned wide as Mary huffed. "Kicked all out of yer hall so we could be alone."

He pulled a bag from his sporran, small like the one he gave his ma.

He fingered it a moment, then spoke softly. "My ma's gift surprised me tonight. My da's stone and hers were something they shared and cherished. I planned to carve ye one of yer own, but with her gift, it makes mine much easier to give."

He upended the bag, and a silver heart—a duplicate of his mother's necklace—fell out. The silver heart glinted in the fire's light. He flipped the heart open, and inside was empty. He placed his father's heart stone inside, rubbed his thumb over it, then closed the case.

He held the case out to her. "Please take my da's stone, Mary. It's my heart ye carry now. It's my love ye hold already." She took the heart stilled by his words. His heart? He closed his hands around hers. "I love ye, Mary. Carry my heart with ye always, and know my love stays with ye."

Mary's eyes filled with tears. "Ye love me?"

He kissed her briefly. "Aye, *mo chridhe*."

She blinked as tears fell. "I love ye too." She held the gift to her heart as her other hand went to her stomach.

Roderick grunted. "Enough, ye will tell me now."

Mary wiped her tears with her free hand. "Tell ye what?"

"Are ye carrying my bairn?" How had he…

Her face must have given her thoughts away since Roderick sat back in his chair. "Ye constantly touch yer belly. Ye haven't had yer courses since ye came here." Mary gasped. To discuss that with a man, husband or not, why she'd never.

Roderick took her hand in his. "Mary, are ye?" She glanced at their hands holding his gift, his heart. Then back at his face. Truth above all else, it's what they'd agreed.

She took a deep breath. "I can't be certain. My…courses were always off, but I could be." His whoop startled her, but she stilled him gripping his hand. "I will wait another week to make certain. Please don't tell anyone till we are sure."

Roderick stood and picked her up as she yelped. He took the stairs as he carried her. "Roderick, ye don't have to…"

He kissed her. "Aye, yes, I do. My wife and bairn.

My family." He reached the top and shifted her in his arms. She still held the heart close to her chest.

Roderick elbowed his way into their room and lowered her along his body. He took the heart from her and kissed her.

He whispered as he set it on the bedside table. "*Mo chridhe*." *My heart.*

When he turned to her, he took her face in his hands and kissed her softly on the mouth. Roderick tilted her head to the side and trailed kisses down her neck till her bodice stopped his advance. He growled low as he reached behind her and made fast work of her laces.

Mary giggled as he worked the strings without looking. "Ye are becoming well practiced at that, husband."

He flipped her around and yanked on the strings until he removed them entirely. He shoved the shoulder down till the garment dropped to the floor. He untied her skirt, and it quickly followed. Mary tried to turn around, but his hand on her shoulder stopped her.

He reached around to her front and untied her shift. As it fell open, his hands covered her breasts, and his lips brushed her ear. "I love it when ye are bare for me." The fabric slipped off her shoulders and dropped to the floor as Roderick brought her body flush with his. His arousal rubbed against her backside as he ran his tongue along her neck.

She reached behind her and brushed her fingers against his bare thighs. His hands molded her breasts and squeezed lightly, sending tingles through her. She turned, and he wrapped her in his arms as he kissed her lips. Roderick pushed her toward the bed till her knees hit it, and she fell back into the coverings. A giggle escaped as she tried to sit up, but he came over her kissing her lips again. Roderick kissed his way to the breasts and suckled one tip hard as Mary arched into his caresses. His kisses traveled lower to her belly, and he kissed her just above her navel.

"Wee babe," came from his lips as he paused there momentarily, his hands rounding her stomach. His chuckle blew his breath on her, and she stirred at the tickle. His kisses moved lower until his gasp blew on her curls, sending shivers over her body. He'd done this only once before but sent her to such heights. She desperately wanted him to kiss her there again.

He spread her legs and inhaled through his nose. A wet lick warmed her, and she jolted at the intimate contact. Roderick growled and licked again, slower this time from bottom to top. His hands grasped her hips and pulled her to the edge of the bed till she felt like she might fall off. He stood and took hold of her knees as his gaze connected with hers. "I enjoy hearing ye call my name, wife. Will ye call my name this evening?" Mary could only smile as she shivered in anticipation of his attention. He spread her knees as he knelt before her, his face level with her woman's parts. The intimate position, so raw for Mary, so erotic.

He licked her again, but this time, it connected differently. Her whole area came under his mouth, all of her kissed by him. She felt naughty and right at the same time—something so deliciously sinful done by the man who was her husband. Mary lay back, closed her eyes, and awaited heaven to arrive. He settled his mouth on her, began sucking, and stars danced behind her eyelids. She tried to close her knees, but he growled and held them open. His tongue ran over her again, this time wet and slippery, but the friction sensation was also there. Roderick's mouth covered her again and sucked over and over. And that energy built like it had the last time. The dam filled behind her, rushing to an end she knew he'd take her to.

She huffed and whimpered as he continued his assault on her body. His tongue, then the sucking, sent chills over her and heated at once. She cried out, but he kept going, attacking her senses. Roderick shifted to the side, his finger slid in her passage, and stars burst behind her eyes as she cried out his name. His finger, his lips, the sucking—it was all too much, and she convulsed against his mouth as she screamed. He removed his hand and mouth. The cold air was a shock to her sensitive area, now heated.

He stripped off his clothing and grabbed her hips. "I must have ye now, Mary." He drove into her to the hilt, the jolt one of surprise and welcome. His fullness filled her as he had before. He stayed there a moment and groaned. "God, ye are so sweet." He pumped again. Her body followed his lead, that pressure building again. He took a frenzied pace as he stood over her, and she lay on the bed. Too taken in pleasure, Mary could only ride with him.

He stopped, grabbed her legs, and wrapped them around him. Roderick grabbed her hips again and lifted her while still joined. He moved with her upon the bed and set her as he kneeled. His face came to hers as he kissed her hard and started his wild pace again. That pressure built, and she came close to that dam again. She cried his name, and he thrust into her once, cried her name, and thrust into her again.

He stayed there momentarily and fell atop her, panting as he caressed her face. "God, Mary, ye are beautiful." He lay there a moment as he caught his breath. Roderick turned and traveled down her body. He rested his head on her breasts as he caressed her stomach. "My wee babe."

She must have dozed off, for the next thing she knew, he'd kissed her and gathered her in his arms. He covered them with the bedding.

He whispered. "Sleep, sweet wife." She fell asleep as he held her close to his heart.

Chapter 14

Mary awoke to a pounding on the bedroom door. Roderick jumped from the bed naked, grabbed his sword from beside the bed, and cracked the door. Whispers came to her as she rolled over with a cramp in her belly. Maybe she was just hungry.

Roderick returned and kissed her cheek. "Dawn and yer father's men are at the gate with a wagon."

She lifted her head as he dressed in the early morning light. "My father's men?" She held her breath as Roderick leaned against his plaid stand and quickly belted the already folded fabric around his waist. *Please say they weren't there to attack.*

His huff came to her. "Aye. My outer guards tracked them for a full day since they entered my borders." Roderick sheathed his sword and swung it on his back. He stopped and smiled at her. "Yer belongings, Mary. Since the snows have held off, yer da has sent yer things."

Mary rose as Roderick moved to the door and paused before exiting. "Take yer time, wife. I'll need to inspect the men, the wagon, the horses. All before I'll let them in the outer bailey."

He went through it as Fiona came inside holding a plate of bread. Roderick took a bite and rushed into the hall.

Fiona set the plate on the bedside table. Carrot

bread again, sweetened with honeyed seeds on top. As Fiona built up the fire and placed a pot of water to heat, Mary turned in her bed till she sat on the side. Another cramp came harder, and she doubled over with a moan.

Fiona was by her side with a hand to help her stand. "Are ye well, Milady?" As Mary stood, a gush of wetness came from her privates. She yelped and rushed behind the privacy screen to the garderobe. *God, no. it can't be.* When she sat and inspected, sure enough, her courses had arrived, announcing her suspicions about carrying Roderick's babe were not true. Tears welled in her eyes as a whimper escaped.

Fiona stood on the other side of the screen. "Milady, I cleaned the blood. There's a basket with some moss and cloths beside ye. Drawers as well. Set there for yer needs."

Mary heaved a silent sob as she bit her fist. No babe. Tears fell down her cheeks. It wasn't the lack of one for the order of the king that hurt the most. It was telling Roderick she didn't carry his babe. The last week he'd spent each night lying on her belly speaking to his son. Telling him of each thing they'd do once he arrived in the world.

Roderick's voice echoed in her head. "Lad, first ye will be the brawest of all. Wide like yer da and his before him." He patted her belly. "Then as ye grow, we'll start yer training with the small wood sword." He gasped. "And a pony. Ye must ride well to be a good warrior."

Mary ran her fingers through Roderick's hair. "What if she's a girl?"

He glanced up at her with a smile on his face. "Then she'll have her mother's beauty and kind heart."

He kissed her belly. "I've even thought of names. Alexander after my da Ian Alexander."

Mary giggled as his breath blew against her belly when he spoke again. "Alexandria for a girl." He slid up to kiss her on the mouth. "Will that do?"

Fiona's voice broke the spell. "Will that do, Milady?"

For a while, it seemed like they were a loved match, husband and wife in truth. A couple eagerly awaiting their first child. Something she often referred to as a gift from God.

Mary wiped her tears and hardened her heart. God would gift them with a child when he felt they were ready. In the meantime, she needed to see to the unloading of her belongings, as meager as they were.

Fiona's voice came again. "Milady, are ye well?"

Mary sniffed and sat up straighter. "Aye, fine. I'll be out soon. And I'll need a sturdy dress today."

Cleaned and dressed she strode into the outer bailey as the wagon and her father's men cleared the gate. Roderick at the lead on horseback pointed them to the side as more of his warriors surrounded them. Mary recognized most the warriors from her father's keep. Each one nodded to her as they rode past.

The Comyn warrior in the front kept his head bowed, but she knew the horse. When he dismounted and walked around the wagon, she recognized his stance and gait. Erik James Sinclair, second son to the laird Sinclair and her father's war chief, raised his face and met hers across the bailey as he slowly smiled. He couldn't be that stupid to come here. Her betrothed, before the king's orders came, turned to speak to her husband, whose rigid stance alerted her of his immense displeasure at having to welcome Comyn warriors into his home. If he found out who it was he spoke with, what would his reaction be?

Rose came up beside her. "Ye da actually sent yer things." She huffed. "And from the look of it, more than just yers."

As Rose spoke, Mary's eyes traveled the wagon stuffed full with an oiled fabric tied over the top. "What all else do ye think he sent?"

Mary stepped forward. "Only one way to find out."

Rose grabbed her arm hard. "Is that—"

Mary shrugged her off. "Aye, say nothing."

Both women strode forward, and as she neared the wagon, Roderick stepped before her and grabbed her arm. "The men will unload the wagon under guard. Ye, wife, will wait in the hall."

She shook her arm free of his grasp. "Nonsense, Roderick. These are my clan members. I wish to welcome them into my home."

She sidestepped him, but he blocked her way. She raised an eyebrow. "It will be fine. We are at peace, are we not?"

Erik chose this moment to speak. "Aye, MacDougall, peace times. Allow her clan to bid her good morn. Let us see her good health and ensure ye have kept yer word."

Roderick stepped aside, but his jaw ticked. He turned away as Mary stepped forward, joining Rose as they greeted the other warriors while she avoided Erik.

Ulrik, a Comyn guard, took her hand. "Ye look well, Milady. Why ye must be eatin' better." She patted his hand and moved on.

Another touched her shoulder, Jim. "Ye look well."

Another guard passed her a bundle from the wagon. "And happy to boot." He stopped and grinned. His name was Edward. "This peace is good for us all." Each one stopped her, all with good wishes and hopes for peace.

First was bedding, followed by trunks filled with clothes. Mary recognized her mother's clothing trunks as well. Farther back into the wagon were wooden boxes she could not identify. As one of her clan's men set one down, she bent to open the lid.

He reached over opening it. "Here, let me, Milady." He lifted it with a smile, and inside were books, many books. She gasped and reached for one on the top.

A voice she knew well came from behind. "Yer mother's books. He sent them all."

She turned and came face-to-face with Erik. The other Comyn men turned away, as she stood on the side of the wagon nearest the castle wall, hidden from view of most in the bailey.

Erik stepped closer as his finger grazed her cheek. She turned away, and he dropped it in a huff. "Mere months ago, ye'd welcome my touch, my kisses." His eyes examined the wall walk. "Now ye are with the enemy two months, and ye already turn from me, from yer clan."

She stepped back. "I do not turn away from my clan. I embrace both. I embrace peace."

Erik sneered. "Embrace peace. I understand ye haven't consummated the marriage. There's still time, Mary. Come away now. Leave this place. Come back where ye belong."

She stood her ground, not wanting to allow Erik to

bully her as he had in the past. "I am where I belong. By order of the king."

Erik slashed his hand to the side. "Not our king. Ye are to be my wife. I am to be the laird of clan Comyn. Come back with me now. Make it right!"

Mary shook her head. "I will not defy the king. I will not defy my husband, my vow, and my marriage in truth!"

Erik grabbed her arms as his voice rose. "Ye have bedded him? A MacDougall has touched ye? Sullied ye?"

As he grabbed her, her hand went to her belly. An involuntary motion he took note of.

He held her arms but stepped back and whispered, "Ye carry his bastard."

Tears welled in her eyes that threatened to spill over. The babe she wanted so badly was gone. "No, I..."

The ring of a sword being drawn came from behind her, and a blade shifted into her vision. Warmth covered her back, and a familiar hand wrapped around her as Roderick's body pressed against her back. "Ye will unhand my *wife*, Sinclair."

Erik's eyes relocated to a place over her shoulder. The breath puffing in her ear told her Roderick's face was to her right. "Aye, I recognized ye when ye first rode up. Not identifying yerself. Not wise in enemy territory." Erik smirked as his eyes traveled from Roderick's back to hers. He held her look for a moment. He wouldn't try anything, would he? Erik was unarmed in a bailey full of armed enemy warriors.

When Erik dropped his hold, she closed her eyes in relief as tears spilled down her cheeks. Archibald and

Hamish came behind Erik with swords drawn as well. Other MacDougall warriors surrounded the Comyn men, all held at sword point.

Roderick lowly spoke by her ear. "Tell me, *wife,* what is it ye and the Comyn war chief discuss?" He gripped her harder, and a cramp hit her belly, making her flinch. He held her tighter as he whispered, "So *intimately?*"

Archibald and Hamish came around Erik forcing him to take a few steps back when they positioned themselves between her and her father's first in command.

Roderick twisted his blade and brought it close to her. "Did I hear ye right? Is he yer betrothed? Yer lover? Ye tell me ye bear my babe, but ye tell him no?" He whipped her around and held her wrist in a crushing iron grip that brought more tears spilling down her cheeks. "Ye play me for false all along? Lie about the babe, spy for yer war chief, and plan to flee. Starting the wars again?"

She cried out as he gripped her harder. "No, Roderick. The babe, I was wrong. I love…"

He pulled her face to his till their noses touched. "No more lies, Comyn." He shoved her behind him into the arms of guards. She came face-to-face with the angry faces of Fergus and Douglas, two of her five guards.

They took her away, as Roderick called out, "Lock her in her bedchamber. She is to remain on guard, indefinitely." As they dragged her away, Roderick called out, "The rest if ye Comyn men, unload the cart, then begone. Ye've made yer delivery. No hospitality will be honored when trust is broken."

As she passed by Rose, Rose shook her head as tears spilled down her cheeks. "I'll see what I can do, Mary."

When she reached her room, she went to the window, knowing she'd have a full view of the bailey and the cart. Roderick had left, but the MacDougall guards remained under Archibald's command.

She stood for a long while watching through the window as she fingered the silver heart Roderick had gifted her last week, with love. MacDougall men carried the heavier trunks as maids came and went helping bring her belongings into the castle. Rose paused and spoke with Archibald, who only waved her away. She followed the maids into the castle.

Erik moved to the front of the cart, and Constance followed, both absorbed in conversation. What would Constance want from Erik? They didn't know one another. The last items came off the wagon, and Archibald called for the Comyn warriors to mount up. He and a group of MacDougall warriors escorted the members of her clan out of the gates.

She heaved a sigh and whispered, "Goodbye."

Roderick's voice roughly spoke. "Is it yer clan ye bid goodbye or yer lover?"

She turned to her husband, who leaned against the closed door. "Ye have it wrong." His hard expression held hers.

She should heed it, but she kept speaking. "We were betrothed and broke it once the king's orders came. Ye know full and well he cannot be my lover. I came to ye a virgin."

He folded his arms and whispered, "The babe?"

Tears filled her eyes as her throat closed. She'd

gotten her courses, but she felt like she'd lost something she'd had, a baby.

Tears spilled as she spoke. "My courses came this morn."

He pushed from the door. "How convenient. Just as yer lover arrives to take ye away."

He pulled open the door as she rushed and grabbed his arm. "It's not true. I don't want to leave, ever."

He stepped through as he shrugged off her grip and paused before closing the door. "Yer wish is my command." Her gaze met his, then Hamish's harder one behind him. He slammed the door. As the echo reverberated, she flinched. Her guard had returned, trust with her husband, broken.

She crumpled into a ball on the floor as tears freely flowed and sobs wracked her body. How had things unraveled so quickly, and how would she piece it all back together again?

****

A few days later the heavy snow arrived blocking the passes as all of the highlands set in for the harder parts of winter. Roderick sat in his study with Archibald going over the accounts and supplies. The supplies dwindled, and they still had months till the snow thawed.

Archibald spoke, and his nagging voice chewed on Roderick's ear, yet again. "Rose has been to see Mary each day, and yer guard denies her entrance. Ye can't lock the lass away like this, no matter how mad ye are at her."

Roderick slammed his hand on the desk. "Enough! Ye sound like a woman, all nagging."

The door burst open, and his mother marched in.

"Enough is right! What do ye mean to keep her locked up? She's Lady of the Castle. We all rely upon her. The kitchens don't know what meals to serve. The maids are lax in their duties. Yer warriors drink the nights away. Ye can't treat her like a prisoner in her own home."

Roderick groaned and picked up his whisky cup draining yet another full measure wanting to welcome the numbness that wouldn't come.

His mother grabbed it from him. "Ye bampot. Stop it!"

He roared back, "She betrayed me, us! She lied about the babe, about everything!"

His mother yelled back as she slammed the cup on the desk. "She did not betray ye! Women who have lived through what she has don't have regular courses. She wasn't pregnant, and from what her maid claims, she cried the whole morn into the next day."

He stood and strode to the fireplace. "What about her lover?"

His ma's bark of laughter rang his ears. "Ha! I've seen the way ye both look at each other, the way ye are. I'd eat my shoe if she loves any other man."

He leaned both hands on the mantel gripping it hard. "I cannot trust her anymore. What if she betrays us?"

His ma came and patted his back. "Ye have spent too long in war. Most yer life." She sighed and rubbed his shoulder. "Robert is someone ye cannot trust, aye. And that war chief, from what was overheard he's angry he lost out on becoming a laird, not the loss of Mary's affections even if he had them to begin with." She sighed. "I know Mary; her heart is true."

Roderick huffed as memories of them together

came to him. Long nights in each other's arms, talk of the babe. Their shared devotion to God, the peace they'd wanted between the clans. But seeing her with Sinclair blurred his memory, hardened his heart, and rage took over again.

"No." He turned away, picked up his cup, and strode to the decanter. He filled it and drained it in one tilt.

His mother stood by the fireplace glaring at him. "Still as hardheaded as yer da." She shook her head hard. "Fine! At least allow her to be Lady of the Castle. The clan needs her. Allow her the honor of being yer wife for the clan even if ye are too pigheaded to allow her to be the wife of yer heart."

He glanced at his best friend and advisor, Archibald, who nodded in agreement.

He set his cup down as he regarded the supply list he and Archibald had just gone over. It was the smallest he'd ever seen for his clan. His ma was right on one account. His clan needed Mary's knowledge and skills to survive on so little. He feared the months ahead and what they would do to his clan. Anger or not, survival was more important.

Roderick rubbed his hands over his face, the headache he'd had for days not going away. "Fine, she may carry on her normal duties."

When his ma clapped and gasped, his hard glare met hers. "She will always remain under guard. Her trust must be earned again."

Elizabeth McIntyre MacDougall stood at full height and glared back at her son, a look Roderick hadn't seen on her since his youth. "She will, and son." She stepped forward, close to him without breaking eye contact. "Ye will regret yer treatment of her. This I know."

She nodded once and moved to the door. She opened it and stopped. "Go back to her bed, son. Stop drinking and work again on the babe. It will rid ye of that nasty headache." She slammed the door, and the sound brought back his pounding headache.

Images of him and Mary making love swirled in his head, affecting him in their usual manner. He sat to hide his arousal, hating her effect on him. He needed to be strong for the clan, not allow some woman to deter his focus on stopping the wars.

Archibald sat before him. "Yer ma's right. Stop sleeping in the study. Yer da always said the best part of any argument with his wife was making up."

Roderick poured himself another drink. "Away an' shite, ye nimpy."

The following morn, he stood ready to begin the morning meal. Mary was absent from her place. Fine. Let it be this way. He'd given her permission to join the clan again, and she denied him.

As he was about to sit, the room turned and stared at the top of the stairs. Mary stood there, back rigid just as she had been the first time. Only today her expression was one of resolve rather than fright. She held her head high and stepped down the stairs, Rose behind, and her guard today, Fergus, followed. She strode through the middle of the clan like a queen, regal and graceful. She rounded the dais and stood behind her chair.

Roderick grunted, pulled his chair out, and sat hard. The room followed his lead. After everyone sat, Mary sat beside him. A maid brought one bowl of oats and two spoons for them both to share.

He stopped the maid. "Ye will bring one for the lady. We will not share a trencher or goblet ever again."

His mother grunted from the other side of Mary. Let her. He wasn't required to share anything with his wife.

Mary stiffened beside him but said nothing as he shoved her spoon to her. The entire meal, she said not a word. Ate her oats, drank her ale, and stared ahead as if nothing were wrong.

Her floral scent teased his nose, as he shoved oats into his mouth. Her profile caught his eye more than once, regal and beautiful. He had to concentrate to not turn his head and stare at her. When he did spy her from the corner of his eye, her complexion was pale, bags rested under her eyes, which were red. Were those tear stains on her cheeks? Certainly not for him likely for her Comyn lover. He huffed.

When the maid took her bowl away, she stopped her. "Tell Bertha I will see her first to direct the kitchens for today. Then Rose and I will inspect the stores and plan the meals." She fingered the silver heart, the one he'd gifted her with his da's stone inside. His gift given in love.

He couldn't be in her presence anymore without touching, kissing, or taking his ease on her. Roderick stood so fast that he knocked his chair over.

Mary jolted but didn't speak.

He strode to his study and slammed the door. He crossed to the whisky and poured himself a drink, hoping to find an escape from the allure of the one woman he loved with all his heart but dared not trust ever again.

Chapter 15

Mary sat still as the clan members moved from their places after the morning meal. The shock of seeing Roderick after all that had happened set her on edge. She took one breath and another as she sat on the dais. Elizabeth stood and marched to the study door, opened it, and slammed it, leaving the sound to echo in the hall. Voices raised in argument between mother and son came, but she couldn't make out the words.

Rose slid into the seat next to her where Mom MacDougall had just sat.

Rose took her cold hand in hers and rubbed it. "It's good to see ye, friend."

Mary took her hand and clasped it. "It's good to be seen, friend."

Constance bent between them. "Oh, Mary. Ye have finally come out of hiding. And at such a great time. Yer bed cold lately?" Mary's heart dropped as Constance's giggle echoed in the hall. "Mine's kept warm by Roderick. Sorry to hear about yer…misfortune. But with no babe, ye'll be gone before the year's out." She stood, grinned widely at both women, and turned away, humming as she went.

Mary's throat closed as tears gathered in her eyes. The idea of Roderick, her husband, the man who only days ago professed his love, was already with another woman stung. This hurt more than she'd ever admit. All her dreams for a family, love, and children—gone. And her husband already—no matter.

Rose grumbled. "She lies. Roderick is not in her bed."

Mary straightened her back and resolved herself to her plight. Roderick or not, the message he'd delivered was that the clan needed her to help them through the winter, and that's what she'd do. She'd always provided regardless of her situation. She'd given her word to him and the MacDougall clan, and she'd keep it. She was Lady MacDougall, and she'd damn well be there for them all.

Mary blinked back her tears and turned to her longtime friend. "Let's start with Bertha, shall we?"

They strode into the kitchen. With a yelp, Bertha turned and ran to her.

Enveloped in a warm hug from the large woman, Mary stood stunned.

She then squeezed once before she was released. "I am sorry about the babe, Milady. We was all a twitter when the gossip came and to be dashed so soon." She patted her arm. "No matter, ye're both so young. Another will come before ye know it."

Mary grinned, but it didn't reach her cheeks. Rose held her hand as Bertha strode around the kitchen, rattling on about the meals, the rationing, and her concern that they may not have enough to survive the long freeze ahead of them.

She stopped mid-stride. "Ye mentioned ye had recipes. Can ye share them? I've repeated so many, and complaints are coming faster than a fart after the meal."

Mary stepped forward and patted her hand. "I'm glad ye asked. My mother always said ye are never too old to learn." She eyed the cured ham on the table. "Let's start with ham stew. And ye still have the salted fish? That's another soup as well. Everyone loves Cullen Skink."

Bertha clapped her hands. "I knew ye'd know what to do."

Mary smirked as one of her ma's sayings came to mind. "Well, ye can tell the complainers, don't bite the hand that feeds you. They should be thanking ye for being creative with yer dishes."

Rose patted her arm. "This afternoon, we'll check on the mending, and maybe ye can work on some shoes like ye did for the clan. The passages are blocked now, and the tinker can't get through."

Mary took Rose's hand. "Thank ye, friend. Aye, keeping busy makes the day pass quicker."

And that's what Mary's days became. Much like her da's hall, a familiar routine settled into her life. The MacDougalls were a warm and caring clan. So many new friends and people sincerely welcomed her as she helped each cope and deal with a harsh winter with so little.

She rose at dawn and ate beside her stoic husband, who spent his days barricaded in his study. He sat and stared ahead at breakfast. Most midday meals he took alone in the room. Dinner was the same as breakfast. Not a word came from him. Not even in greeting.

Sundays were her favorite days. He permitted her outside the gates, even if only to the chapel for prayer. She'd tread the path with Rose, her ever-present guard marching behind and Archibald behind him. The routine was always the same. Rose and Archibald would pray in the rear of the chapel, and she would pray in the front pew. Mom MacDougall sat in the back and eyed them but said nothing.

Sometimes Mary would read from her Bible that came with her belongings. All put away perfectly for her use. Her mother's books even found their own shelf in the study. A few minutes into her prayer, the door would open, and Roderick would slip in. She always kept her head bowed. But she would peek behind her as he would take a pew near the door and pray. Somedays, he whispered, moving his rosary beads through his large fingers. Other times he'd sit and stare ahead. He never made eye contact with her, and she wished each day he would.

This Sunday, after church, Mary went to her room to retrieve a book for the reading lessons to share one of her ma's sayings with the women.

Upon entering, she came up short. Roderick stood over his chest, rummaging through it, tossing clothing here and there. She cleared her throat, and he came up fast. He was shirtless, and the day she'd come to him on the training field popped into her mind. When his broad naked chest filled her sight, her knees went weak. She couldn't remove her eyes from his chest. He took a breath, and the muscles undulated much as they had that day.

He growled and picked up a shirt. "I came for my clothes. Nothing more."

He strode past her, and she reached out, touching his chest. "Roderick, I am sorry."

He jolted and grabbed her wrist. "Do not touch me."

He shoved her back, and she stumbled but righted herself. He stood glaring at her, then strode from the room.

Mary hardened herself and resolved to make things work between them. Her only ray of hope was a plate of carrot bread that came to her room each morning, and she'd think of her and Roderick sharing the treat. She'd sit and eat it with her hot tea, hoping he'd come around. Winter would be over soon, then summer. Before they knew it, Christmas and a reckoning with the king. Mary had to be pregnant by then to save her father, and her husband, her true love.

****

Another week passed, on top of the one before that and the one before that. Roderick stood staring at the women in the hall surrounding Mary as they read together. With the snow set in they'd taken to reading a couple times a week now. Some days it was King Arthur's stories, ones he recalled as a child. Other times it was a scripture from the Bible, and damn Mary for always choosing his favorites. Today it was a book of those sayings she claimed her ma liked. Damn it all; he enjoyed them too.

Constance strolled by him again, her hand on his chest. "Roderick, ye look so…lonely. Care for some company?" He grabbed her wrist as his eyes caught Mary's across the hall. Her expression showed shock before she quickly lowered her face with a bright blush.

Roderick pushed Constance away, angry with her and himself. "Yer advances are unwelcome, and yer harassment of my wife must stop. Archibald tells me ye taunt her with lies. Yer cousin's keep is inside the valley, easily reachable in the snow. I'm sending ye to Archibald's da."

Archibald walked to them at the perfect moment.

"Actually, I've sent a missive, and it's already had a reply. Pack yer bags, Constance. Ye leave on the morrow."

Her eyes glittered as she straightened her back. "Ye will regret this, Roderick."

He huffed. "What I regret is not forcing ye to leave when Mary first came."

Constance strode off with a huff, and Roderick smiled. His first in so many days.

His best friend leaned against the doorframe. "Ye sit here and brood each day. Somedays ye stare her down like a bitch in heat, others ye glare at her with hate in yer eyes."

Roderick grunted as Mary rose and moved among the women, bending over, helping each to read, her cleavage teasing him from across the hall. He had to shift his plaid to hide the rise in the front. Damn her and damn this mess.

His mother strode by and used her book to whack him in the head. "Come to yer senses, son, and act like a man."

She stood glaring at him as he made eye contact with his ma. " 'Tis good ye're getting rid of that nasty Ross chit. She's dishonored herself by her advances and insulted yer wife."

His ma strode away. She knew how to get under his skin and irritate his nerves. Her "birds" flew fast. He'd only decided to send Constance away last week. Hell, he suspected she knew more about his clan than he did.

As Mary lifted her head and their gazes connected, her hand went to the silver heart at her chest, his gift to her.

Roderick growled and shuddered. He wanted so badly to cross the hall, take her in his arms, and make mad love to his wife. He punched the doorframe and stormed into his study.

Archibald followed and shut the door. "Ye can't keep up like this. Ye not only have broken Mary's heart, but ye have a duty to the king. Not bedding yer wife is no way to get her pregnant by next Christmas. Hell, ye were supposed to have a wean by then."

Roderick picked up his goblet, filled it again, and drained it.

Archibald folded his arms. "Shite, are ye even sober enough to bed her?"

Roderick threw the metal cup into the fireplace as liquid flew out, and the crash echoed through the castle. "I can't trust her. What if she's conspiring with her da, and they attack when the snows first melt? Then where are we?"

Archibald yelled back, "How can she conspire with yer enemy, ye eejit! Ye've had her under lock and key since that day her da sent her things. She's only been outside the castle on Sundays, for Christ's sake, Roderick."

Fiona peeked into the room. "Mary sent me to clean the spill, Milaird. I'll only be a moment."

Archibald nodded as Fiona crossed the room carrying a bucket. She knelt and wrung a rag out.

Roderick stood and heaved his breath. He'd lost control and didn't know how to regain it. He'd lost his wife, and he'd soon lose his mind.

Archibald glanced between Fiona and Roderick. A smile spread as he brushed his plaid and sat in the chair before the desk. "Fiona, ye still tending to Mary each day?" Now what was his captain up to?

She stood and curtsied to both men. "Aye, each day like I have since I came here. Love her I do, like my own sister. She died years ago. Mary's kind like her."

Roderick sat hard in his chair. Of course, Mary was kind. She was kind to everyone.

Fiona knelt again, blotted the spill with a rag, and threw it into the bucket she'd brought as she stood.

She stepped to the door, but Archibald raised his hand. "Just a moment, Fiona." She turned and waited as her look moved between both men.

Archibald set his hands on his knees. "The day she woke and lost the babe." Oh, God, Roderick couldn't think of that day. Why had Archibald brought this up now?

Fiona's eyes teared up. "Aye, a right sad day that was. She cried but hid it well." She lowered her face to the floor. "She cried for days."

She cried for days for the babe. The one they not only needed to save both their clans but one they both desperately wanted together—husband and wife, mother and father. Two people rejoicing in the life their love created.

Fiona crossed to the door, and Roderick groaned. "Stop."

Fiona turned and stared wide-eyed as Roderick's face met hers. "Her days, how are they spent?"

Fiona tilted her head to the side. "Always the same. Rise at dawn, tea, and bread. She tends the clan well. Sundays are worship and spent teaching reading. She's even mended shoes better than the cobbler used to." She sighed. "But can't mend her own, run out of sap."

Mended shoes, his Mary. *The cobbler always*

wears the worst shoes—one of her ma's quotes. He'd picked up one of her books and read it one sleepless night. He rubbed his face. Hell, all nights were sleepless without Mary. She'd saved his clan from starvation, provided in times of need, and taught many to read. What could she not do?

Roderick cleared the lump in his throat. "Her nights?"

Fiona dropped her gaze to the floor as a blush creeped up her neck. "Well, I leave her after she's changed. A guard is at her door all night as ye ordered. She's alone, Milaird." She paused as uncomfortable silence filled the room. Fiona shifted from foot to foot.

Her head came up. "Candles, she goes through candles like no one I've seen. Says she reads at night."

Reading at night, teaching to read during the day, like her ma. Roderick had to look down as tears gathered in his eyes. His gruff response came out hoarse. "Thank ye."

The door opened and closed. Archibald's chair squeaked as he stood. "I'll leave ye to yer thoughts, Roderick, but a word of advice from yer friend. Let the war go. Stop drinking and make up with yer wife."

He opened the door, and Roderick raised his head as his eyes connected with Mary's across the hall.

Archibald stood there a moment before he spoke again. "Everyone in the whole damn clan has accepted her—knows she's not the enemy. Why can't ye?" He left the door open and strode away.

Mary stared at him momentarily, then her shoulders sagged, and she returned to helping a woman read. His people, she'd help his people survive, and all he'd given her was mistrust. His treatment was no better than what his clan had done when she first came. How the hell would he fix this mess?

Chapter 16

Dawn warmed the room as Mary sat before the fire. Fiona handed her tea and the bread plate. Plain bread and not carrot bread sat on the plate.

Mary looked up at Fiona. "Not carrot bread?"

Fiona shrugged. "There was none, Milady."

Mary sat back in her chair. Roderick wasn't gifting her with the sweet treat anymore—yet another tie from their relationship, broken.

A commotion came from the bailey. Mary stood and went to the window, curious who would be up and about this early making so much noise. Dawn edged its way across the still skies, pink then orange that faded into lapis purple—the beginning of another day, married but alone.

Her eyes moved down, and in the outer bailey, guards prepared for travel—a full dozen by what she saw. Strange, the snow had set in. There wasn't any place outside of the valley where anyone could travel. Who would need to leave with so many?

The answer to her question flounced out of the main hall and down the castle steps. Constance Ross stomped to a mount, and her maid, Ester, followed. Archibald came around the horse, and they exchanged heated words. Constance's whine carried, but Mary couldn't determine what was said. Ester dutifully mounted her horse as the guards did as well. Constance stomped her foot, and Archibald shook his head as he folded his arms. They stood there momentarily, and Constance's look shot to her window. Mary stepped back, but she caught Constance's eye. The expression held nothing but malice and hatred.

So, Constance had finally worn out her welcome.

Fiona peeked out the window. "Aye, about time she's gone. Caused nothing but trouble since she walked into this place. Many are happy the laird finally kicked her out."

Mary's gaze shot to Fiona's. "Roderick did?"

Fiona nodded. "Aye, sent her to Archibald's father. Poor man's gonna have his hands full with that conniving bitch."

Fiona curtsied. "Pardon me, Milady."

Mary huffed. "Ye speak nothing but the truth, Fiona." Her observation returned to the bailey. Constance glared at her window, and a chill spread up her spine.

"Yes, well, better the devil you know than the devil you don't." Mary spoke one of her mother's sayings without thought.

Fiona grinned. "Aye, that's a good one. Let's get ye dressed for today."

Mary's day passed much like any other. Rise, break her fast with Roderick's brooding next to her. She helped in the kitchens ensuring the rationing continued while still seeing that all had enough to eat—the midday meal stew. Roderick and Archibald had gone to an outer village to deal with an issue. Her ever-present guard trailed behind her all day. Today it was young Robbie.

That afternoon she hoped to do some mending, but

an issue from the pigs had her there all afternoon—a troubled birthing that had the castle in an uproar. Agatha came, and with a little push and shift, the birthing went well, and all piglets were saved.

Mary stayed behind to watch the piglets enjoy their first meal, then snuggled into mamma for a nice nap. New life's first step brought tears to her eyes. What she would do to have a baby, the one she and Roderick wanted so badly.

Rose came up next to her. "Did ye see Constance leave this morning? Archibald said she threw a fit, but he finally sent her to his da's. Good thing that bitch is gone."

Mary nodded but wasn't in the mood to discuss Constance, no matter how happy she'd been to see her leave.

They stood there a moment, and Rose elbowed her. "Cute, aren't they?"

Mary nodded, not wanting to give away how much the piglets' arrival had affected her.

Rose smiled as one rooted for her ma's teat. "Well, at least we don't have to have them by the dozen."

Mary sniffled, having a hard time controlling her emotions. She held the silver heart that rested near hers. "Roderick's heart" was what she'd called it, imagining she carried his heart near hers.

Rose put her hand on her shoulder, and the tears fell freely. Mary turned to her friend, and all the things she'd bottled up to keep going came rushing out. "Rose, what if I can't give Roderick the baby he needs? The one the king demands to save his life?"

Rose took her in her arms. "Mary, don't talk like that! It's just one time. Ye'll have another chance."

Mary stepped back. "Really, I doubt it. Roderick isn't interested in speaking to me or taking me to his bed. How will we keep the king's orders if we aren't even trying to get pregnant?"

Rose took her hands. "Aye, Roderick is stubborn but will come around soon."

Mary teared up again. "What if it's me? What if I'm not able to have children?"

Rose squeezed her hands. "Stop it! It's not ye. Nothing is wrong with ye. Have patience, Mary. I know deep down he loves ye. I know how ye feel about him. Ye both need to try again. I'm sure soon ye'll make up."

Rose pulled a cloth from her pocket. "Now, dry yer eyes. It's time for the evening meal, and Roderick and Archibald rode in only a little while ago."

Mary dusted her skirt. "I smell like the pig pen."

Rose took her hand. "Well, we'll run up, freshen up, and be at the table in no time."

Rose dragged her through the main hall as the maids set up the tables for dinner. Robbie had to jog to keep up. At the room, he waited in the hall.

Fiona helped her quickly wash and change into a fresh gown in her room. Mary stepped through the door. Rose stopped Fiona, both whispering momentarily, then joined Mary.

Rose took her hand with a big smile. "Come, Mary. I am certain things will return to normal this evening for you and Roderick. I can feel it."

Dinner progressed much the same as any other meal spent next to Roderick. He stared ahead, never spoke to anyone, and his response to any conversation directed at him was a grunt.

Mary turned to him. "More soup, Milaird? Cullen Skink, it's yer favorite."

He grunted and shifted in his chair. Well, so much for trying to be polite. The grunts were his usual response to anyone. This evening his grunts were heavier.

Archibald spoke between bites. "Roderick, the days are shorter. Hopes are the snow will melt early this year."

Another grunt came from Roderick.

Rose smiled as she held her spoon. "Roderick, ye should have seen the new piglets born today. Quite a sight."

Roderick huffed and grunted.

Rose rolled her eyes and elbowed Archibald, who only shrugged.

Rose smiled wide. "Why, Roderick, ye sound like ye spent the day with the pigs. Tell me, did ye?"

Archibald barked a laugh. Rose snickered as she stared at Roderick.

Elizabeth spoke from beside Mary. "Not only does he sound like an old pig, but he acts like one too."

Mary nearly spit out her soup. The grunts did sound like an old pig. She coughed but giggled after. Rose and Elizabeth's jokes were funny, and the way Mary stared at Roderick so expectantly, like he would truly answer her, near sent Mary into hysterics.

When Mary giggled, his face turned, and those eyes bore into hers. "Something funny, wife?"

The low rumble of his voice warned her not to comment. His temper lately had been short.

Mary bent her head. "Nothing, Milaird."

When she glanced up, he'd bent to his soup. Rose

and Archibald had done the same. The light banter, while welcome, ended too soon. The mention of the piglets' birth soured Mary's stomach, the reminder of the babe she'd lost dampening her mood.

Mary rose and whispered, " 'Tis been a long day. I'm off to bed."

As she passed, Roderick grunted. Well, so much for a good night from her husband, but then again, the grunts were more than she'd heard from him in the weeks since their separation. The thought brought tears to her eyes, but Mary held her head high and made her way through the hall filled with clan members, up the stairs, and to the laird's bedchamber, alone again.

Fiona waited for her in her room to undress and ready her for bed.

After her routine, Fiona stopped at the door. "Yer book is by the bedside table. Oh, and I tidied the room. Night, Milady." And shut the door.

Mary sighed as she sat before the fire. Another day passed, and nothing had changed between her and Roderick. Her conversation with Rose echoed. Could things be mended between them? She stared into the flames. Orange and yellow hypnotically danced before her eyes.

She jolted in her chair, and the fire had burned low. She must have dozed off. Mary stretched her taut muscles from sleeping in such a strange position, then rose and brought a taper lit from the fire to her candle by the bed, lighting it for her evening reading. She'd usually read until she fell asleep. Tonight, she looked forward to finishing her latest—the King Arthur stories she reread. The stories of lore, chivalry, and fantasy were always an escape for her.

She picked up the book and curled onto her side, her favorite position for reading by candlelight. But when she opened the book, it wasn't King Arthur but a study of weaponry. Strange, she'd not picked up this book. She slid from her bed and crossed to the stack of books nearby; the pile wasn't there. She glanced at her chest, and that stack had gone as well.

Fiona's parting words echoed. "I tidied the room." Damn, she'd likely put them all back in the study.

Mary grabbed her arisaid, wrapped it around her, and picked up the candle, intent on finding a book to while the hours till dawn or hopefully fall asleep on.

She stepped through her door to the hall, and her night guard Hamish came to her. "Milady, it's near midnight. Ye all right?"

She sighed. "Aye, I only go to the study for a book."

Hamish's eyebrows rose. "The study, are ye sure?"

She moved past him and descended the stairs before he caught up with her.

At the bottom, he caught up and opened the door with a smile. "Ye be careful in there." She glanced at him as she went through the door. He winked just before he shut it.

She stood there momentarily, allowing her eyes to adjust to the dim room. The fire burned low but didn't provide much light.

She stepped to the bookcase, held the candle high to read the spines. Then chastised herself. Her mother's books were on the other side of the fireplace.

Mary crossed toward the other side, her focus on the stack of books there. Her foot caught something, and Mary fell forward. As she fell, the doused candle disappeared from her hand, and strong arms swept her into an embrace against a man's chest. She squeaked and pushed against him.

The arms tightened, and she came flush to a naked chest as a whisper came to her ear. "Is this a thief come to steal from me in the middle of the night?"

Roderick's voice sounded like smooth silk and sent chills through her. His musky scent of sweat and sandalwood enveloped her.

Her voice cracked when she replied. "N-not a thief." He set the outed candle down.

Roderick held her closer as his breath brushed her ear. "My wife roaming the halls in nothing but her shift? Meeting someone?"

Mary jerked. "No!" But he held her hard. His muscles moved with her. The shift of a caress against her body made butterflies tickle her stomach.

"I only want a book, my book. Hamish is in the hall."

Roderick released her so fast she fell forward.

He caught her hand. "Steady, Mary." She glanced over his body. He was only in his plaid, rumpled as if he'd slept in it.

Roderick kept hold of her and guided her around what she'd tripped over. She glanced down, stepping over the bedding before the fire. Her gaze rose to his, and he grinned in the dark. His teeth glowed white as he helped her to the other side of the bookshelves. His other hand reached for the book atop the stack left there, and he handed it to her.

She took it and read the cover in the firelight—the King Arthur stories. Her eyes connected with his.

His thumb rubbed the top of the hand he still held.

"It's what ye were reading, is it not?"

She glanced at the book. "Yes, but…"

He smiled again as his other hand rose to her cheek. "I've seen it on the bedside table in yer room. Ye read it most days to the women. It's a favorite of mine as well."

Mary set the book down and waved at the bedding. "This is where ye've been this whole time?" He caught her hand as she brought it back. "Not in Constance's bed?"

He brought both her hands to his lips. "Never another's bed, Mary." He brushed his lips against her fingers.

She sucked in a breath. "Roderick, I…"

He stepped forward and brushed his lips over hers. He lifted his head and whispered to her lips, "Please, Mary, forgive me. I've been a crabbit fool."

She blinked. "Ye aren't still angry?"

He sighed and caressed her face. "I was not happy to see ye with another man. I can't describe what came over me." He took a deep breath. "I wasn't ready for how much it affected me. The thought I'd lose ye to another." He rested his forehead against hers. "Then the news of the babe." He sniffed. "It tore my heart out." When he lifted his face to her, tears welled in his eyes. "I can't lose ye, Mary."

Her throat closed as her eyes watered. "Roderick, I won't leave. I love ye."

He kissed her hard as he brought her close. She returned his kiss fully as she wrapped her arms around his neck.

He chuckled into the kiss.

She smiled and whispered on his lips, "What's so

funny, husband?"

He kissed her and spoke into the kiss. "My da always said the best part of an argument with yer wife is making up."

She stepped out of his embrace, but he held her hand. "We are making up, husband?"

He pulled her back into his arms. "God, I hope so."

Roderick slid her arisaid off her shoulders as he kissed her neck. Mary stepped into his embrace as tingles shot down her spine.

"What about Hamish? He's at the door."

Roderick growled. "And if he knows what's good for him, he'll stay on the other side."

He stepped back and untied her shift and allowed it to drop.

His eyes roamed her body, and he whispered, "Mary, I missed ye."

She stepped toward him and unbuckled his belt. "Fair's fair, husband." As she pulled the belt away, his plaid dropped.

Roderick smiled as he kissed her. He lowered himself to his knees and kissed her stomach as she threaded her fingers through his hair.

She tilted her head to the side, noting his expression, soft and caring.

He pulled her down with him as he cupped both breasts, taking one nipple in his mouth and suckling. Tingles spread through Mary as she tilted her head back. His hand came around her head, bringing her lips to his, and kissing her hard.

He whispered into the kiss, "My wife." She pushed him till he lay down and crawled atop him, straddling his hips.

She kissed him and whispered, "My husband," as she rocked against him. He growled and kissed her again. She sat up, still rocking herself against his staff. His hand moved to her breasts and massaged them, rubbing his thumb along one peak. Mary rocked again as her head dropped back. They'd done this position once before, and she truly loved being in control. She rose a little and grabbed him, hard and moist between their bodies.

She sat back and pumped him once. He threw his head back and groaned as he squeezed her breasts harder. She nudged her hand again, and his breath hitched. She leaned over to kiss him, and he closed his eyes, but she stopped shy and whispered, "Something ye want, husband?" She pulled her hand on him again, and he rocked his hips with another groan. "Ye, Mary, I want ye."

Mary rose over him, positioned him at her opening, and slid slowly down, wrapping herself around him. He groaned again and ended it, whispering, "Oh, Mary."

She stayed seated for a moment, enjoying him filling her. She loved having her husband connected to her intimately again. He sat up and took her by the neck, shifting them a little till his feet came flat. He slowly moved as he kissed her, his eyes connecting with hers.

He continued his slow movements as he watched her. "God, Mary, I missed ye, missed loving ye." He picked up the pace but shifted again, flipping her under him. He took them to soaring heights in full control as he made love to her at a maddening pace.

The familiar pressure built, her passage contracted, and she closed her eyes as she screamed his name.

Roderick continued his mad pace as she floated in the heavens. The pulse against her drove her to new heights. Panting, Roderick drove hard into her and roared her name. He froze and pumped once, then again, and warmth filled her.

He collapsed beside her and held her close as he panted, his body wet from his efforts.

She shifted and pulled his plaid over them.

He wrapped his arms around her, kissing her softly. "Next time I act the bampot, wife, just play a thief, and we'll make up. Agreed?"

Mary huffed. "I shouldn't have to play the thief to steal yer heart, husband."

He opened his eyes and gazed at her. "Aye, no ye should not. Ye have my heart already, wife."

She kissed him. "And I shall never let it go."

Chapter 17

Someone prodded Mary from her slumber, and strong arms embraced her. Ice-cold feet and legs brushed against hers, bringing her fully awake. She lay against a somewhat chilled Roderick as the fire blazed before them. He wrapped his plaid around them. "I had to build up the fire, Mary. Damned cold in here."

Mary giggled. "Aye, I'm lying against ice."

The study door burst open, and Elizabeth strode in carrying a tray. "So glad ye two have made up." She eyed them. "And glad all yer nether parts are covered. Break yer fast, and then it's off to the hunting cabin with ye." She poured tea, the steam rising from the cup a welcome sight to Mary.

Elizabeth strode over, and Roderick reached for the cup, but his ma handed it to Mary. "Shame on ye, Roderick—scaring the clan like this. When Fiona didn't find Mary's guard or Mary in her room this morning, she had a near panic attack—sent Archibald all over searching. Even woke me and I told them all ye had to do was check and see if Mary's guard was at the study door. Fools, all of them."

Mary sipped her tea, almost too hot to drink. But it warded off the chill. "The hunting cabin?"

Roderick rose naked, and his ma swatted his arse. "Cover yerself, son."

He flinched and shrugged. "With what? Mary has

my plaid."

Elizabeth retrieved a shirt and plaid from the stack of clothing in the corner and tossed it to her son.

He caught them as he sipped his tea. He set down the cup, slipped on his shirt, and bent on the floor, pleating the fabric. "Aye, a cabin in the mountains used for hunting for stores and a favorite winter hideaway for my parents."

Elizabeth leaned on the desk. "Aye, I love that cabin. So many good memories."

Roderick lay on the floor, wrapped his plaid, belted it, and stood clothed. He winked at his ma. "Aye, and it's why all my younger siblings are born between October and November."

He belted his sporran Elizabeth handed him. "Great idea, ma. Ye already seen to packing for the stay?"

Elizabeth huffed. "Of course."

Archibald opened the door and peeked around it. "Everybody decent in here?"

When Elizabeth nodded, he opened the door wider. Fiona and Rose came in with clothing for Mary.

Mary glanced between Elizabeth and Roderick. "We're going on a trip? What about the kitchens, the meals, the reading lessons, the clan?"

Elizabeth herded everyone out but Rose and Fiona. At the door, she paused. "I'll tend to the clan. Ye, my dear, need to tend to yer husband." She strode out.

When the door clicked closed, Rose turned and giggled. "Swept off to the privacy of the hunting cabin." She sighed. "What I wouldn't give for that. So romantic."

Mary turned back to her friend and glanced between Fiona and Rose as everything fell into place.

"My books moved yesterday. Ye! Ye both planned this!"

Fiona smiled and placed her shift over Mary's head. "I was only doing as ordered."

Mary's head popped through the opening, and she glared at Rose, who shrugged. "I don't have this level of planning or slyness. And to get the whole clan to go along with it…"

Mary stood from putting on her skirt. "Elizabeth!"

Both women giggled as Mary shook her head. "I wish I had her skill. This was impressive."

Rose smiled as she picked up and folded the bedding from the floor. "Wait till ye see what they planned for the cabin. That's impressive."

In just over an hour, Roderick lifted Mary onto a dapple-gray stallion. He mounted behind her and gathered her close in his arms. Archibald handed him a fur, and he wrapped that around them both, tying the ends with attached leather ties. His war horse shifted.

Roderick patted his neck. "Easy, Merlin."

Mary gasped. "Ye named yer warhorse after Arthur's wizard?"

Roderick grinned. "Aye. Claimed he carried magic, and at times he does."

Archibald patted Roderick's leg. "Ye both head out before it gets too late. Don't want to be out after dark. The cabin's readied and stocked for a month."

Roderick tensed behind her. "If any change…"

Archibald's gaze shot at her and back to Roderick. "I'll come personally. Ye'll have a guard rotation for the perimeter as usual. Present but not seen."

Elizabeth spoke from the doorway. "Heed yer ma's orders. Work on that babe. I need my grandbabies."

Mary blushed as Roderick snorted behind her.

Rose stepped beside Archibald. "Mary, ye'll have such fun. Tell me all about it, friend, when ye return."

Mary reached out and took her hand. "I will, Rose."

Her face rose to Elizabeth's, who nodded and winked at her—blessings from them all, her family, her clan.

Roderick kicked his mount, and they rode through the gates to what she hoped was some well-earned private time with her husband.

Roderick kept a hard pace, traveling farther north into the mountains. He skirted Loch Etive and slowed when the sound of rapids filled the air.

He leaned into her ear. "If ye look out over the loch, the rapids are the Falls of Lora." He shifted in the saddle. "The loch is a *U* shape here, and the falls are a shallow part." They stayed there momentarily as the rush of the water filled the air, a relaxing sound.

She fingered her heart necklace as Roderick's whisper came near her ear. "Ye wear it still?"

Mary blushed. "Aye, always. I carry yer heart, Roderick."

He hummed in response as they stayed there a moment longer.

Archibald's earlier comment, combined with more scouting groups and more practice with the warriors, weighed on Mary's mind. Had the wars not ended?

She tapped his arm. "What Archibald said, it's the clan war again, isn't it?"

Roderick tensed, and his arms tightened around her. "What do ye know of it?"

She turned in the saddle to face him. "I only know

what I see at Dunstaffnage. Yer increased patrols, frequent sword practice, we already ration. Ye prepare for an attack, but why? With our marriage and Malcolm with my father, peace is promised. Word given."

Roderick blew a hard huff. "Archibald mentioned ye and Rose recognized the preparations. I had hoped ye'd not."

He turned the horse and headed toward the mountains at a walk. He didn't say anything for a while, and Mary feared he'd shut off again, refusing to discuss her clan, her father.

But his voice came stern. "The wars threaten to start again, aye. And I share with ye in caution."

She spun to face him. "I think I've proven my loyalty. I haven't had any missives from my father or clansmen. And I haven't sent one nor asked to."

Roderick stared at her for a moment, then kissed her cold nose. "Aye, I know." He gazed forward. "Archibald reminds me of it often. That I should never question yer loyalty but yer father's."

Mary faced forward and snuggled into his embrace. "Aye, I agree with him. My father isn't to be trusted." She rubbed his hand. "These 'issues' at yer villages. Are they attacks?"

Roderick sighed. "Aye, always in yer clan's plaid. But they come and go so fast. No descriptions of men, just sudden attacks wearing the Comyn plaid." He cleared his throat. "Yer da and I have exchanged messages. He claims I attack him and accuse him out of turn."

Mary jolted. Her father sent Roderick missives but not her. Did he even ask about her? She sniffed. Well, no matter. She'd gone from his life.

Roderick whispered in her ear. "Dinna fash Mary. He doesn't have to ask about ye. And I don't have to ask about my brother, Malcolm—spies we both have. But aye, he does ask about ye. Fondly even."

Mary blinked back tears she'd not known gathered in her eyes. Her father cared.

Roderick turned the horse to go around a tree. They both had to lean to accommodate the movement.

When righted, Roderick huffed. " 'Tis why I was confused when Sinclair showed as he did. Yer da was all for our marriage once the king became involved. And Malcolm, Comyn calls him his 'second son.' " She imagined her father was much happier with the son he always wanted, not the daughter he had.

It was Mary's turn to huff. "Well, Erik always took his orders a bit too far. He used them for his own gain, much as it angered my father. He pushed for the betrothal and the promise of laird." She sniffed again. "Second son" hurt. "I went along thinking I'd done a good thing for the clan."

Roderick kicked the horse into a run and mentioned nothing more. But it still sat in Mary's mind. If they were both for peace, why still raid each other?

As gloaming claimed the skies, the cabin came into view—a small stone two-story dwelling nestled into the forest. Private and quaint reminded Mary of Fae tales of a crofter in love with a Fae he kept on land as his wife only to have her escape to the sea again.

Roderick lifted her from the saddle, and she stumbled as her legs gave out. He held her till she stood solid.

He handed her the fur wrap. "Go on into the cabin, Mary. Warm by the fire while I tend Merlin."

Mary stepped carefully through the snow to the cabin door. Light glowed from within. Archibald said they'd readied the place, and Rose claimed it was impressive. Mary opened the door, and the fireplace burned with a roaring fire. She went to it and warmed her hands. As she turned to warm her backside, she noted a kitchen area sat beyond the seating area around the fire. Bundles of food stores sat on the table, the shelves. She crossed into the cooking area and spotted a box. She lifted the lid, and wrapped ham, cheese, and lamb were inside.

Mary lifted the ham and cheese. Found bread in another bundle. A wooden trencher in the cabinet and a knife, and she made quick work for a simple dinner making sure to pile the serving tall as she knew Roderick ate two to three bites to her one. She picked up her offering for their meal and went to the chairs before the fire. She set the food on the table and turned back to the kitchen.

Her eyes caught the wine bottle already opened with goblets beside it. She poured two, returned to the chair before the fire, and sipped her wine as her feet warmed. It wasn't long before her husband entered and stomped the snow from his boots. When his eyes met hers, he grinned wide. "Ah, wife. Ye read my mind."

She rose and handed him a goblet of wine. "I am completely capable in the kitchens, ye know."

Roderick sipped the wine as he sat before the fire. "Aye, I am well aware, and yer Cullen Skink is my favorite." He smiled as he popped a piece of ham into his mouth. " 'Tis why I didn't protest this trip. With yer cooking, I'll not starve."

Mary rolled her eyes. "Ah, so that's why ye agreed

to this trip. For my cooking."

He stood and grabbed her hand. " 'Tis not the reason." He kissed her hard, and heat flashed over her body. He grabbed the food and his wine. "Come, let me show ye the reason for our visit. We can eat later."

Mary grabbed her wine as Roderick led her up the stairs. He pulled her to the right into a bedchamber where the fire roared as well.

But he stopped in the doorway, blocking her entrance. "For ye, my wife. Close yer eyes."

Mary blinked. "Why?"

Roderick chuckled. "A surprise. My ma insisted, saying ye will enjoy this."

Mary closed her eyes, and Roderick moved away. She reached out, and his hand took her wine goblet. He went away again, and when he returned, he stood behind her. He took her in his arms and shuffled them forward.

When he stopped, his whispered breath tickled her ear. "Open yer eyes, wife." Mary did, and dried red rose petals covered the bed, the floor, and in front of the fireplace on top of a fur.

She blinked and turned to Roderick. "Where did ye get these? The garden's still frozen."

Roderick caressed her cheek. "My ma has the largest rose garden I've seen and collects them every summer." He bent and kissed her. "She swears making love on top of rose petals will always give ye a bairn. And she says it's highly romantic."

Mary pulled back. "Ye brought me here for the king's order, the bairn?"

Roderick held her tighter. "I brought my wife here to spend time with her." He kissed her again. "I brought ye here to make mad love to ye without interruption, anytime I wish." He backed her up from the bed till she fell, and he came over her. "I brought ye here, Mary, because I love ye." He kissed her till their tongues danced, and his hand roamed her, bringing butterflies to her stomach. He whispered into the kiss. "Aye, I want a babe, but not for the king, Mary, for us."

Growling, Roderick stood and pulled her up with him. "I want ye bare on the petals." He untied her laces with surprising speed as he grunted. The bodice flew off her, the ties to her skirts came loose, and the fabric pushed to her ankle as he knelt before her. When he stood, the shift came over her head, and when her face came free of the material, her husband's heated gaze caught hers. He pushed her back, and she stood still, her hands working his belt.

Roderick's chuckle filled the room. "Aye, both bare on the petals." He kicked his boots off as he unbuckled his belt. The fabric of his tartan followed with the clatter to the floor. In one motion his shirt came off, and he bent to pull his socks off as he stopped and blew on her curls.

Mary shifted, but his hands took her hips firmly as his tongue darted out, licking her...there.

He pushed her to the bed, and she fell back again. The rose petals puffed, and a fresh scent of roses filled the room. His hands held her hips, and he positioned her on the bed. Roderick's hands trailed the back of her thighs and lifted her knees. He knelt before her as he spread her legs wide. As she moved on the bed, the petals rubbed against her skin, a little rough from the fact they'd dried over the fall months.

He growled as he licked her again, this time

connecting at her woman's place displayed in full view to him. Mary was so open and vulnerable, entirely under his control. Curiosity won over her inhibitions, and she fisted the bedding in anticipation of what play her husband had in store. He licked her again, and her head turned, the scent of roses coming to her from the petals on the bed. His mouth covered her, and he sucked her nub, and heat flushed her body. The sensation of his warm mouth and her hot body shot tension through her. She grabbed his head and ran her fingers into his hair.

With his next suckle she gripped his hair and rocked her hips against his mouth. The pressure built in her against that familiar dam, and she wanted more. He hummed as he licked her again, and heat shot from her core. He shifted and slid a finger inside her as he sucked her harder. Mary's hips bucked as he drove into her, the sensations glorious as she cried out. Roderick suckled her nub and slid in another finger. He lifted his head, and she released his hair as his fingers worked her. She threw her head back and gripped the covers, her panting heavy as he continued his assault.

His voice came her to in the haze. "Mary, let go, love. I want to see ye come undone."

At that moment her world exploded, moisture filled her as Roderick continued his play, and harder and harder he pushed her to a place she'd never been. Her passage tightened, and he thrust once hard and held it there as she screamed his name. He slowly withdrew, and she sensed his body shift. Her panting made it hard to come back, her head spun, and the haze of her mind was still in another place. Her legs fell and strong arms lifted her, moving her on the bed. The crunch of rose petals sounded, and the fresh scent wafted to her. Limp like a doll he took her in his arms and held her till her breathing became normal.

Roderick kissed her. "Did ye like that, wife?"

Mary nodded. She wanted to give him the same rapture he'd given her when he kissed her…there. She wondered; would a man enjoy it as much as a woman? She kissed her way down his chest, his hands gathering her hair to the side. She licked his stomach, and the muscles contracted as he gasped. She moved even lower kissing as she went, and his hands fisted her hair. Arriving at her destination, she giggled, and her hand wrapped around him.

Roderick lifted his head, and her eyes connected with his. "Is it a kiss ye want, husband?"

She kissed the tip, and Roderick threw his head back releasing a groan. She licked his rod as she squeezed it, and he gripped her head. She placed the tip in her mouth, and his hips bucked as he groaned. She released him, licked her lips, and came over him again. She pushed him slowly into her mouth, allowing his size to fill her. His long groan as she did so told her he liked her special kisses. Her head lifted and went back down again, mimicking the motion of making love as Roderick's hands on her head guided her, showing her how he liked it. His response gave her confidence, and she craved the control she had over him. Wanting to see him come apart from her kisses, she continued her play, following his lead.

Soon Roderick halted her with his hands as he scooted back. "Dear God, woman. I'll not be able to hold out. Ye must stop."

Mary grinned as he lay there panting, trying to gain

control over himself again. He blew out a few hard breaths as he gripped the bedding. His control was nearly gone, like hers before.

She crawled over him and positioned herself atop him with his rod near her entry. The crush of rose petals combined with the fresh flowery scent, made her more daring, more playful.

Roderick's hands rose to her hips, and he lifted her guiding her over his shaft as a groan escaped when he filled her. "God, Mary, ye are beautiful." He guided her as she rode him slowly.

His hips helped the motion, the friction between them. That heat flushed her again, and the tension built quicker this time, the familiar feelings consuming her again. She rested her hands on his chest for support, and he growled as he flipped her and lifted her knees. He drove into her as he kissed her. His hips created a faster pace, going deeper into the new position. The bed rocked, and the petals crunched. The scent of roses enveloped them as Roderick drove into her over and over. Heat consumed her. A hot flash flew over her as she broke into a sweat. Roderick thrust once hard, then again. He froze, and his body flushed red. Heat filled her core with a slight sting. He panted as he rested his forehead against hers, their bodies still joined.

Mary made to move, and his firm arms held her. "Don't move, lass." He lifted his head and caressed her face. "I want to make sure my seed has set. To create a babe for us, Mary."

Tears filled her eyes. "Not for the king?"

He shook his head. "No, lass. For us."

He rolled them to the side, still joined, and held her, her head resting against his chest, his heartbeat steady in her ear. Eventually, their bodies slid apart, and she shivered from the chill in the room. Roderick rose and threw a plaid over her. When he returned, the petals crunched, and the scent of roses filled her nose when she returned to lie on his chest. Mary fell asleep to the sound of his heartbeat and the hope they'd made a baby tonight.

****

Awake into the night, troubling thoughts plagued Roderick as he held Mary. She shifted in her sleep, and Roderick brought her closer to his heart.

He kissed her head as he whispered, "Mary, what a fine mess we are in, eh?" He huffed. "If ye knew what a trouble marrying me and coming here would have been, would ye have just let the king's men kill me?" He ran his fingers up and down her arm. "Nae, ye wouldn't have. Not my Mary. Kind as ye are, ye are wise as well." He chuckled. "That's what the king's agent said. I remember it well. 'Lass, you are the wisest in the room.' "

Roderick recalled that day well, playing it repeatedly in his mind. Both clans unwilling to meet the king's demands for peace, but the Comyn daughter brought peace with one sentence. A woman he knew his parents wanted as his bride taken for peace.

His da had said they'd wanted it that way since her birth years after his. Upon seeing her beauty that day in battle, then up close in the abbey—aye, he'd wanted her body and soul. He'd see them through this, have peace with the Comyn, and keep Mary safe.

****

Mary fell into a comfortable lax routine at the cabin. The days blended into the nights, and the nights blended into the days. Their love grew into a comfortable companionship filled with lively debates, friendly conversations, and heated love in their bed—a near-perfect marriage.

Some days they only left their bed for food, and often, Roderick brought one dish they shared while snuggling. He'd tend to Merlin each day, and some days she'd follow with an apple for the sweet horse.

Merlin nudged her shoulder, and Roderick caught her before she fell over. "He looks for his treat, wife. Ye will turn my well-trained war horse into a pet."

Roderick warned, "Take care around him, he can be as feisty a lad as his namesake."

Mary patted the horse's head, who bent into her enjoying the attention.

Some days they'd ride out along the mountain range together to exercise the war horse. Others, a guard would have to take him out and exercise while Roderick insisted they stay abed, working on a babe, "for us."

But as another week passed, the days grew longer and the air warmer. No more snow fell, and when she stood on the ridge, the dotting of snow in the valley grew smaller and smaller. Heavy winter was soon at an end. Mary feared their treasured paradise would quickly come to an end as well.

This morn, Mary woke to a cramp as tears gathered in her eyes. No, it couldn't be. She slowly rose and sniffled as she crossed to the privacy screen hiding the chamber pot. Sure enough, her courses had arrived meaning no babe. She bit her fist, but a sob escaped. Tears flowed, and her throat closed. She heaved a breath and another as a sob let loose.

A bundle scooted toward her from the other side of the partition.

The dawn's light cast Roderick's shadow against the screen as he sat on the floor. "I saw the blood on the bedding, Mary." The package was familiar to her—her "woman's items" of moss, cloths, and drawers for her courses. Seeing it brought dread to her heart. No babe, again.

Roderick passed her a clean shift. "Dress, Mary, then we'll talk." He rose, and she sat there waiting to see what he'd do. Would he rail against her? Yell and call her a failure? She sat and waited. His shadow traveled around the room as the rustling of fabric came to her. He changed the bedding.

Mary cleaned herself as more tears fell. She set her woman's items in place and stood. She removed her shift and threw it on the ground as a cry came out. She picked up the clean gown and pulled it over her head, which got stuck. As she pulled on the fabric, she yelled. It didn't move, and she screamed loud and hard. Hands softly untangled her. With the garment in place, her head popped out, and Roderick stood before her. Tears fell again at his turned-down expression.

He picked her up, carried her to the bed, and held her as he lounged. He said nothing. Just held her and rubbed her back. As a sob and more tears returned, he'd "shh" her as he rocked her.

When she'd felt she'd gained control, she whispered. Knowing the need to face what she'd feared all along. "What if I'm unable?"

Roderick caressed her face. "What do ye mean by that? Ye're a woman."

She pushed him on his chest, so they came face-to-face. Tears fell again. She wanted to give him a baby so badly.

"What if I can't produce a baby? What about the king's orders?"

She folded her arms and leaned against him. "I should go to the king, beg for an annulment. Ye deserve a wife who can give ye babies. The clans can still have a union through Malcolm. But I can't be a true wife to ye if I can't give ye a family."

Roderick shook her. "Nonsense, Mary. Ye are my wife in truth. Ye spent the last weeks proving it over and over." He ran a hand through his hair. "I'd lie like the devil before I'll allow anything to come between us. If faced with it, we'll find an orphan, a babe, and take him on as our own son."

She whimpered. "Really, ye'd do that?"

He caressed her face. "Or maybe a girl. One ye could dote upon." His expression hardened. "But ye will not go the king. Of all the things, Mary, especially after the last few weeks. Don't ye know I've move heaven and earth, just for ye?" He sighed. "We will continue to try for a babe." He kissed her. "I love trying again and again."

Mary snuggled into his embrace.

"Rest, Mary. We'll try again soon." As she slipped in and out of sleep, he whispered, "Ye only need rest."

A pounding on the door woke her. Roderick jumped from the bed, belted on his plaid, laid pleated and ready to don.

He grabbed his broadsword and bent, kissing her. "Ye wait here. The only person who'd disturb us is Archibald." His feet thumped down the stairs, and the door opened and closed. Hushed voices floated to her, and she rose and wrapped a blanket around her. Archibald here meant only one thing. Her father attacked, and the wars started again.

Mary tiptoed down the stairs and found Archibald speaking lowly to Roderick. Neither noticed as she hid in the stairwell, listening to their conversation.

Archibald cut a piece of lamb and shoved it in his mouth, speaking as he chewed. "Aye, rode all night. An injured crofter came stumbling into the bailey yesterday." He swallowed and chugged some ale. "The attacks start again. Comyn plaid, men come and go fast." He paused and took a breath. "But this time, they killed two men. There's a message to MacDougall. Prepare for war."

Roderick cursed lowly.

Archibald spoke faster. "Comyn sent a missive."

Roderick growled. "Now, what from the bastard?"

"He claims ye attack his villages. Lay waste to food stores and kill livestock to ensure his people starve."

Roderick slammed his hand on the table. "It's not us! I swear it."

Archibald put his hands up. "Aye, ye and I both know this. But who attacks in our plaid and why?"

Mary stepped from the stairs into the dawn light.

Her face connected with her husband's angry one. "We must return. Ye must send a reply to my father."

Roderick crossed to her and took her hand. "Mary, ye should not worry about these things. Ye aren't even dressed and in yer condition."

Archibald grinned. "Am I to congratulate ye both?"

Mary glanced away. "No, no babe." She wiped a tear from her face and returned her gaze to both men.

"Ye must send word to my father. Ye are not behind the attacks, but someone is." She stood tall. "I would like to include my own message and beg him to stop raiding *my* clan, *my* kin." She heaved a sigh. "Maybe he'll take mercy upon his only daughter and listen."

Roderick caressed her face. "No wonder ye have such a hard time making a babe. So much stacked against us. The threat of war, the burden of peace. Ye working yerself to the bone keeping our clan from starving. All this and the pressure to produce a wean." He bent and kissed her. "Ye are a treasure, Mary."

Chapter 18

Mary stood on the wall walk as she gazed at the loch and mountain range. She'd stood here most days as the landscape transitioned from winter into spring. The snow melted, the sun came out, and rain came and went. She watched daily as the valleys quickly changed and grew into the lush green that rolled before her. The land stood against it all, changing and conforming to the challenges nature put against it. Spring was upon them, and Mary felt much like the land—transformed and fitting to her new life as Lady MacDougall.

She brushed tears away. This morning her course had come again, still no babe, and they already neared May and summer. Roderick demanded she meet with Agatha and discuss the lack of a babe with the clan's healer, but Mary knew the problem. She was the failure. Soon, she'd have to face the fact. She'd go to the king and throw herself upon his mercy. Beg he did not kill her husband, her love.

She made her way down the stairs and into the bustling bailey. Many stopped her along the way with well wishes. So many were happy to have survived the brutal winter and looked forward to a bountiful crop and spring. The clan, back on its feet again, prospered. Mary should smile, but today, it wasn't in her.

Agatha approached her, her typical basket in hand. "I almost had to climb those dreaded steps to come get ye." She smiled. "Come, let's have a sit in the garden, Milady."

They strode into the garden, and Mary went to her favored spot, Marlin's tree, she called it. A weeping willow with a bench under it. When she'd first spotted it the day with Alister, now in the summer, she welcomed its embrace—a place to collect herself and find comfort.

Agatha sat and took her hand in hers. "Roderick told me yer news this morning." She sighed. "I am sorry. But let's not dwell on that. We need to see what's keeping ye from 'getting up the duff,' eh?"

Mary huffed a laugh, knowing Agatha only tried to lighten the mood.

Agatha patted her hands. "Aye, that's the spirit, Milady. Now on to what's ailing ye."

Mary blurted out what she had on her mind for so long. "I don't understand. Minus our tiff after Hogmanay, Roderick and I are…quite active."

Agatha put her hands on her hips. "Aye, castle gossip is ripe with how he keeps ye up at night." She grumbled. "The men whine as the women make more demands to make them happy if ye ken what I mean." She sighed. "So, does he do it right? Some men, they like…other things."

Mary blushed. "Aye, he's doing it right, and his seed is as well."

Agatha nodded. "The act is right. On to ye, dear. What do ye eat each day?"

Mary shrugged. "Oats, bread the same midday, and dinner as the rest of the castle."

Agatha sighed. "Ye sure? Was something coming special just to ye."

Mary sat and thought a moment…just to her. "Wait, before our argument. There was bread. Carrot bread we shared each morning."

Agatha grabbed her arm. "Carrot bread. Did it have seeds in it at all?"

Mary nodded. "Aye, little seeds on top sweetened with honey. Roderick and I shared it."

Agatha cursed long and loud. "Ye said it stopped coming to ye with yer argument."

"Aye, the day we made up."

Agatha rose and paced. "Damn her to hell and back again. I can't believe she'd stoop so low." Who'd stoop so low, and who would do this to her?

Mary fisted her hands in her lap. "What is it? The carrot bread is the issue?"

Agatha's gaze connected with hers.

Her expression changed as she sat again and took her hands in hers. "Carrot seed. It's an old trick but works to keep a wean from taking root. When Constance asked me for the remedy, I thought 'twas for her. She'd slept with so many men. I took it as she didn't want a wean out of wedlock." She huffed. "Unless it was Roderick's."

Agatha's expression softened. "Had I known her true purpose, I wouldn't have told her. The day ye and Roderick were found in the study nearly naked was after he'd sent her packing."

Carrot bread. The treat Mary thought Roderick sent to her was a trick. Something from Constance to keep her from becoming pregnant with Roderick's child. A plan to thwart any effort to keep their marriage a true one. All this time and it was the bread. Tears filled her eyes, and her throat closed.

Mary sighed as Agatha squeezed her hands. "Yer courses, they've been heavy and painful, haven't they?"

Mary nodded as a tear escaped. Damn Constance.

Agatha handed her a cloth from her basket. "Dry yer tears, Mary. It's been months, and I suspect they get easier each time yer courses come, am I right?"

Mary dried her tears as she thought over her last courses that came regular now. They had eased since that first one after her arrival here. The day her ex, Erik Sinclair, came with her wagon of belongings from her father.

Agatha dug in her basket and retrieved a wrapped bundle. She opened it, and inside were dried stalks with a crystal coating. "I have to fight Bertha for sugar, expensive as it is. I coat the young stalks so people can tolerate the taste."

She wrapped a few into another cloth and handed it to Mary. "Scots lovage, like a celery or leek, but has a more pungent taste." She blew a laugh. "Funny how all the healing plants taste like shite."

"Licorice root? I am to eat licorice root?" *It can't be that simple.*

Agatha patted her hand. "Well, aye, but making sure yer husband 'tends yer womanly needs' each day, well, that's how ye get with a babe, Mary." Agatha smirked as she gathered her basket and stood. "Trust me. Ye will be carrying in no time. The carrot seed should be out of ye by now, and with Roderick as active—" She laughed. "By next month, I tell ye."

****

The following day Mary's mount followed Roderick atop Merlin as they wound their way through the woods.

In the woods, out of the sun, chilled Mary and she wrapped her Comyn arisaid tighter around her shoulders. "Where do we go, Roderick?"

He turned and grinned at her. " 'Tis a surprise, Mary."

She snorted. "Not much of a surprise when ye said, 'Mount yer horse. We go for a ride.' So, we travel. But where and why?" She glanced around, noting how alone they were. "Roderick, with the attacks, are we safe?"

He turned Merlin before her, stopping her horse. "There are two warriors who follow out of sight. The attacks on MacDougalls are outer villages and to the north only. Ye are safe, I promise."

He turned Merlin, and her horse came alongside him. They rode silently for a while as they went out of the woods into the open. Birds chirped, and the flowers were in full bloom. The air carried a sweet scent and blew warm against her skin. Mary closed her eyes as her horse kept a slow pace with Merlin. She lifted her face to the sun, and the world fell away.

A hand brushed hers, and she took hold. Roderick hummed as he gripped her hand. She turned her head and opened her eyes to her smiling husband. Husband. Who would have thought she, a Comyn, would find comfort with a MacDougall after all this time?

They wound their way near Loch Etive, and Roderick pulled Merlin to a halt. "Here we are."

Mary stopped beside him. "Here is where? There's nothing here."

Roderick smiled. "I wanted to get ye away from the castle. A break from all the responsibilities." He'd led them to the outcropping, and her view was of the

Falls of Lora, the marina, and the back of Dunstaffnage framed by the Firth of Lorn as the ocean opened from the point.

She glanced at him. "A distraction from the clan wars?"

His gaze shot to hers. "Not wars, just petty attacks here and there."

She turned to him. "Two of MacDougall's crofters died. Not petty attacks." She shook her head. "And my father doesn't acknowledge his part in this, his treachery."

Roderick huffed. "Ye eavesdrop too much, wife. I should not have involved ye."

Tears stung her eyes. "Well, no matter. My father doesn't even reply to my pleas for peace. It's as if I don't matter." She blinked them away. Her father's lies hurt more than his blatant refusal to reply to his only child.

Roderick reached over and took her hand in his. "To me, ye matter." He kissed the back. "To yer clan, the MacDougalls, ye matter."

He released her hand. "Come. I only planned to have ye out till noon meal." He turned Merlin back toward Dunstaffnage.

He called out as he grinned over his shoulder, "Race ye back."

Mary kicked her mount till she came alongside him. "Oh, 'tis not a fair race. Merlin's a war horse. I'm on a mare."

Roderick kneed Merlin, who reared at the promise of a good run. "First one back gets the prize."

Mary's mare pranced at Merlin's actions, both mounts ready for a run.

Mary held her reins tight. "What's the prize?"

Roderick turned Merlin in a spin. "Me!" Then he took off at a gallop.

Mary's mare sprung after, and Mary let her have her head as she leaned low over the horse's mane. Merlin kept a fast pace, and Roderick glanced under his arm and smiled as he spotted her.

He slowed as they neared the marina and village. She came closer to Merlin's backside. They both made the turn to Dunstaffnage. A whiz flew past her. The guards behind her called out a warning, and she sat up. The whir came again, and pain shot through her left shoulder. Something knocked her to the side. The jostle of the horse tipped her, and everything went black.

****

The guard's yell brought Roderick to a halt. As he turned Merlin, Mary's mare flew past. Empty of its rider.

God, Mary!

He rode hard toward his men as one dismounted and bent over a body on the ground. He flew off Merlin, who stopped when his rider came out of the saddle.

Mary lay on her side with an arrow protruding from her shoulder. Hamish knelt near her. "Milaird, she's been shot."

Roderick turned her a little, and she cried out.

His scrutiny went to his men, Hamish and Robbie. "Who? Who shot her?"

Robbie, still mounted, searched the land. Roderick's eyes followed, and a man stood at the forest's edge holding a bow. "Ye there!" Robbie took off at a gallop.

Roderick examined his wife. Blood soaked her arisaid at the shoulder where the arrow came clear from front to back. "Hamish, we must get her to Agatha soon. The blood, there's so much."

Hamish nodded. "Aye, Milaird. Break the arrow. Leave it in so she won't bleed out."

Hamish bent to take her in his arms.

Roderick stopped him with his hand. "No! I shall hold her. Ye break the arrow."

He swallowed hard as bile rose in his throat. "I don't think I can cause her pain without dying myself."

Roderick sat and placed his legs around Mary as he cradled her. God, he'd held her so many times, but this time, with her hurt, tears filled his eyes. He shifted her to have a good grip in case she jolted, and she moaned low and long. The painful sound tore his heart.

Hamish took hold of the front part of the arrow. "Hard and fast, Milaird." His eyes met Roderick's. "Forgive me the pain I cause." He gripped the bolt with both hands and broke the shaft.

Mary screamed hard, then fainted in Roderick's arms.

Robbie rode up with the man from the forest before him in his horse, William, a fisherman who dismounted. "No, it's not true." He gaped between the three men. "I was told ye were under attack by a Comyn, that I had to save ye." His eyes fell on Mary. "Not the lady. Oh, Lord, forgive me. I saw the Comyn plaid chasing ye and acted. It has more green then the red like ours." He fell to his knees. "Please, Milaird, have mercy."

Roderick rose with Mary in his arms. "It is not me or the Lord ye should beg mercy from. It's yer lady."

He handed Mary to Hamish and mounted Merlin, who stood still when cued with his knees. Hamish handed Mary up to him.

He nodded to Robbie. "Have William held under guard at the castle till I can question him more." He adjusted Mary and took hold of the reins. "Hamish, ride to the village, find Agatha. I don't care who she tends. She comes at once." His gaze dropped to Mary, pale and limp in his arms. "Tell her she comes to save my love."

Hours later, Roderick stood at the end of their bed as Agatha wrapped bandages around Mary's shoulder, the grueling task of removing the arrow and stitching the wound now complete. He thanked God Mary stayed passed out through the entire ordeal. Twice he'd broken down in tears as he held her while Agatha worked. The heavily bruised wound and the skin ripped from the arrow killed him every time he saw it, and now he pictured it over and over in his mind.

His mother took his hand in hers. "She's strong, Roderick."

Agatha finished tying off the cloth and covered her with the bedding leaving her unclothed. She turned and eyed his clothing. He'd not left Mary's side since he carried her into their room. Blood stained his plaid and shirt, her blood. He didn't care. All he cared about was her.

Agatha moved toward him and patted his shoulder. "Ye, go clean up." Her face connected with his ma's. Elizabeth took his arm, but he refused to move.

"I will not leave her." His voice came out gruff from the lump in his throat.

Agatha turned, wrung out a cloth, and placed it on

Mary's forehead. "Ye get cleaned up. I won't let ye near her in yer filth." She spoke over her shoulder. "Roderick, the worst is yet to come. She'll have a fever, and ye need to be ready."

Tears filled his eyes, spilling down his cheeks in the same tracks as before. "Will she...die?"

Both women stared at him.

He fisted his hands. "I don't ask for the king, damn it. I ask for me. Will I lose her?"

His ma took his arm. "Not if Agatha or I can help it. And I bet ye won't either. Come, son, clean up and then we'll see how Mary fares."

Time came and went in a blur. Her fever rose, and Agatha's teas, rank-smelling ointments, and constant care hadn't abated her illness. Roderick refused to leave her side. He even took to holding her mistletoe as he prayed.

Rose came and spoke with her about their friendship. Archibald came and took Rose away. Agatha gave him tea which he dribbled into her, thankful when she swallowed at his begging. His ma came and went. Reverend O'Donnell sat with him for a long time, holding Mary's hand with his as he whispered prayers.

When she wasn't delirious babbling about not being the son her da always wanted, she lay still as death. While those times scared him, he took advantage of them. He read to her. First, her Arthur stories hoping she'd respond. Something to tell him, she remained with them. As her fever rose, he switched to scriptures, begging her to say something, blink even.

On the third day, well after midnight, her fever rose higher.

Agatha's voice as she whispered to his ma echoed. "Her fever must come down soon. If not, I fear she won't ever be the same. Why, some don't even wake."

Roderick picked her up, bedding and all. "I'm taking her to the loch to cool her."

Agatha trailed behind. Her nagging voice carried in the hall as they passed sleeping clan members. "The cold may harm her. The water may irritate the wound."

Not listening, Roderick stepped from the castle. He only cared about her, and instinct told him to take her to the loch. He stopped at the sea gate and roared since it stayed locked. His ma fumbled her keys, unlocked it, and opened it for him. He strode to the water's edge, not stopping, and waded in fully clothed till he came waist deep with her in his arms. A chill of the water gave him shivers even though they were well into summer. He turned her till the bedding floated away.

He floated her naked in his arms, allowing her hair to spill out around her head, reminding him of the day he'd first seen her from the battlement. The memory flashed as her hair floated on the water. Her golden-brown locks flew about her as she floated above him like a siren from mythology, half-woman and half-bird. His heart thudded, and he sensed he drifted. She opened her mouth but said nothing. He felt a connection, something ethereal and unearthly. "My soul mate" floated through his mind.

Agatha's yell brought him back. "I have a blanket and a fur for her when ye come out."

When Mary's cheeks turned red from the cold, and a shiver began, he carried her from the water. He sat down at the base of an oak tree overlooking the loch and mountain range beyond and held her. Early dawn lit the sky purple as Agatha wrapped Mary in the blanket and then the fur. "Let's get her inside, Milaird."

Roderick gripped Mary to his chest. "If it is to be her last sunrise, we will watch it together." He wiped the water from her face. Cool to the touch.

Agatha stood her ground, and Roderick barked at her, "Leave us."

A short time later, his ma appeared carrying a pitcher and two wooden cups. She had his plaid folded over her arm. She set the drink items to his right, pouring liquid into the cups. He sat forward from the tree as she wrapped one of his plaids around his shoulders. The warmth was welcome against his damp clothing.

She pulled his flask from her sleeve and set that next to the pitcher and cups. "Tea for Mary and yer flask I swiped from yer sporran." She stood and stared at him for a moment.

He gazed at the sunrise of a new day and what he prayed wasn't Mary's last.

His ma huffed. "Ye just as hardheaded as yer da. Enough will for both of ye, ye have." She laughed. "I wouldn't be surprised if ye have enough will to force her to survive." She blew a breath. "I pray like hell ye do, son."

She turned as Roderick spoke. "Me too, ma. Thank ye."

They finally left him alone. With his wife in his arms, he watched the sunrise. Gradually, the purple faded into blue then the red melted into orange. The sun washed across the mountain side. The green and blue blended with the sky until the sun's light came fully upon them.

In his mind and his heart, he silently begged God, "Please don't take her from me."

Mary stirred in his arms.

He nearly jolted at her movement and glanced at her face. With her eyes closed and a blush on her cheeks, she smiled.

Mary whispered in a cracked voice, "Warm."

Roderick choked on his breath as tears fell down his cheeks. His hand brushed her face. "Mary, are ye awake?"

She cleared her throat as she squinted her eyes.

Roderick grabbed the cup filled with tea. "Here, lass, drink."

She sipped, sighed, and blinked open her eyes, gazing at his face. "Tears?"

Roderick smiled through his tears. "Aye, lass. Happy tears. Welcome back, wife." He had her drink more. Then he set the cup down.

She shifted and moaned. "Back, where have I been? Feels like hell."

Roderick choked on a sob. "Ye have been, but the sun has risen to a new day."

Mary glanced at the sunrise and then back at him. "We are outside?"

He wiped his face with his hand, drying his tears. "Ye've been ill. I had to dip ye in the loch. No matter, ye are back. That's what matters." He sighed, and one of her ma's quotes came to mind. "The darkest hours are always before the dawn."

Chapter 19

Mary shuffled back to her bed with the help of Rose and Agatha. She'd quickly recovered over the last two days since Roderick dipped her in the loch to reduce her fever.

As she climbed back into bed, her shoulder only pinched a little. Rose took the MacDougall arisaid from her shoulders and offered a solemn grin when she folded it. Roderick had taken her Comyn arisaid away as he begged her to wear his colors.

He'd stood beside her bed, holding his colors. "Mary, I know it's tradition the wife wears her family colors. But lass, I near lost ye." He hiccupped a sigh. "William made an honest mistake and one he keeps trying to make up for by bringing us near every fish he catches." He glanced at the plaid in his hands. "Ye must wear my colors for yer protection, lass."

As he wrapped the arisaid around her shoulders, he brought the ends together and bent slowly kissing her. "I not only ask for yer protection but for me, for my love. I want ye in my colors because ye are truly my wife." He patted the plaid. "Wear them for me, please?"

She smiled at Rose as she placed the plaid on the chair beside the bed. "Where is Elizabeth this morning? She's normally here."

Rose and Agatha exchanged glances, and Mary wondered what was wrong. The creak of castle gates opening, and a large group mounted on horseback moving through them came to her.

Mary sat forward. "Who could that be, and so many?"

Both women froze.

Mary shifted out of her bed intent on getting to the window to see what the ruckus was.

Rose came forward taking her arm. "Mary, ye shouldn't be out of bed."

Mary brushed her off. "What? Agatha just gave me a lecture about getting out of bed more to strengthen my legs." She hobbled to the window, and the sight stole her breath. Her father dismounted from his war horse in the outer bailey amid a small group of warriors from her clan. Malcolm MacDougall was with them, looking fit and happy. Erik Sinclair was not in sight.

MacDougall warriors surrounded them fully armed. Her eyes shot back to her father. He was unarmed.

Archibald strode forward and waved her father into the main hall as Mary's heart dropped. "Oh no! He heard I was injured. He's here to see for himself." Her eyes connected with the women in the room. "I must dress now. Hurry."

Agatha stepped forward her hand out. "Milady. Ye are in no condition to dress and waltz down to the main hall."

Mary stepped toward her clothing and grabbed the bed to steady herself. "It doesn't matter. If I don't, my father will either report to the king who will kill my love or run him through himself." She grabbed her bodice. "I have no choice."

****

251

Roderick sat in his chair at the dais, higher than where Laird Comyn stood now, keeping the upper advantage. He'd had two days to prepare for this meeting. Word of Comyn's group traveling under a white flag of truce came to him the day Mary woke from her fever.

As her father's group traveled closer and closer, Roderick had time to prepare for his response to why Mary lay in bed, near death. Her speedy recovery over the last two days boosted his confidence in what he'd say. But the simple fact remained, Laird Comyn's daughter was seriously injured in Rodericks's care. A violation of the peace agreement put his life at risk. It all came down to what Robert would do when he learned what all had happened.

Robert shifted his weight from foot to foot, his glare tilting into anger. "I'll ask again, MacDougall. I've heard rumors about my daughter. Rumors say she's dying or dead. Here I stand in yer hall with yer brother beside me healthy and hale." His eyes bore into Roderick. "Where is my daughter Mary? Where are ye hiding my jewel?"

"I'm here, Father." Everyone in the room gasped as all turned to the stairs. At the top stood Mary, hastily dressed with Agatha and Rose on either side of her.

Roderick stood so fast his chair fell over. He came around the table and jumped from the dais. "Mary…"

She waved him off, and he stood frozen next to her father who stood with his mouth agape.

She lifted her head. "I bid ye welcome to my home, Father."

Mary took a step, and the women on either side moved with her, their arms around her waist.

Her father whispered, "Good God, they carry her."

She stopped halfway, out of breath. "Ye see, father…I am…fit as a fiddle."

Roderick crossed to the bottom of the stairs, worried she'd fall flat on her face. But she continued slowly, step by step and stood before him. "No need…to confront my husband. I am treated…well."

Her father spoke from behind Roderick. "She's as white as new fallen snow."

Mary fainted, and Roderick swept her in his arms. The people in the hall gasped and broke into shouts and heated conversation.

He turned and bellowed, "Enough!"

Everyone froze and stared at him as he yelled. "She's sacrificed enough for yer peace!"

He took a deep breath and spoke lowly. "Comyn, follow me. The rest of ye take yer ease."

Agatha and Rose moved up the stairs before Roderick as he carried Mary to their room. Comyn followed quietly behind. The rest of the people in the hall took a seat, the Comyns off to a table of their own as maids served ale. At the top of the stairs Roderick paused, caught Archibald's eye, and tilted his head to the Comyn warriors. Archibald nodded. They'd be guarded.

Roderick placed Mary in the bed, and Agatha and Rose stripped her to her shift. Her father stood at the end of the bed beside Roderick. He felt awkward standing beside his enemy in silence. But together, they worried over Mary.

Comyn spoke as the women shifted her bandaged shoulder. "It heals?"

Roderick grunted. "Aye, she's recovered fast."

Her father sighed. "She always has." The women finished, and Agatha covered Mary. "We'll leave ye men. Don't disturb her." The door closing announced the men were alone.

Comyn lowly spoke as he stared at his daughter. "I'd heard she'd been shot. An arrow."

Roderick replied, his anger rising. "An accident that wouldn't have happened if ye hadn't been raiding. A man shot her for the plaid she wore!"

Robert turned to him. "Me, what about ye!"

Roderick raised his voice. "I am not raiding ye!"

Mary's voice came from the bed. "The enemy of my enemy is my friend."

Both men froze and turned to her. She lay still but stared at them both.

She sighed. "Elizabeth is right. Ye both are thickheaded." She tried to sit up and winced. Roderick came to her side and helped her to sit up. He offered her a cup, and she sipped.

He set it aside and kissed her forehead. "Ye are more than a jewel, Mary. Ye are a treasure."

Her father huffed from the foot of the bed. "Ye can stop pretending. The rumors claim ye are in love, but I don't believe it."

Roderick tensed. "I don't give a damn what ye believe."

Mary audibly sighed. "Are ye both going to argue like little boys or listen to what I have to say?"

Roderick waited as her father waved to her. "Ye spoke one of yer ma's sayings, so what of it?" She had. The enemy of my enemy is my friend.

Mary rolled her eyes. "It's a wonder this war has gone on so long. Ye both don't attack the other, but someone attacks ye in the other's plaid. Ye have a common enemy. Either one or more works against ye both."

Roderick crossed the room and paced. "What she says has merit. We both claim there are no raids, but raids occur in our plaids. I must admit I had a hard time figuring out how yer clan made it through a snow-blocked pass to raid me. But what if they were already in my valley?"

Her father put his hands on his hips. "Ye have a point, Roderick. I wondered the same." He rubbed his neck. "So, who is our enemy, eh?"

They stood there a moment, and Mary sighed again. "Do I have to do all the thinking? Who in yer clan has reason to have ye at each other's throat? What would someone gain from the wars?"

The Comyn growled. "Well, I know who has good enough reason and kept nagging me to keep the wars going. When I refused, he acted and raided yer village shortly after the wedding. *Against* my orders."

Roderick stopped his pacing. "Erik Sinclair?"

Her father nodded. "Aye, kicked him out just after the snow melted. He near ran me through when I announced I wanted Malcolm as the laird."

Roderick's glare shot to his enemy, but he didn't see an enemy but a weary older man standing before him.

Comyn's shoulders dropped, and he fell into the chair beside the bed. "Aye, I need to secure the clan, ensure they prosper after I am gone. I'm tired, tired of fighting, tired of starving. Mary only has young female cousins. The eldest, still younger than Malcolm, I planned to ask for a betrothal for him. Have them take over the clan."

Mary smiled. "Ye did? That's nice, Father."

Comyn smiled at her. "Mary, ye are a rare one, ye are."

He turned to Roderick. "So, who in yer clan has a reason for this folly?"

Roderick paced before the fire. "I don't know. It would take a warrior to lead raids. All are loyal. I've not denied anything that's due to them. I'd have to think about it. But in the meantime, we need to work together."

Comyn snorted. "No one would believe it. A MacDougall and Comyn working together."

Roderick grinned. "Aye, that's why we work in secret." He rubbed his hands together. "We track the raids, try and not only find their camp but work together to catch them in the act."

Comyn shook his head. "I don't know, lad."

Roderick stood tall. "Is this the man who's raided my lands so well?"

Comyn laughed. "It was Erik who planned it all."

Roderick paced again. "I send one man to ye, and ye send one man to me. They ride with our men to stop each raid. That way, they could identify the other clan's men parading in the enemy's plaid."

Mary shifted as she spoke. "But ye'd have to keep it a secret. Today ye must leave in an argument, but, Father, ye leave behind one man, and Roderick sends one with ye. They trade plaids."

Comyn stood. "Agreed." He put his hand out to Roderick, offering a shake. "Secret partners, to end in peace?" Roderick glimpsed Comyn's hand outstretched to him—a peace offering, a way to end the wars for good. He glanced at Mary, who smiled and nodded to her father.

Roderick shook the hand as one of Mary's ma's sayings came to mind. "Honor among thieves."

Comyn shook it back. "Aye, that we are boy."

Mary's father smiled and nodded. "I'd like to visit the chapel before I depart then return and have a private word with Mary. But we'll ride out tonight, seeing as you'll deny me hospitality after our argument."

Roderick nodded as he bellowed, "Ye'll do what?"

Comyn's grin went wide. "Ye'll not harm my daughter, ye bastard!"

Bastard? Well, Roderick could do better. "Look here, ye boggin levvy head. I love her."

Comyn strode to the door and hit it. "Love her, ye gowk! MacDougalls don't know how to love!"

Comyn opened it, and Rose and Agatha fell to the floor at his feet. Roderick had to cover his mouth to stop from laughing.

Roderick bellowed, "Archibald! Ye guard the Comyn. He'll leave after his prayers and a private visit with his daughter."

Her father smiled as he whispered, "Ye get well, Mary. I'll be back to say my goodbyes."

With that, he strode out, head high with a smile. An enemy made a friend, and they'd get to the bottom of the raids and ensure peace. Roderick had never felt so good in his life.

****

Elizabeth retreated to the chapel with the intent of avoiding Laird Robert Comyn. The wars were enough for her to cope with. She doubted she'd be able to face him after what he'd done and not run him through.

She fingered her heart necklace, thinking of her Ian as the stone glowed no longer.

The door creaked open, and a heavy footfall came up behind her. She'd know him anywhere, sense his presence no matter the place. He had a lot of nerve to come to her after what he'd done to her and to his longtime friend.

Robert Comyn's voice cracked as he spoke. "I knew I'd find ye here, Lizzie."

Her head snapped to the side. "Don't call me that!"

He huffed. "We all called ye Lizzie. Ye all called me Robbie. We were younger back then." He sat down next to her on the pew. "It's Rob now to those familiar with me."

Elizabeth shifted in her seat. "Well, *Robert*, don't worry, we aren't young anymore."

"Ye loved me once."

"A young, foolish girl who didn't know what love was until she met her true love."

Robert grunted. "Not yer love. I was yer love."

Elizabeth turned to him. "Both loved her and fought over her. Endlessly. But ye miss the most important part of the fable. The Stone of Love never glowed for ye."

Rob turned, facing her. "Ian and his stupid magic stones. His stupid Fae fables. A man by a creek spotting his love and the stone glowed for him."

Elizabeth stood and paced. "If ye are going to quote the fable, quote it right. 'Confused, he snuck off to his spot by the stream. As he sat, he saw a maiden approach the stream.

'She had glowing cream-colored skin and an inner beauty he had not seen in a woman before.

'Her light-brown hair glimmered in the sunlight, seeming as if to cast the threads of a pure gold halo around her head. Her soul called to him in a way he had never felt before.' "

Robert grunted. "Yer hair is dark brown, like a walnut."

Elizabeth rubbed her hand over her hair. "Was, it's silver lined now."

He rose and reached to take her hand. "Come with me, Elizabeth, please. I love ye, always have."

She stepped back avoiding his hand. "What of Mary? Ye professed love for her."

He dropped his hand and sat hard on the pew. "I did, loved ye both—differently."

Elizabeth stood and stared at the man she'd once called friend, her Ian called best friend. "Why did ye have to fight over me? And for so long, even when ye were married to Mary?"

Rob stood and strode to the other side of the chapel. His voice rose as he spoke. "I never loved Mary the way I loved ye. I fought for ye. I fought for our love that Ian stole from me with a stupid rock."

Elizabeth yelled back, "A magic Fae stone and one that glows when my true love is near." She held up her heart pendant and flipped it open, revealing the dark red heart-shaped gem that rested inside. "The Stone of Love never glowed for ye, Robert. I never loved ye!" She breathed hard as she stared at the man she once knew, now old and weary looking. "I never asked ye to start the wars for me." She blinked back tears as she yelled, "Ye killed my true love. *Yer best friend*, for a war to try and gain my love! What's wrong with ye?"

Robert's face went red as he roared back, "I didn't

kill Ian! Ian was my friend! We discussed peace and the betrothal! My stupid war chief stabbed him! It wasn't me!" He sobbed the last. "It wasn't me."

She stared at him. "The Sinclair boy? Please tell me ye ran him through." She huffed. "Of course not. He was here with Mary's things. Ye and yer war is more important than anything."

Robert barked at her, "I banished him for going against me, his laird!"

He sat on the bench away from her and spoke in a fatigued voice. "Forgive me, Elizabeth. I have wronged for too long and am here to make it right."

She closed the pendant and held it to her heart as she sat on the bench on the other side of the room—so close yet so far apart. "Ye speak to Roderick and Mary? Ye stop the raids and speak of peace?"

Rob nodded. "Aye, a partnership in secret to oust a common enemy making the raids we both haven't done." He sighed. "And it was Mary who figured it out. Ye women, always the brains behind the brawn."

Elizabeth dried her tears. "It's time to pass the clans to the youth. Young and innocent needing to be mature too fast."

Rob mumbled, "Youth is wasted on the young."

Elizabeth raised her head. "Ye picked up Mary's sayings."

He shot back, "My daughter speaks them to me endlessly to abuse me."

Elizabeth whispered, "I meant yer wife." She sighed. "She lives on in yer daughter, such a beautiful girl. Smart and clever."

Robert turned and smiled. "When ye sent Rose, that was a huge help. Thank ye."

Elizabeth turned to face him. "I couldn't leave Mary's girl alone in yer hall of warriors. She needed a companion." She sighed. "They still do not know, and I want it kept that way."

Robert nodded. "Malcolm is a bright lad. Strong and a good fighter." He heaved a sigh. "Ye'll find out soon enough. I'm making him laird of clan Comyn, marrying him to a cousin." He sighed. "Brought him with me. I thought ye'd like to visit since the king denied yer goodbyes."

Elizabeth nodded as tears filled her eyes. "Thank ye. I'll see him before ye leave."

Elizabeth's gaze met his. "Ye are? Ye truly mean it. Peace."

He nodded. "Aye, peace."

****

Mary's door opened, and her father entered the room, looking older than she'd ever seen him. Archibald nodded and closed the door, leaving them alone. She didn't know what to say now that the man stood before her.

Laird Robert Alan Comyn stood by the door and stared at her.

He glanced down and sighed. "I suppose ye have no love for me after all that I've done." He tapped his hand on his thigh. "Bartered ye off in a farce of a marriage to save my own arse." He huffed. "Used ye like a servant to keep my clan from starving, from going without."

He had, but she'd do it all over again. They were her clan, too—people she loved. Tears gathered in Mary's eyes as her father blurred before her.

He took a step toward the bed. "I know ye may not

know it, but I love ye, Mary. Raised ye as best I knew how." A memory of her as a child flashed in her mind—her father, younger. Laughing and lifting her above his head. Her squeal of delight and her mother's fair face smiling at her. Mary's throat closed, and she swallowed the lump there.

She opened her mouth to speak, but her father raised his hand. "Let me finish before I lose my nerve."

He stepped closer and sat on the bed next to her. A scar rubbed her hand as he took it. "Ye are smart, canny like yer ma." A tear trailed down her cheek. For the first time, her father spoke to her as his daughter. She'd hoped for this moment all her life.

He blew out his breath. "For so long, I couldn't look at ye. Ye are so like her." He smiled. "And here ye are. Married and in love." Roderick's face flashed the day she woke in his arms in the sunrise. His tears and expression of love moved her.

Mary smiled. "Aye, I am."

He nodded. "Please forgive me for all the wrongs I have done. Once this war business is over, please allow me a chance to be a better father to ye."

Mary hiccupped as more tears fell. "I'd like that."

He patted her hand. "I am so proud of ye, Mary."

They sat together in silence for a while, Mary taking in all her father said, hoping against hope he meant every word.

He patted her hand and stood. "How lucky am I to have someone to say goodbye to, that hurts me to say it."

Mary squeezed his hand. "It's not goodbye. We'll see each other again."

"Aye." He bent and kissed her forehead. "Ye are a

jewel, Mary."

Her father released her hand, turned, and strode to the door. Before he opened it, he stopped and said over his shoulder. "Ye will get to work on a babe? Not for the king, but for yer old da. A grandson, maybe?"

Mary blushed. "I'll try."

He winked as he opened the door, stepped through it, and closed it softly.

Mary sat and prayed. Prayed for peace, prayed for both clans, but most of all, she thanked God for giving her back her father.

Chapter 20

Roderick studied the missive from Comyn again, made in the code he used to speak with the tinker who carried the messages under the guise of "gifts" between Mary and her father. Roderick smiled. Over the last month, each package from the Comyn contained coded messages between lairds folded into real letters between Mary and her father. This week the gift from father to daughter was a set of hair combs made of simple bone. They made Mary happy—something from her father to her. The accompanying letter was a response to her previous one. Their regular correspondence kept her spirits up. Comyn stuck to his promise to Mary to be the father he hadn't.

Archibald stood and paced. "I don't get it. Comyn says a hooded rider leads the raiding party on his southwestern village near the pass between us. Repeated raids to the same village. We know yers is centered to two north of here near my da's land, the MacArthurs."

Roderick shook his head and focused on the message. "I'll reread it. Maybe another meaning will come."

He cleared his throat.

Hail the Gowk youth.
News from the common land.
My "friend" has a settlement of followers near the

north, basking in the glory of nature among the oak land forest near the captain clan. The hound lies in wait, but for the hunt or the treat, one doesn't know.

As to yer "friend"...maybe one who "holds with the hare and runs with the hounds." A fighting leader who hides in full daylight is an ode to danger. The hooded one walks the line and appears in the north and the east like the Gae, coming and going with the mist. Be wary, boy.

The crafty ol' dodger

Archibald spoke from the mantel. "Erik has a camp in the oak forest near my clan, living off the land. So, that's an easy one to raid and capture. But the other is the puzzle."

Roderick blew a laugh. "The part where he calls me a *fool youth* since he opens each missive with a new insult or the one where he calls me boy knowing I'm a man or the part about the hooded one?"

Archibald laughed. "The one where he called ye a wee nilly bahookie. Well, that's my favorite so far."

Roderick grunted. "Good to know ye both are having such fun at my expense. And I don't have a small arse."

He paced as he stared at the parchment. "To 'hold with the hare and run with the hounds' is to deceitfully remain on good terms with both sides of a conflict. But to come and go with the mist and appear in north and east?"

"Must mean the hooded one leads both raiding parties."

"We must catch them in the act. No more witnesses after." Roderick crumpled the paper in his hands. "I want them caught, especially the hooded one. That's the betrayer from the MacDougalls."

Archbald strode to the map on the desk. "We start with the easy prey. Erik, in the forest near the MacArthurs." He pointed to the forest near his clan. "If we capture him, we can question him and find out who the hooded one is."

Roderick threw the missive in the fireplace, ensuring no evidence of the partnership was left for anyone to find. As he watched the parchment burn, he worried about what to say to Mary. He was headed to ambush and take her former betrothed hostage. He'd likely have to brutally question him to gain the answers he needed, they needed. She wouldn't take it well.

****

Mary barked a laugh from her chair as she sat dressed for bed. Roderick stood before the fireplace in their bedroom. "I appreciate yer concern, husband, but as far as I'm concerned, torture the Sinclair all ye want. I want this war ended and our life without it begun."

The past month flew by, and her healing from the arrow was nearly complete. Only a pucker of a scar where the arrow's entry and exit remained from her ordeal. Her health improved with the spring's bounty, and the clan food stores were back to usual levels.

The newfound relationship with her father promised a happy future. When she'd learned Erik was the one behind Ian's death, she'd begged Roderick to launch a search and exact revenge for his da. Even in Roderick's rage, he held firm. They needed to draw him out and catch him in the act of raiding the MacDougalls in the Comyn plaid. Now that the opportunity was open to Roderick, she didn't want him to hold back.

Roderick chuckled. "Yer bloodlust makes me

ensure I shall never cross ye, wife." He knelt before her. "But ye realize this means I head out to war. I must not only lead the MacDougalls, but I must catch Erik in the act. Question him myself so I can carry the message to yer da and the Comyn clan."

Tears filled Mary's eyes. "Why must it be ye? Ye have warriors for this."

He took her hand in his and kissed the back. "To rally the clans together, Comyn and I must work with and for each other. For Erik's capture, yer da brings information and sets the bait. I will attack and bring the guilty to him."

She huffed as he kissed her lips then sat back as he spoke. "The clans must see us as partners, together. It must be the lairds leading. 'Tis the only way the clans will follow."

She hiccupped a sob. "When do ye leave?"

His head bent till their foreheads touched. "Dawn."

He kissed her hard, and she responded with all the love in her heart. New tears fell, and the salt on her lips reminded her of the sting of their upcoming separation.

Roderick picked her up and carried her to the bed. He laid her on it and came full over her. "No more tears, wife. Come, love yer husband, and not worry about the wars." He pulled on the hem of her shift, and she rose helping him remove it. Bare before him she reached for his belt. He stood and stripped his clothing as he beheld her.

Naked he came over her and kissed her as he shifted above her. "I wish to love ye, wife. Show ye my heart."

He slid over her sex, the folds already damp in anticipation of the rapture she'd find in his arms.

Tears filled her eyes as she whispered, "Roderick, I love ye." Hoping and praying this wasn't the last time she'd lie in his arms. He moved within her, slowly as he kissed her. His gaze held hers as he brought them bodies, minds, and souls together as one.

No other words were spoken. The act of love, the joy of giving herself to the one man she loved with all her heart and soul fulfilled her more than anything. His hand caressed her face, his other lifted her leg, so he could love her better, deeper. Each slow thrust a caress to her soul.

She wrapped her arms around him, trying to draw him closer, closer to her heart. He bent into her and kissed her neck as his thrusts came harder, intense. Soon, her world split apart, and she cried his name as tears spilled down her cheeks. He soon followed with an arch and a cry of her name to the heavens. He huffed as he rested his head against hers, their bodies still connected in love. He stayed there for a moment, then slowly shifted. He bent and kissed her belly. Roderick rolled to her side as he cradled her in his arms.

He pulled her to him, close to his heart, and whispered, "My true love."

Mary held her husband, as tears flowed silently. Soon, his breath changed, and the deep soft breathing of sleep consumed him.

Mary lay on her husband's chest, his heartbeat steady in her ear. She drifted off to a restless sleep of nightmares filled with screams of warriors in battle. Swords hacked away at men in the MacDougall plaid red with a hint of green and blue. Blood soaked the colors into a black stain that faded into blackness before her.

She turned and ran but came upon more warriors fighting in the Comyn plaid of green with red, soaked in blood. Both clan warriors blended into one mass of fighting. Men fell at her feet, bleeding as they reached for her, begging for mercy.

Her father's panic-stricken face flashed before her. Another roar from a warrior and Erik Sinclair's menacing face came at her. She raised her hands to protect herself, and he slashed his sword at her, but it wasn't Mary he hit. It was Roderick atop Merlin. Her husband's roar combined with Merlin's scream filled her head. He fell hard, and blood poured from his leg. When her eyes moved to this face, his eyes lay open, gaping in death's stare.

Mary came awake with a jolt. She panted in her damp shift. Her hand went to her side where Roderick slept and encountered bedding. Sounds of warriors preparing for battle came from the bailey, and her gaze flew to the window. The pink of dawn lit the sky.

"No!" She grabbed her heart pendant, the one he'd given her for Hogmanay, and fled. She ran down the stairs and nearly fell over her shift at the end as she cried out. She had to speak to him one last time. She needed to ensure he came back safely to her.

She opened the doors and screamed, "Roderick!" All in the bailey stopped and stared at their lady who stood in her shift, gripping her pendant to her heart. She didn't care. She ran down the castle steps and farther into the bailey.

Tears fell freely as Roderick approached and halted before her. "Mary, what is it? What's wrong?"

She ran to him and launched into his arms. "Ye can't leave without saying goodbye."

269

He held her for a moment, then lowered her to the ground. "I didn't wake ye to avoid this. I don't want ye upset."

She gripped his plaid as she held the pendant. "Never leave me without saying goodbye, and I love ye."

He brushed the hair from her face as he whispered, "I love ye."

She pulled back, opened the pendant, and handed him the heart-shaped Iona stone, the one his da carried for luck. "Ye must take it. Ye need it for luck."

He shook his head and handed it back. "Mary, I gave ye this so ye'd always carry my heart with ye."

She fumbled and tried handing it to him. "No, I had a dream. Ye must take it."

He shook his head, but Mary wouldn't stop. He needed the stone to come back to her safely. "No, please take it."

Roderick growled, "I want ye to carry my heart."

Mary cried back, "I need ye to carry mine."

Roderick placed the stone back in the locket and held it against her heart. "Here is where I need it. With ye so ye know how much ye mean to me." He bent and kissed her hard.

He whispered into the kiss, "I love ye always, but never goodbye." He backed away. "Till I see ye again."

He brushed his fingers on her face and turned. "Mount, we ride now!"

Mary heaved a sob as Rose and Elizabeth came up on either side. The men mounted, and Roderick, next to Archibald, led them toward the gate. Rose, Elizabeth, and Mary stood on the castle's steps, holding each other as the men rode into the dawn.

When they crested the hill and were no longer visible, Mary crumpled. "He's not coming back. I've seen his death."

Elizabeth bent and picked her up. "It's yer worry for yer love that has ye at wit's end."

Mary rose with her knowing she needed to be strong.

Rose held her other hand. "We'll do as we usually do."

Mary nodded. "Keep busy."

****

A week passed, and no word came from the raiding party. Mary spent time on the wall staring to the north, MacArthur land. A guard, Hamish, paced by again on his regular pass. "Milady, I promise to send word once they are spotted. Roderick would have me cleaning latrine shoots if he knew I let ye up here."

She sighed. "I know, but I can't help myself."

Elizabeth came up beside her. "I know. I stood here many a time waiting for Ian's return." She rested her hands on the edge. "Worrying never did anyone any good. And it's too early to return from MacArthur land. Another week, Mary."

Mary nodded, knowing Elizabeth was right. But it didn't help the emptiness in her heart and the fear that rested in her dreams.

The following morn, Mary woke ill and barely made it to the chamber pot before she upended her stomach into it. She came out from the screen and sat before the fire. "I've worried so much and made myself ill." Fiona bustled in with her tea and bread, and Mary ate it, feeling nearly starved.

Fiona eyed her as Mary spoke. "Is there more?"

Fiona nodded and fetched her more.

Mary's days came and went, one after another and another. Each day she'd rise with the sun and a queasy belly, eat two pieces of bread, work herself till she nearly fell into bed, and spend the night passed in fitful sleep plagued with nightmares of blood and war.

On the fourth morning, Elizabeth came with her tea and bread followed by Fiona and Rose.

Elizabeth set down the tray, and with two slices of bread there was a slice of ham and an ale. She sat in the chair next to her and rested her head on the back. As Rose built up the fire, Mary shoved the bread into her mouth as she drank her hot tea, not caring that it burned her mouth.

Fiona hummed as she made the bed. The ham she ate slower, but the hunger pains wouldn't abate. She swallowed the ale and burped as she sat back in her chair.

Elizabeth clapped her hands and laughed. "I knew it!"

Mary jolted in her chair. "Knew what?"

Elizabeth sat forward. "How long has it been since yer last course, Mary?"

Mary sat up. "What day is it?"

Elizabeth smiled. "Eighteenth of July, the year of our lord 1718."

Mary counted on her fingers and then threw her hands up. "I don't know. I lost count."

Fiona spoke from the bed. "Ye be three weeks overdue."

Rose turned from the fireplace and smiled.

Elizabeth snorted. "Based upon yer illness in the morn and that appetite ye have, ye are carrying."

Mary huffed. "The illness is worry. The appetite, who knows."

Elizabeth barked a laugh. "Ye ate two servings of Cullen Skink at midday and three large pieces of lamb at dinner yesterday alone. I ate everything in sight when I carried Roderick."

Mary sat up, and her hand went to her belly. Was it too much to hope for? Would it be real this time? Stick with her?

She turned to Elizabeth. "How do ye know for sure?"

She smiled. "Well, Agatha can look at yer piss, but I'd bet my best shift ye are carrying."

Mary stared at Elizabeth's excited expression and whispered, "I'm carrying Roderick's babe." She broke out into a grin and spoke louder, "I'm carrying Roderick's babe." She stood and yelled at the top of her lungs, "I'm carrying Roderick's babe!"

Rose clapped her hands as Fiona covered her ears. "Ye don't have to shout it."

Elizabeth stood and took her hands in hers. "Aye, dear. Good things come to those who wait."

Chapter 21

Roderick led his warriors through the forest wearing blackened plaids and dark mud dried on their faces. Erik's group camped deep in the woods with no fire or lights. Their horses were tied in a line between trees, fully tacked, ready to ride out at any moment.

Roderick's men moved through the horses, covering their noses as they patted them to keep them calm not to alert the men that someone approached.

Roderick opened a saddlebag and spotted two distinctive plaids—the red of the MacDougalls and the heavier green of the Comyn. So, Sinclair led the attacks on both clans—the proof he needed to take to both clans to show both lairds were innocent and provide swift punishment to the guilty. But first, Roderick needed to question Sinclair. Who was the MacDougall betrayer? Who worked against him?

He signaled Archibald, who sent the sign silently down the line—surround the camp and wait for the call to attack. Roderick shifted into a place where he kept an eye on Erik, ensuring his prey could be reached when the fighting started. All knew to leave Sinclair to him. He wanted him captured alive.

Roderick was about to give the motion when one of Erik's men moved to the horses. Roderick's men froze and waited.

Erik's man who stood next to the horses directly in

front of Robbie lifted his plaid, and pissed on Robbie, who shifted back.

Erik's man's eyes connected with Robbie, and he yelled, "We're under attack!"

Sinclair rose and gave the Comyn war cry. *Fhad's a bhios maide sa choill, cha bhi foill an Cuimeineach*, as long as there is a stick in the woods, there won't be deceit from Clan Comyn.

All hell broke loose as Roderick found the war cry ironic. Sinclair was a stick in the wood and was about nothing but deceit. The wars ended today.

Roderick roared as he emerged from the bushes and attacked Erik.

Sinclair drew his sword and parried with Roderick. "MacDougall, fitting, ye think? Come to make yer death that much easier for me?"

Roderick blocked the attack and drove forward with a swipe overhead, then another at Erik's feet.

"Come to expose the deceitful stick in the forest. I spied both plaids in the saddle bags. Yer trickery is at an end."

Sinclair blocked above as he grunted. "Mary was mine." He stopped the lower pass as he shifted backward. "She was to bring me to greater heights."

Sinclair ran at him with his sword aimed at Roderick's middle. He barely sidestepped it but took a slice to his side. He grunted as he dodged away and turned back to Sinclair.

Sinclair grinned as he came close. "But that won't matter now. Another will bring me all." Sinclair's blade flew at Roderick.

Roderick pushed back on Erik's sword, disengaging them both. "The other promises more than he can deliver."

They stood panting, waiting for the other to attack.

Sinclair smiled. "Ye don't know who betrays ye."

He swiped at Roderick's left, which he blocked. "I know enough. I have enough to prove to both clans ye are the traitor."

Sinclair swung right then left, and Roderick's blade caught his as he pressed closer, bringing their faces close.

Roderick barked, "Who is my traitor?"

Sinclair smirked. "The serpent within will be yer undoing." Roderick paused. The serpent? Who could that be?

His temporary halt was his mistake. Sinclair took advantage of the moment and lowered his sword, disengaging the blade's lock. As Sinclair drew back, he swiped a deep cut in Roderick's right thigh.

Roderick roared, and he fell to his side. "Who, damn ye?"

Sinclair laughed. "Someone who will give me all."

Pain burst across Roderick's face as he fell to the ground. Men screamed around him as he lay in a daze. Erik's boots retreated as the world tilted and blackness consumed him.

Someone lifted him, and he roared in pain. Archibald's voice spoke nearby. "Wrap the wound. Get him on his horse."

He turned and rasped, "Arch, Sinclair."

Someone patted his shoulder as Archbald's voice spoke in his ear. "Angus, Fergus, and Robbie follow and will report. Ye rest, Milaird." A cloth tightened around his thigh, and Roderick roared in agony.

Multiple hands placed him on a horse as pain shot

through his right leg. The familiar shift under him told him he sat on Merlin. He fell over the mane, not caring that the saddle pommel jutted into his belly. He stirred and would have fallen off if not for the hands that caught him.

"Tie him to his horse. We must get him back soon," Archibald whispered near him. "His ma and Mary will have a fit if he bleeds out."

Roderick whispered as he hugged Merlin's neck, "Take me home, boy."

****

Mary stirred in her sleep as an awareness overcame her, like someone was in the room with her. She blinked, sat up, and glanced around the chamber. Waves from the firelight danced around the room. A chill spread over Mary, and she pulled the bedding closer. The shadows shifted again, and a glowing green woman materialized at the foot of her bed. Mary's hand went to her belly, the instinct to protect her babe.

The woman, dressed in older clothing, floated at the end of the bed. The frame of the fireplace and fire Mary saw through the apparition. A low murmur sounded in the room that moved through Mary. It changed into a whimper, then a sob. Mary's gaze went to the woman's face, and she cried. The woman's mouth opened. Then continued to open larger than her face as it morphed into a black abyss as a scream echoed. Mary threw herself down and covered her stomach with both hands.

Pounding hit her door hard. Hamish's voice yelled from the other side. "Milady, ye must come fast. The men are coming in the outer bailey now."

Mary sat up in an empty room. Bam! Bam! Bam!

277

"Milady, it's Roderick. Come now!"

Roderick? She threw the covers aside, grabbed her arisaid, and opened the door to Hamish's worried expression.

Down in the outer bailey, it seemed all hell had broken loose. Injured men dismounted horses, and women and other warriors rushed about frantically.

Archibald's voice rose above it all. "Cut him off his horse." Rose was beside him as he held her in his arms. Her eyes followed Archibald's, and that's when Mary spotted Roderick hunched over Merlin, the horse's dapple-gray coat covered in blood under the saddle. Men hefted Roderick from his horse. He lay in their arms unmoving with a blood-soaked bandage on his right leg.

Mary rushed to his side, her hand on his sweaty face. "Oh, my love. What have they done to ye?"

Elizabeth called from the castle steps, "Get him inside. Call for Agatha."

The men moved their laird up the steps and into the castle as Mary stood numb in the bailey.

Elizabeth called for her. "Mary, come on, dear. Now is the time yer husband needs ye most."

****

Someone shook Mary awake. She moaned and lifted her head from the bed as she held Roderick's hand.

Elizabeth stood over her. "Come, ye need yer rest."

Mary shook her hand off her shoulder. "No, I'll not leave him."

Elizabeth sighed. "Ye have more than yerself to think of these days. Come to the bedroom next door. We'll wake ye if there's a change."

Mary gripped Roderick's limp hand with both hers. "He didn't leave me. I will not leave him."

Elizabeth stood there a moment with her hand on Mary's shoulder. "Ye know, the men are supposed to be the stronger of the sexes. Ian always said he was strong as steel, but I don't believe that's what God intended. The women birth the babes. Raise them, tend to the clan, and care for all within their reach. All the men do is protect." She hummed. "In all my years, what I've seen. It's the women that are stronger."

Agatha sighed from the chair before the fire. "Put her in bed with him. It'll make it easier for me to care for them both."

Mary stood and removed her arisaid. Elizabeth pulled the covers away, and Mary snuggled into her husband's left side to not disturb the injured right one.

Elizabeth smirked. "Ye'll regret this, Agatha. Roderick is never down long with an injury. It's why we always sear his wounds, so he's up and about quicker. I hope he doesn't wake and decide to see to his wife's *needs* while ye are in the room."

She patted the bedding as she smiled at Mary. "Rest. Ye helped through the wound's cleaning, searing, and bandaging." Elizabeth moved to the door. "Ye're a good wife, Mary, and will make a better mother." She sighed. "I'm off to bed. I'll be back in the morning when Roderick wakes."

Elizabeth shut the door with a click, and Agatha shifted in the chair, settling in for a nap. Mary lifted her head. "Agatha, is what Elizabeth said true? He will wake soon?"

She sighed. "Usually does. Sleep, Mary."

Mary rested her head on Roderick's shoulder but

wasn't tired. She kissed his bare chest and rested her head next to his heartbeat, steady and strong.

Soon Agatha's light snores filled the room, and Mary whispered to her husband, "I have the most exciting news, husband. I'm to have our babe." She glanced up at his face, younger looking in his rest. She sighed. "Yer ma, well, she swears it's a boy. She tells me I eat like she did when she was pregnant with ye. Everything in sight." She sat up and stared at his face, but still nothing. She kissed his chin. "Please don't die. I'm to have our bairn. Not one for the king, but one for us."

Mary fell asleep to the beat of Roderick's heart like she'd done many nights. The comforting, steady pulse reassured her he lived.

Large hands roamed her body as warmth covered her. His hand moved to her rear and squeezed it as he pulled her closer to him. His breath blew into her ear just before he kissed it. "Is this a dream, or is there a Fae in my bed?"

His hand cupped her breast. Mary came fully awake and jolted. "Roderick, ye are awake."

He grunted at her movement but held her to him. "Don't move. It hurts."

She froze. "Are ye in pain?"

Her husband chuckled. "The pain I have will take movement to cure, and my leg hurts too much for bed sport, wife." He kissed her. "I am happy to wake with ye in my arms." His arms tightened around her as he whispered, "Did I dream it, or did ye say ye are having our babe?"

Mary sat up and pushed against his chest. "Ye were awake!"

He yelled out at her movement. "Aye." The rest came out through clenched teeth. "Stop moving."

Mary lay back down. "Sorry, husband."

Agatha came beside the bed with a cup in her hand. "For ye, Milaird."

Mary took it as she and Agatha helped Roderick sit up. He grunted and sipped the cup Mary held for him. "Agh, more of yer nauseating brew. Where's my ale?"

Agatha shook her head. "Willow bark tea with healing herbs is all ye'll get for now."

He pulled Mary closer as she helped him drink more. "If my Fae is here to serve me, I'll drink any shite ye give me."

Agatha strode to the door. "I'll give ye two some privacy. I expect Archibald will come with a report when he's up." The click of the door shutting told her they were alone.

Mary reached over Roderick as she put the cup on the side table. When she returned, he held her face and kissed her deeply. She returned the kiss, thankful he was awake and healthy.

He rested his forehead against hers. "A babe, finally." He set her back, a hand moving to her belly. "How long till he comes?"

Mary moved back to his side, her hand covering his. "Who says she's a boy?"

Roderick rested his head back against the headboard and sighed. "I give it seven, maybe eight months, *mo chridhe*."

Mary sighed as she lay in his arms. "Such an expert now that he's to be a da."

Roderick pulled her to him and kissed her again. He sat back and gazed into her eyes, brushing her cheek with his fingers. "The night before I left. I knew we created a babe. I felt it as we came together." He kissed her again. "I dreamed of the Dunstaffnage ghost visiting me, smiling."

Mary sat up, ignoring Roderick's grunt. "The ghost? I saw her!"

Roderick pulled her to his side. "Green and smiling, aye. That's our *brùnaidh*. A wee brownie she is."

Mary shook her head. "No, she cried. Wailed just as ye came back last night."

He shifted her in his arms. "Crying, well... The ghostie appears and reveals what's to come for the MacDougall family. Smiling is good, and crying..." Mary hugged him closer, and he squeezed her once. "Dinna fash, I am well."

A rap sounded at the door, and her husband called, "Enter, Archibald."

The door opened wide, and Fiona came in carrying a tray as Archibald followed and shut the door. Fiona set the tray on the bed and handed Mary her bread with a slice of ham.

Roderick reached for it, and Fiona held it away. "Agatha said tea only for ye." She handed the meal to Mary. "This is for the lady. Feeding two now she is."

Mary sat back and wolfed down the respite, surprised she had not woken to a queasy belly this morning.

Roderick chuckled. "Eating for a boy, I tell ye."

Archibald smiled. "Congratulations to ye both."

Roderick bent forward with a groan and swiped the ale off the tray. At Fiona's gasp, he held it to his chest. Fiona moved away and picked up Mary's wrap. As

Fiona helped her into the wrap, Mary stood. Fiona led her to the chair before the fireplace.

Roderick gulped ale and spoke. "Ye will please tell me my men follow the bastard traitor."

Archibald stood beside the bed. "Angus, Fergus, and Robbie track Sinclair and the surviving men. Last I saw, they headed east."

As Fiona handed Mary her tea, Roderick burped. "Good choices. Robbie will come back with the news. Good punishment for him giving us up too early."

Mary froze as she listened in on the report. So, Erik survived the attack that didn't go well. She hoped no MacDougall warriors died.

Roderick's voice took on an edge. "In the meantime, I need ye to work on something." He sighed. "Erik said the traitor to MacDougall is the serpent within. Claimed I didn't know who betrayed me."

Archibald huffed. "Serpent. Who would Erik call a serpent, and who does he know?"

Mary turned in her chair. "I am the only person he knows here. Maybe it's a reference to Adam and Eve? But I am not yer betrayer."

Roderick's gaze connected with hers. "Fiona, please take Mary to the bedchamber next door while Archibald and I finish our business."

She stood. "No, I want to stay and help." Pushed aside, she wanted to help bring the wars to an end.

Roderick's expression and tone brooked no argument. "Ye, wife, will protect our babe by not getting involved."

Mary stomped her foot as Fiona took her hand. "Come, Rose prepares a bath next door. Soak for a while. Then ye can come back and harass yer husband."

Mary followed Fiona out. Roderick nodded, and she moved through the door.

****

Roderick sighed as the door closed behind his wife. "Damn, I have to make sure she doesn't get involved."

Archibald sighed. "She's a woman. Getting involved where ye don't want them is what they do best."

Roderick huffed as he eyed his empty cup. "Sinclair mentioned her as we fought—claimed her as his own. I fear he may come for her."

His first nodded. "Guards doubled already. For now, we wait for Robbie's news. And give ye time to heal."

"Aye, but who's the serpent?"

Chapter 22

Mary helped Roderick back to their bed. His steps seemed more even today, and he leaned less on her for support. Roderick seemed to be getting better, and Mary smiled to herself.

He grunted as he sat and swung his injured leg over. "Is this what our relationship has reduced us to? Ye helping yer crippled husband to the garderobe and back again."

She situated the covers around his body, leaving the injured leg exposed. "Well, if it sees my husband up and back to his normal active self, then it is."

Her husband crossed his arms and frowned. "Another week confined to the bed. I have work to see to—a clan to run."

Mary suspected this was what he looked like as a young boy denied a treat. She snickered as she picked up the small jar of salve. She scooped out a large portion and bent to rub it on the burn where Agatha had sealed the wound.

Roderick grabbed her wrist. "There are other places ye can rub that salve, wife."

Mary blushed and tugged her hand away. "Agatha said no strenuous activities." Her fingers rubbed some on his thigh. "And she was quite specific about bed play, husband."

Roderick sat back. "Spend the day in bed and no

bed sport. I'm in hell, and ye women bedevil me."

Mary rubbed along the scar covering it more as Agatha had shown her. She said it was to reduce the scarring and allow the wound to stretch and heal so that Roderick could use his leg while fighting without pain. Mary set the jar aside and wiped her hands on a cloth.

Roderick smiled and patted the bed beside him. "Come, wife. Keep yer prisoner company in his confinement."

Mary slid into the bed beside her husband, arranged her skirts, and leaned back as he took her into his arms. "Ah, now it's not hell but heaven."

He kissed her head as she snuggled into him. Her eyes traveled the long burn scar on his leg. Mary felt under the fabric of her shift at the arrow scar—the pucker of the wound mere bumps compared to the long burn on her husband's leg.

"If searing the wound makes it heal quicker, why didn't Agatha do that for me?"

Roderick's fingers followed hers to the scar. "Mm, it's healed nicely." His fingers lightly brushed the area. "Searing a wound is extremely painful. I could not stand it when ye was in pain from the arrow." She recalled his bellow of pain, the scent of burnt flesh, and her tears as she watched. The process seemed so brutal at the time, but now seeing the results of quicker healing the payoff made the pain worth it.

Mary brushed his fingers with hers. "But if it heals faster…"

Rodericks's hand grasped hers. "Searing leaves a mark, a larger scar." He brought her hand to his lips and kissed the fingertips. "I did not want yer beauty marred. Or a permanent reminder of the clan wars."

She glanced at his leg, then back at his face. "But ye will have a scar. A reminder of the clan wars."

Roderick chuckled. "Ah, lass. Scars on a warrior are a testament to his bravery. They mark him as a survivor of battle. We wear these with pride. Each one carries a story with it." He shifted and showed her his ribcage with a long white scar running from front to back. "This one. Well, I go this one the day we laid siege to Comyn's castle."

Her fingers ran the scar length. Roderick jolted as she tickled him.

He grabbed her hand with a chuckle and kissed it again. "That was the day I saw ye. On the battlements." He held her hand to his chest. "Aye, ye floated above me like a siren from mythology, half-woman and half-bird." He released her hand and caressed her hair. "Yer golden-brown locks flew about yer head."

Mary stared into his eyes, blue like the ocean, and a memory flashed of him on the ramparts.

She smiled. "I recall a time I saw ye on the battlements as well. When we attacked Dunstaffnage." She sighed. "The blue of yer eyes stopped me—so bright—and yer intense expression. Had me rooted to the spot."

He smiled. "My eyes, eh?"

Mary glanced down. War seemed to be a way of life still. They were supposed to be in a time of peace. His confinement made for a nice respite. And while necessary, it was temporary. He'd return to a battle again and sooner than Mary wanted to admit. Her eyes watered, and her vision blurred.

Roderick's finger came under her chin, bringing her gaze up until it met his. "Ye are sad. Why, *mo ghràdh?*"

Mary blinked back tears. "Ye will go back, back to fight."

His hand brushed her cheek. "Aye, it's what warriors do, Mary."

She huffed as a tear fell.

Roderick's thumb caught it. "Tell me what yer worries are."

Mary swallowed. "I-I am afraid. What if ye don't come back, or they bring yer body back and not ye?"

"Aw, Mary." He bent and kissed her. "I will always come back to ye. 'Tis why I do not say goodbye. That way, my spirit carries me back to ye."

Mary shook her head. "This time, ye came back injured. What if ye come back in pieces or not at all?"

He took her head in his hands. "Mary, I will come back. Whole." He sighed and took her in his arms. "I have so much more to come back to now." His fingers ran up and down her arm. "I have not only the clan but ye. Ye and the babe. My spirit will guide me home to ye, where it wants to be."

Mary dried her tears and shifted till her head rested on his chest. His heartbeat thumped strongly against her ear—her favorite place to be, in his arms with his chest as her pillow.

They lay like that for some time, each silent, left to their thoughts.

Roderick hmpfed. "I want ye to go to the woodworker and ask for a cane. Tell him like my grandda had. While I like spending the day with ye in my bed, not being up and around drives me daft."

Mary sat up. "What about Agatha's orders?"

He waved her off. "She always errs on the side of

caution. I'm fine as long as the wound doesn't reopen."

The following day Mary came to him with a wooden cane, thick with a round, smooth ball for the top. Agatha followed her into the room. Mary handed her excited husband his newest toy while Agatha stood with her hands on her hips.

Mary suspected the war between healer and laird was about to begin.

Roderick swung his legs onto the floor and used the cane to help lift him off the bed. He stood there steadily as he smirked.

Agatha shook her head. "Aye, so ye can stand. Ye start to walk and open the wound, undoing all my hard work, I'll brand yer backside while I sear it shut again."

Roderick lifted his shirt, baring a naked butt cheek. "Will ye now? Can ye make the brand an *M* for Mary?" He dropped the fabric and grinned at Mary. "That way, anytime I swing my tartan, all will know who my arse belongs to."

Mary giggled as Agatha shook her head. "Try walking, Milaird."

He took a few steps, the cane thumping the floor with each uneven step, his limp pronounced.

Agatha turned and strode through the door. "Ye mind yerself on the stairs and no fighting for another three weeks." She stopped at the door. "And if I brand ye, it will be *A* for Agatha!"

Roderick called as she moved into the hall, "Not *A* for arsehole?"

Mary didn't know whether to be happy or not. Roderick up and around meant he'd be back to fighting sooner.

****

Roderick sat at his desk with a cane beside him as Robbie stood before him at attention, covered in dirt, wearing a serious expression on his face. He exchanged a glance with Archibald, who nodded to Robbie. The lad looked close to falling on his face.

Roderick huffed. "Damn, near four weeks, Robbie. What the hell took ye so long, and why aren't Hamish and Fergus with ye?"

The lad didn't balk at Roderick's gruff manner. Good, the boy had learned to be a man.

Roderick had to stop the grin from filling his face as Robbie spoke. "We tracked them to the pass to the east—the one to Comyn land. I personally snuck up to their camp on foot. Their main camp is in a cave on the ridge. A place they can hold up for months at a time." He held his shoulders back. "Hamish and Fergus lay in wait on our side of the pass by the river and will send word if Sinclair moves to our lands."

Roderick moved his cane and stood up, thumping to the fireplace as he walked. While his healing took time, he kept as active as possible wanting to be ready to fight to end the wars. Robbie eyed the cane but said nothing.

"Ye spied on the camp. Did ye ever catch sight of a hooded man? One in all black?"

Robbie shook his head. "No. Only Sinclair, the survivors from our attack, and a few more. All in Comyn plaids."

Roderick whacked his cane against the fireplace. It was the third one Mary had the woodworker make for him since he kept breaking them.

Robbie jumped at the sound but sighed and stood still. Good, the boy knew he'd ruined the raid, lost them the advantage of surprise. It seemed he'd done his penance.

Roderick nodded to the door. "On with ye to the kitchens. I imagine Fiona is waiting with a full meal and a kiss for ye."

Robbie's mouth fell open. "No punishment for botching the raid?"

Roderick waved his cane to the door. "Ye've done well, Robbie. Take yer ease tonight and be back on duty tomorrow."

Robbie strode to the door, opened it, and stopped. "I'm glad yer leg is better, Milaird. I am sorry."

The door shut with a slight slam. Seemed Robbie was eager to get to Fiona.

Roderick sighed. "In the pass all this time and still no sight of the hooded one."

Archibald stood and stared at him. "I swear every time I see ye stand there with yer cane, ye look more and more like yer grandda."

Roderick growled, "Enough with the old man cane jokes. I'll be rid of it before ye know it."

Archibald chuckled. "Aye, old man."

Roderick had had enough between the old man, ye'll be a father, ye look like yer grandda. But the friendly banter was welcome from his good friend.

Archibald stood and bent over the map on the desk. "The tinker's due today. We need to formulate a plan, send word to Comyn and yer men. Bring this to an end."

Archibald traced his finger east and north along the mountain ridge to the pass leading to the Comyn lands. "We need to trap them. Where they'd have no place to go."

Roderick limped over and leaned over the desk. "Aye, but if we draw them out through the pass—" He moved his finger from the Comyn castle to the pass. "—have Comyn men push from behind and above and we wait on our side. They wouldn't know we'd be working together and wouldn't expect it." He tracked his finger through the pass to the river on the MacDougall side. "We capture them all and expose who all is a part of this. Hooded one and all."

Roderick sat, set aside his cane, and drew out a parchment and a quill. "What insult do ye think I should open with to the Comyn?"

Roderick spoke as he wrote. "Greetings, claddy Jackie."

Archibald sat before him in a chair. "He might like being called a messy chronic drunk."

Roderick smiled. "Aye, it's a compliment. We need to mend the family ties."

Archibald chuckled as Roderick continued with the missive. By the time he was done, he was quite happy with the message. He stood and read it aloud.

Greetings, Claddy Jackie.

News from the land of Macs.

The lame stallion mends quickly as the mare breeds and will drop her foal before the spring showers.

The fallen war chief and his band of flies rest in yer hills. Like a bowel movement, I suspect after a good push through the pass which comes with a new moon. The nobbers will find themselves caught like the flies in a web woven of red and blue.

An unknown serpent still crawls in our midst. Beware.

Ur Athair, new father.

By the time Roderick finished reading it, Archibald laughed so hard he had tears in his eyes. "Yer reference to bowel movement and the pass I don't think will gain ye any literary respect. And referring to yer wife as a brood mare may upset her da."

Roderick waved the parchment to dry it. "It's fitting. He used her that way to begin with. I only use it to remind him of our duty to the king and how we've met it."

Archibald wiped his face. "Aye, but never let Mary see that. Ye'll never live it down."

****

The morning of Roderick's departure had arrived. He'd promised Mary he'd allow her a moment before he left—for her.

They stood in the outer bailey as his warriors prepared to depart. Some stood awaiting the order to mount. Others whispered lowly to women they bade farewells too. He'd never think of this as a goodbye. Archibald held Rose close and kissed her. Time was upon them. He must leave soon.

Roderick pulled Mary to him and held her close as dawn pinked the sky. She held the heart-shaped pendant in her hand. She'd try to get him to take it again, but he wouldn't have it. The stone was his heart, and she held it always.

She held the pendant before her as she whispered, "Never leave me without saying goodbye, and I love ye." He huffed a laugh at her repeated statement.

He brushed the hair from her face as he whispered back, "I love ye."

She pulled back, opened the pendant, and handed

him the heart-shaped Iona stone. "Ye must take it. Ye need it for luck. Last time ye came back injured, this time…"

He shook his head and handed it back. "Mary, I gave ye this so ye'd always carry my heart with ye."

She handed it to him. He shook his head, but Mary wouldn't stop. "No, please take it so ye come back to me safely!"

Roderick growled, "I want ye to carry my heart."

Mary cried back, "I need ye to carry mine."

A repeat of the same as before—he couldn't have this. Mary needed his heart, and she wanted him to have hers. And damn, he *wanted* to carry her heart with him.

He took the stone from her and strode to the smith's anvil. He placed it on the surface, drew his sword, and struck the rock with a roar. The ring of the impact echoed in the dawn as everyone stood frozen.

Roderick sheathed his sword, grabbed the stone pieces, and returned to her.

He held his hand out, and two even halves of the heart stone lay in his palm. "We each carry the other's heart. Apart we are only pieces of a soul." He handed her half and fisted the other. "Together, in our love, we become whole." Roderick kissed her hard and held her there a moment.

He whispered into the kiss and said the same as before, so she'd know he'd come back to her, "I love ye always, but never goodbye." He backed away. "Till I see ye again."

"Mount up! Time we end the wars!" He mounted as Mary backed away. Rose took her hand, and they stood there together, tears streaking down their faces.

****

After a week and a half of travel, uniting with Hamish and Angus, another four days till the new moon, and Roderick and his warriors lay in wait at the base of the pass—hidden from view awaiting the plan's outcome to oust the traitors.

He gripped his half of the stone. Mary's tearstained face came to him. It was his last view of her.

Roderick clutched his stone as he prayed. "Please, Lord. Let me come back to Mary. I have so much more to come back for now."

Shouts alerted him as the men approached from the pass. Comyn kept his word, and the foul outlaws who betrayed them all would walk into the net. He signaled his men, and all waited ready to come from hiding at the right moment.

Sinclair led his men out of the pass. Near two dozen followed. Roderick waited till he spied the first Comyn warrior following and signaled his men. The MacDougall warriors easily surrounded the men with the Comyns. The traitors had no place to go. Sinclair dismounted and made a run for the mountain, but the Comyn warriors caught him. Robert Comyn rode forward and joined Roderick as they faced the betrayers united.

As they brought Sinclair forward, Roderick felt capturing came too easy. Everything fell into place too well. His eyes trained on the ridge, searching for treachery but found none.

His gaze returned to Robert Comyn, who grunted. "I gave ye my word. Ye are married to my jewel. She loves ye. I'd not risk her heart for anything."

The Comyn's men brought Sinclair before the lairds. He fought against their hold, and they had to bind him to control him.

Roderick stepped forward. "The hooded one. He's not here. Who is he?"

Sinclair spit at his feet. "Ye are so blind, MacDougall." His eyes went to Robert Comyn, then back to Roderick. "The hooded one outsmarted ye all—still lays in wait and will rescue me. I will have it all and…"

The whiz of an arrow flew and landed in Sinclair's eye in a deep thud. Roderick jolted as warriors around him took the offensive by drawing swords. Those holding prisoners held them before them. Sinclair fell at his feet, dead before he hit the ground.

Roderick turned to the hillside where he suspected the shot came from. "Archibald, to the hills!"

Archibald waved to Hamish and Angus. "With me." And the three mounted and took off searching for the archer.

Roderick moved to mount his horse, but a hand on his arm stopped him.

He turned, and Robert stood before him. "The hooded one didn't want ye to know. Took out his man before he told ye." His gaze went to Sinclair, dead on the ground. "We'll have to be on alert."

Four hours later Archibald returned with Angus and Hamish. "Nothing, Milaird. Tracks, but there's too many. We have nothing we can follow."

Roderick had to lean on a rock to rise. His leg ached, and the day wasted away.

Laird Comyn approached. "Nothing, eh? Well, the day's near spent." He eyed the tied-up Comyn traitors. "They'd be best with yer clan. Let the traitors spend time with the MacDougall clan in hard labor." He smiled. "Hopefully, they'll come around to peace." Comyn's glare grew hard as he spoke louder, so the men heard. "And if not, ye have my permission to kill them."

When Robert glanced at Roderick, he winked. Not really an order to kill. Roderick hoped these men came around to peace.

Both clans went about packing up and preparing for travel. The duty was done, and the plan was seen to its end. Roderick didn't know how to feel. The wars were finally over, and a new alliance formed. He hoped all would go well in the future, not just for the clan but for him and Mary as well.

As the warriors from each clan loaded up, Robert and Roderick came together.

Robert offered his hand to Roderick, who took it, and they shook hands as allies.

Roderick smiled. " 'Tis good, coming together as one."

Robert grinned. "Aye, an ally for sure ye are, MacDougall."

They stood there a moment, released their hands, and turned to mount their horses.

As Robert rode away, he called over his shoulder, "Ye wee nilly bahookie, call my jewel a breeding mare again and I'll run ye through."

Roderick huffed a laugh. "Now look here, ye Claddy Jackie, I'll not have ye speaking like that to my son when he comes!"

Robert called as he entered the pass, "A visit to the land of the Macs. I'd love to! Make sure ye have enough whisky for the Claddy Jackie!"

****

A lone cloaked figure sat on horseback overlooking the valley as the two groups of warriors rode in separate directions. Who would have thought enemies hell bent on hating each other would come together like this? Years of planning, years of manipulation, years of waiting, and the plan failed. Thanks to *Mary*.

The blackness of hate built inside her as her emotions seethed and swirled as a new plan formed. Constance Ross set her bow in its holder on her saddle, removed her hood, and glared at Roderick's retreating back as he rode toward his home and *wife*. They'd get what was coming to them, especially Mary. God made Roderick for her and her alone. Nothing would stop Constance from getting what was due to her—nothing.

Chapter 23

Mary stood at the Chapel in the Woods door, ready to enter to renew her vows to Roderick.

She adjusted her cream wedding dress again as her father huffed beside her. "Ye look beautiful." She patted her veil again, her hair worn loose down her back, as Roderick asked her to wear it. A real wedding dress, her hair done, and her maid of honor, Rose, was inside the chapel, decorated for Christmas—the wedding of her dreams.

Her father sighed. "Everything is as ye wanted it, Mary. So much mistletoe decorates the church, I can't see the greenery beneath."

Mary did her inventory one more time. Something old, her grandmother's veil, her father brought to her. Something new, a new shift from Elizabeth. Something borrowed, Rose's bracelet Archibald gifted her with last Hogmanay. Something blue, Forget Me Not flowers she grew in her room specially for the occasion. Kept out of the cold but placed in the sun. Roderick joked he'd forget them before the ceremony ended, but she held firm. She wanted these. She even had the mistletoe sprig from a year ago tucked in the bouquet for luck. Her shoe pinched. Oh, and a sixpence in her shoe.

Robert chuckled as Mary whispered, "What's so funny this time? 'Tis the third time ye laugh while we wait."

Her father grinned. "Aye, well, the first time was the king's agent when he saw yer plump belly. The look of surprise was priceless. He suspected ye both would kill each other before the year's out. Not fall in love."

Mary smiled. "The second laugh?"

He barked a laugh. "How drunk we got the king's agent last night. Yer husband's whisky trade flourishes, and now I know why. Damn stuff is smooth." He adjusted his dress jacket. "Promised me a barrel to take home he did."

Mary tugged his arm. "The third time?"

Her father sobered. "Well, that was one for yer ma. The best-laid plans of mice and men oft go astray. Here we are a year later, on MacDougall land, and both glad to be here." He smiled. "Ye are not only a jewel. Ye are as Roderick says—a treasure." He bent and kissed her cheek as tears gathered in her eyes. "Yer ma would be proud." He huffed as tears gathered in his eyes. "I am proud, Mary. Ye serve yer clan well."

The chapel doors opened, and the bagpipes performed a wedding march. Mary's gaze took in the chapel, fully decorated for the Christmas Eve ceremony. Greenery filled with mistletoe bowed along the ceiling as well as the end of each pew. The altar also held foliage with mistletoe. Elizabeth and Rose had promised her a perfect Christmas wedding, and they didn't disappoint. Her eyes landed on Roderick, who stood before her at the end of the aisle. His expression held hers, and her stomach fluttered. A year later and she was still newly in love.

A tug at her arm had her turning to her father. His wink had her smiling. Robert stood tall and escorted her to her love, Roderick. Archibald was at Roderick's side as best man. Rose stood on the left, as her maid of honor. Elizabeth sat in the front row. As her father passed, he winked at her. Soon she stood before her husband.

Reverand O'Donnell spoke clearly. "Who gives this woman away in matrimony?"

Her father replied. "I do." Under his breath, he whispered, "Ye weak-kneed willy arse. Ye don't treat her well, I'll be back."

Robert handed her to Roderick, who took her hand and bent to her father. "Look here, ye sippy bampot. I love her."

Mary rolled her eyes. The offenses from their letters carried on into every conversation between the two. It was as if they each tried to outdo the other with insults.

Her father started to speak.

Mary kicked him as she whispered between her teeth, "Enough, Father. I want to be married on Christmas Eve, not Christmas Day!"

He jumped and backed up as he laughed then turned and sat beside Elizabeth.

Reverend O'Donnell chuckled as he held his Bible. "Welcome all to the renewing of marriage vows between Mary and Roderick MacDougall. They have selected special vows they will recite together." He nodded to them both.

Mary handed her bouquet to Rose, who smiled when she took it. Mary turned to her husband, and they both held each other's hands.

She whispered before they began. "I hope I get it right."

Roderick whispered back. "Just like we practiced,

mo ghràdh, my love."

Together they took a deep breath and spoke in unison.

I take you in my heart
at the rising of the moon.
And the setting of the stars.
To love and to honor each other,
through all that may come.
May our vows be reborn
That we may meet, know, and love again.

Reverend O'Donnell spoke loudly. "And with that, marriage vows renewed. May I present Lady and Laird MacDougall!" The chapel erupted in cheers, and Roderick bent to kiss Mary. It was the wedding of her dreams, finally coming true.

Later in the main hall, as the feasting carried into the night, Archbald stood and wavered as he held his chalice up. Mary and Roderick held the MacDougall celebration goblets up, the red heart-shaped gems glittering in the light.

The hall cheered, and Angus called out, "Another toast? I'm near pissed as it is!"

Archibald waved everyone to calm down, and they did.

He raised his cup. "To the wedded couple and to peace!" Everyone cheered as he pulled Rose to stand next to him. "And ye may all congratulate me! Rose has agreed to be my wife!" The hall erupted into cheers again, and many warriors banged their cups or pounded on the tables in approval.

Mary sipped and set her cup down. Roderick leaned in as he held a mistletoe sprig before her. "A kiss for good luck, wife?"

Mary grinned. "That's for Hogmanay, husband."

Roderick hmpfed. "Aye, but today's special."

He held the mistletoe between them. "Mary, we may have begun as enemies, but now we are family."

He held it above her head and kissed her. "Once for luck."

He kissed her again. "And again, for peace."

He kissed her longer this time. She responded as he deepened the kiss.

When he lifted his head, he whispered, "For love."

****

Christmas day started cold as Mary and Roderick walked together to the chapel. Mary wrapped her newest gift from her husband close—a wrap in the MacDougall plaid with fox fur on the collar for extra warmth.

"What does yer mother want with us so early on Christmas morn?"

Roderick smiled. "Ye will see."

Mary glanced at him and had a feeling he knew what Elizabeth was about this morning. He wasn't giving any hints.

As he opened the door to the chapel, he stopped her. "Mary, I have faith in ye, in our love. Please remember that, always." He kissed her quickly and waved her into the nave.

The chapel, still decorated for Christmas, held greenery and mistletoe all around. The sight warmed Mary's heart all over—a tradition she planned to continue for years to come.

She and Roderick walked down the aisle they'd just walked yesterday in their wedding vow renewal. The memory brought tears to Mary's eyes.

Elizabeth sat in the front pew and rose when they came beside her.

She smiled as she took Roderick into an embrace. When he pulled back, she patted his cheek with tears in her eyes. She turned to Mary, hugged her hard. Held her for a moment, and released her.

She held her silver heart pendant in her hand as she faced them both. It was the one she claimed held the Stone of Love, the one her husband Ian had given her.

She took a deep breath before she spoke. "The time has come. The young grow old, learn, and mature." She handed the pendant to Roderick. "My time as guardian has come to an end. While my love for Ian will live forever, the stone no longer glows." She stepped back as her gaze moved between the two.

Mary started to speak, but Elizabeth held her hand up. "Roderick will explain all." She patted his cheek. "I leave ye to it, son. The duty is now yers." Elizabeth turned and strode out of the chapel. Mary stood speechless, not knowing what to think.

She glanced back at Roderick, who stood smiling at her. "Mary, ye remember the Fae fable story I told ye?"

Mary nodded. "Aye, the one from the book in the study. The one in the case."

He stared at the pendant in his hand. " 'She had glowing cream-colored skin and an inner beauty he had not seen in a woman before. Her light-brown hair glimmered in the sunlight, seeming as if to cast the threads of a pure gold halo around her head. Her soul called to him in a way he had never felt before. So caught up in his examination, he had not noticed that the Stone of Love glowed red.' "

Mary smiled. "Ye quote the story."

Roderick nodded as he opened the pendant.

Mary glanced down, and inside sat a dark red gem in the shape of a heart.

He whispered, "For generations, the Fae have entrusted the MacDougalls with a task. I share with ye a family secret ye must keep till the grave. Or until it is our turn to pass the duty to our son." Mary's hand went to her swollen belly—their son. She loved it when he spoke it aloud.

Roderick kissed her cheek. "We guard the Iona Stones for the Fae to keep them safe for all mankind. The three stones, Hope, Faith, and Love, we protect." He glanced at her and back at the stone. "For generations Lady MacDougall has protected one of the stones; the others are hidden. This is the Stone of Love. When we touch it, we will become their guardians. Our love will protect the stones."

Mary's gaze shot to Roderick's. "Ye mean, the magic stone. It's real?"

He smiled. "Pick up the stone, Mary, but don't be afraid. Ye'll see soon."

Mary shifted her hand under the stone, its weight caught in her hand. The dark red stone lowly glowed from the inside. She brought her other hand to the stone and gripped it. The stone warmed and glowed brighter. A sense of peace washed over her. All the love she felt for Roderick flowed from her heart. Roderick set the pendant on the pew and wrapped his hands around hers. The red light pulsed, and a new feeling of love filled her.

Her eyes connected with his, and he smiled. "It's my love ye feel."

He held them there for a moment. Then he whispered, "For love to bind, faith is a prerequisite. Ye have faith, Mary." She nodded.

"And one must also have hope. Have hope, Mary."

She whispered, "I have hope for us, my love."

"The greatest of these is love. I have faith and hope we shall love for all eternity."

Mary sighed. "For all eternity."

A word about the author…

Margaret Izard is an award-winning author of historical fantasy and paranormal romance novels. She spent her early years through college to adulthood dedicated to dance, theater, and performing. Over the years, she developed a love for great storytelling in different mediums. She does not waste a good story, be it movement, the spoken, or the written word. She discovered historical romance novels in middle school, which combined her passion for romance, drama, and fantasy. She writes exciting plot lines, steamy love scenes and always falls for a strong male with a soft heart. She lives in Houston, Texas, with her husband and adult triplets and loves to hear from readers.

You can email me at:
info@margaretizardauthor.com